MORE THAN A PRETTY FACE

A PRIDE & PREJUDICE VARIATION

FRANCES REYNOLDS

Quills & Quartos
PUBLISHING

Edited by Mary McLaughlin and Debra Anne Watson

Cover design by Carpe Librum Book Design

ISBN 978-1-956613-25-4 (ebook) and 978-1-956613-26-1 (paperback)

To Mom, who taught me to love and honour the written word, and to laugh at the notion that 'a woman, especially, if she have the misfortune of knowing anything, should conceal it as well as she can'.

CHAPTER ONE

Charlotte Lucas had once told Elizabeth Bennet that a woman had best show a gentleman even more affection than she felt if she wished to secure him. As the ancient Bennet carriage rumbled over the miles between Meryton and London, Jane Bennet was fiercely glad she had not heeded that second-hand advice. Her abandonment by Charles Bingley six weeks prior was the talk of the village—and, regrettably, of her mother's parlour—but her own actions were far less frequently canvassed than his. The public and private humiliation of having been thrown over for reasons unknown was indeed painful, but she found some solace in the certainty that her behaviour in the matter had been entirely proper.

However, weeks later, as the door closed behind Caroline Bingley and Louisa Hurst, who had returned Jane's prompt attentions with a belated call to Gracechurch Street, she was prepared to concede that all her hopes of Mr Bingley had been for naught. Indeed, she was beginning to suspect that his sisters had spoken against her. She had been sincerely attached to him and his defection still caused her pain, but she now realised that she had much rather attract a man who was firm in his affections. This, more than anything, eased her bruised heart.

As Easter approached, further distraction came in the form of a slight indisposition on the part of her aunt, who confided that there would likely be an addition to the family in the autumn. Mrs Gardiner's mornings were therefore not as tranquil as she would like, nor her energies as abundant. Jane willingly took on the tasks her aunt was accustomed to completing early in the day, that she might dwell quietly in her chamber until the most trying hours had passed.

In April, when Elizabeth joined them in London, Jane found herself more distressed by her sister's account of Mr Darcy's arrogant and insulting proposal than by the information that he had colluded with the Bingley sisters to end Jane's brief romance.

"Oh! I had not meant to disclose that!" Elizabeth exclaimed in chagrin seconds after the revelation escaped her. "I am sorry, Jane. My anger at Mr Darcy's insufferable presumption overrode my intentions, and now I fear the information has caused you pain."

Though the confirmation of her suspicions about the Bingley sisters did give her a pang, Jane smiled serenely at her sister. "Indeed, I believe they have most inadvertently done me a great favour. I understand now that to be truly happy in marriage, I must have a man who knows his own heart and mind and will put his wife above all others in his consideration, as I would my husband. As amiable as Mr Bingley is, we can only conclude that he is not such a man. He has wounded my heart, but it is healing. I shall be contented again."

Elizabeth squeezed Jane's hand. "I pray it might be so, dearest Jane, and that our mother has gotten over her disappointment half so well!"

Jane laughed and grimaced simultaneously and, knowing that she did not wish to revisit her mother's lamentations, hastened to change the subject. "But Lizzy, this news about Wickham's character is most shocking. And yet it seems it must be true, from the evidence Mr Darcy provided."

It was Elizabeth's turn to grimace. "How wrong I was! I meant to be uncommonly clever in taking so decided a dislike to Mr Darcy without any reason. It is such a spur to one's genius, such an opening for wit to have a dislike of that kind. One may be continually abusive without saying anything just, but one cannot be always laughing at a man without now and then stumbling on something witty."

"When you first read that letter, I am sure you could not treat the matter as you do now," said Jane.

"Indeed, I could not. I was very uncomfortable—I may say unhappy. And with no one to speak to of what I felt, no Jane to comfort me and say that I had not been so very weak and vain and nonsensical as I knew I had! Oh, how I wanted you!"

Jane wrapped a comforting arm about her sister's shoulders. "How unfortunate that you should have used such very strong expressions in speaking of Wickham to Mr Darcy, for now they do appear wholly undeserved."

"Certainly. But the misfortune of speaking with bitterness is a most natural consequence of the prejudices I had been encouraging. There is one point on which I want your advice. I want to be told whether I ought, or ought not, to make our acquaintances in general understand Wickham's character."

"Surely there can be no occasion for exposing him so

dreadfully," Jane replied. "To have his errors made public might ruin him forever. He is now, perhaps, sorry for what he has done and anxious to re-establish a character. We must not make him desperate."

She paused for thought as her own situation caused her to see the matter in a new light. "Perhaps... It occurs to me that our first concern must be for our fellow ladies. The gentlemen might gamble with him or extend him credit as they choose, and they ought to know enough of the world to comprehend the dangers. But if he is such a scoundrel and—" Here she stuttered over a word she had never thought to utter. "And s-seducer, perhaps Papa ought to be told, and he might have a quiet word with the other fathers in the neighbourhood. It will do the ladies of Meryton no harm to be watched more closely, and if Mr Wickham has reformed, it shall do him no harm either. What is your opinion?"

Elizabeth stared at her sister as though seeing her for the first time. "I had thought it ought not be attempted, but you have given me cause to reconsider. I shall tell Papa all, with the exception of Miss Darcy's identity, and beg him to see to the protection of the ladies. I only hope he will be moved to act."

"Surely he will. I shall add my voice to yours, if necessary. We return home in three days and shall set upon him immediately, if it pleases you!" As Elizabeth laughed at the image these words conjured, Jane added, "I shall be glad to go home, Lizzy. This time with my aunt and uncle was just what I needed to settle my spirits, but I miss our family and Longbourn and our friends and neighbours."

"As do I," her sister agreed. "Enough has occurred these last months to satisfy my desire for novelty for years, I think! It will be wonderful to return to our home and our usual habits once more."

Their planned departure for Longbourn was delayed by a sudden worsening of their aunt Gardiner's health. The poor lady was confined to her bed as the sickness which had plagued her mornings increased in intensity and claimed all her waking hours. Jane and Lizzy, along with Maria Lucas, who had accompanied Elizabeth from Kent, divided their time between Mrs Gardiner and her children, who were kept from their mother that they might not also fall ill. The children were too young to readily adapt to the illness and absence of their doting mother, and Mrs Gardiner rested better and more happily when she knew they were contented.

Little Arthur, at fifteen months, was the most vocally distressed by the separation, for unlike his elder brother and sister, he did not yet understand what it meant for one to be ill. Young Jonathan, called John by the family, had, at four years of age, some concept that his mother suffered from a stomach-ache and could not leave her bed, and he strove mightily to be a good boy for her sake. Six-year-old Evelyn was old enough to be frightened by the notion that her mother was so afflicted that she could not be seen, and she clung to her elder cousins for reassurance. Maria Lucas, who had younger brothers of her own, was soon a firm favourite with John and Arthur and cheerfully devoted many hours to their amusement and comfort. The doctor was called on the fourth day, for Mrs Gardiner's symptoms were growing worse rather than better. Shortly after he departed, Mr Gardiner summoned his nieces to the sitting room.

"My dears," he began, "I know you have been worried for your aunt, as have we all. Mr Melsome has just informed us that she is indeed increasing, and it is the babe making her so dreadfully ill."

Though aware that many women felt some distress early in pregnancy, neither of the Bennet sisters had ever heard of anyone being laid so low as their aunt. "Shall she be well, Uncle?" Elizabeth asked.

Mr Gardiner rubbed a hand over his face, and when he looked at his nieces again his eyes swam with tears. "It is most devoutly to be hoped, but you are both old enough to bear the truth. He says that while it is rather more likely than not that she will recover, it is not uncommon for such a violent reaction to end in the loss of the babe…and possibly the mother."

Jane gasped. "Is there aught we might do?"

Elizabeth cried, "Oh, yes, Uncle, tell us how we may be of use to my aunt!"

Mr Gardiner smiled through his tears. "I know you are both longing to be home, but I confess I had hoped that at least one of you might stay until your aunt is feeling better."

"But of course, Uncle! I shall be happy to stay for any length of time," said Jane instantly. She turned to her sister, expecting a similar response, only to find Elizabeth quiet and thoughtful.

After a moment, Elizabeth spoke. "If I were to consult only my own wishes, I would gladly stay, but I have recently learnt that there is an officer among the militia near Longbourn who is a danger to any decent woman. I feel I must communicate this information to Papa, and knowing how he allows his correspondence to languish, I do not think it wise to rely upon a letter." She sighed. "I must return to Longbourn and ensure that the ladies of the neighbourhood are not taken in by a scoundrel."

Her uncle, though patently disappointed, nodded gravely. "Indeed, you must. However, if you are willing, you might send me a note when your mind is easy on the matter, and I will reply with a carriage to bear you hence."

Elizabeth flew from her seat to embrace Mr Gardiner. "As soon as ever I may, Uncle. Though duty to my sisters and friends calls me away, be sure that my heart will not stray from Gracechurch Street until I am returned."

CHAPTER TWO

lizabeth and Maria Lucas departed for Longbourn the next morning, the former eager to complete her business there. With her she carried a short letter from Jane to their father, urging him to heed Elizabeth's information and act accordingly. Mr Gardiner saw Miss Lucas off with not only his thanks for her assistance in the preceding days, but also a dress-length of fine pink muslin as a more tangible token of his appreciation.

Jane continued to divide her time between her aunt and the children, who were now allowed to see their mother for a few minutes each morning and afternoon, but only if they were on their best behaviour. Though the nursery maid did her utmost to fill the time, her charges were used to spending with Mrs Gardiner; when they became fractious or anxious, it was Cousin Jane who could best soothe them.

Jane also undertook the management of the household and was thankful every day for the excellence of the Gardiners' housekeeper. Even with that able lady's assistance and the willing hands of all the Gardiner servants, Jane was stretched to the limits of her endurance by the constant demands of an unsettled household. Mrs Gardiner continued to be very ill; she was shrinking at an alarming rate and spent most of her time either sleeping or casting up her accounts. The physician came by every third day, prescribing vast quantities of ginger syrup for his patient, who seemed incapable of keeping anything else down.

A week after Elizabeth's departure, Jane received a letter from home, though she had no time to read it until she staggered to her room for the night.

Dearest Jane,

Papa has now learnt all, excepting that one piece of information which is not necessary for anyone to receive, and has somewhat reluctantly begun to act upon it. I was required to give him your letter, I regret to say, but you may be content to know it was that which finally spurred him to action. He said to me, 'If Jane is resolved that measures must be taken against someone, then it must be so, for she would forgive nearly anything.'

Every day I must urge—I might almost say harangue— him from the house to make two or three calls on other gentlemen, so the business proceeds slowly. I encouraged him to visit Sir William Lucas early and have high hopes that garrulous gentleman will take it upon himself to spread the news further.

Mama and our sisters are all very well, excepting the lack of your presence. They send their greetings to you and our relations in town. Nothing at all has changed here since you went away, except that the orange cat in the stables has gifted Longbourn with six kittens, every last one of them black as night.

How I long to return to you and Aunt Gardiner! I must assume that she is not much better, or you would have written to relieve my anxiety. How does my uncle? But I should ask you no questions, for I do not wish you to take time away from my aunt to answer them. You shall tell me all when I return, please God it shall be soon.

Your loving sister,

Elizabeth

Jane sighed as she folded the letter and tucked it into her little lap desk. She was happy to know that all her family in Hertfordshire were well, but she had hoped her father would be more energetic in his efforts. Her eyes freshly opened to the failings of more than one gentleman, she conceded to herself that his indolence in even such a crucial matter should come as no surprise.

Days passed before Jane found half an hour to pen a brief reply to her sister, assuring her that their uncle was well and had settled some of his more common business concerns on his head clerk for the time being, that he might spend more time at home. Her aunt, she was sorry to report, continued much the same. She did not add that Mr Melsome looked increasingly grim with every visit or that her own fear for her aunt's health grew daily, as that bright and clever woman became more listless and confused and her appearance more skeletal.

Several days after posting her reply, she received a thick missive from Longbourn.

Dearest Jane,

Did I not tell you that you must not waste your time writing to me? And yet it lifted my spirits considerably to receive word from you, though I had hoped for better news. Therefore, I will allow that if you have leisure, you may continue to send me a short note on occasion. I am dreadfully selfish, am I not? But I miss you so, my Jane.

I hope I may soon be able to join you. I wait only to be convinced that our parents' extraordinary resolve shall persist —but I am running ahead of myself. I dare say even you shall hardly believe what I am about to relate!

A few days after I sent my last, Lydia began twittering on at the dinner table about how handsome and charming and good Mr Wickham is, and Mama prattled right along with her, agreeing with every word. Mary attempted a sermon on the subject of flirtation and the brazen girls who engage in it, and Kitty told her to be quiet, throwing her agreement in with Lydia and Mama. I looked at Papa while this occurred and cannot describe his expression. It seemed to me he had finally realised the consequences of his neglect of our younger sisters' education.

Jane, he slammed his fist down on the table and shouted that he had heard quite enough! We were all stunned into silence, and he proceeded to declare that Mr Wickham is a rake and a rogue who has been known to trifle with both gentlewomen and those of the lower classes. He added that to his own certain knowledge more than one tradesman's daughter in Meryton had lost her virtue to the cad (which came as a surprise to me, though perhaps it should not have done) and that there would be no more talk of him or any other officer in Longbourn henceforth.

Mary and Kitty were horrified, and Mama of course began to loudly lament that such a scoundrel had ever been admitted to her acquaintance and her home. Lydia, however, was stubborn to the end and declared she did not, would not, believe it. As she shrilly expounded on the subject, such a look of defeat overspread Papa's countenance, I trembled to see it. I knew what would come next—he would give in, if only to have peace.

And now I come to the part of the tale that I think you will suspect me of inventing for my own amusement. Indeed, I can hardly credit it myself, and I was there.

Mama stood from the table and slapped Lydia across the face! This had the blessed effect of silencing her at last. She pulled Lydia from her seat and shook her. 'You foolish girl,' she cried. 'You shall not ruin your chances of a good match by dangling after a scoundrel! My girls will marry respectable men! Our acquaintance with Mr Wickham is at an end, do you hear me?'

Lydia attempted to object, and Mama shook her again and declared that if she could not be trusted to find a good husband, she should not be out in society. 'Mr Bennet,' she said, 'I believe our youngest needs to return to the nursery until she learns to heed the good counsel of her elders.'

Papa, I think, was too shocked to speak, for he only nodded. Mama marched Lydia upstairs and locked her in her room. The next morning Lydia came down for breakfast with her hair in braids and wearing an old dress of Mary's. She looked every inch the girl of fifteen that she is, and she complained bitterly over her 'childish' appearance. Mama only said that if she will act like a child, she will be treated like one. We all, Papa included and Lydia excepted, looked upon Mama with new respect.

Papa mentioned, rather diffidently, that these days seventeen seems to be the more usual age for a coming out, and perhaps they might plan on following this new fashion with their youngest. Lydia choked on her toast, but Mama nodded approvingly. Lydia was locked in her room for two days after the tantrum she then threw.

Kitty is much subdued—whether due to the shock of having been in company with such a cad or fear of being punished like Lydia, I cannot say. Perhaps she is simply lost with no Lydia to follow. She has taken up sketching again, knowing she will not now be mocked over it, for Mama keeps Lydia upstairs much of the day and will send her there on the slightest provocation when she is with us. Papa begins to talk of hiring masters for Kitty and Mary to help them along with their chosen accomplishments.

Papa now joins us in the parlour whenever gentlemen come to call, and if they are officers, he ensures that they stay not so much as a minute beyond the strictly proper length of an afternoon visit. How glad we all are that the militia removes next week! The Forsters came yesterday to make their farewells, as they depart tomorrow to see to their new quarters. Mrs Forster asked if Lydia might visit her in Brighton, but Mama said that Lydia is needed at home.

Lydia in Brighton with only Mrs Forster to watch over her —can you imagine it, Jane? I shudder at the very thought.

You may infer from the above a new composure in Mama's manner. As much as she enjoyed Lydia's noise and constant motion, I do think it exacerbated her nerves. With Kitty now so quiet and complying that she might almost be mistaken for you, our parlour and our table are quite civilised and there is little for Mama to fret over or for Mary to sermonise upon. Lydia's frequent bursts of temper do not overset Mama as they used to do, for it seems her determination to see us all well and respectably married is sufficient to overcome both her nerves and her favouritism!

Our parents appear united in their desire to curb Lydia's wildness and to pay more and better attention to Kitty and

Mary. I remain only to assure myself that this alteration will not reverse at the first hurdle. I do not know what shall convince me, but let us hope it happens soon. Give my love to my aunt and uncle and cousins, and be sure I am

    Your astonished sister,

    Elizabeth

Jane's surprise at these events was such that it could scarcely be contained, and she found herself in agreement with her sister that it was hardly to be believed and difficult to trust. She allowed herself a moment of resentment that her family had seemingly reformed only after performing so badly to the Bingleys, but then determinedly set the thought aside as unprofitable.

To her prayers that night she added a most fervent wish that Elizabeth might soon return to Gracechurch Street, for she had begun to fear that they would not long enjoy the company of Mrs Gardiner, and she did not know if she could endure that sad event without her sister by her side.

Her dearest wish was answered a few days later when notes arrived for both Jane and her uncle, the latter requesting that he send a carriage to Longbourn. It was dispatched within the hour.

Elizabeth's letter to her sister was brief.

Dearest Jane,

    Two nights ago, Lydia escaped the house by exiting her bedroom window on a length of sheeting. Uncle Philips happened upon her at the post house in the morning, trying to cajole a driver into allowing her aboard the coach to London without paying. It transpires that she intended to make her way to the militia camp at Brighton and impose upon the Forsters for lodging.

My uncle was forced to drag her, thrashing and wailing, to his home, to the delight of all the gossips in the village. Papa retrieved her and is now at least as angry as Mama. He has declared that though we are to be the last Bennets of Longbourn, we shall not end ten generations under a cloud of scandal. Mary and Kitty will not speak to Lydia and say they are humiliated to be connected to her. Lydia's windows have been nailed shut, and Father has hired two maids to keep watch over her, one during the day and one at night. They are both sensible girls and much stronger than our sister.

Given these events, I feel my presence is more needed in town than at home. I shall be with you soon and shall relate to you all the little details I have not put down here.

Elizabeth

Hearing the sound of a carriage stopping before the house the following afternoon, and seeing that her aunt slept peacefully, Jane slipped from the room and flew down the stairs to launch herself into her sister's arms the moment she stepped through the doorway.

"Oh, Lizzy!" she cried. "My aunt has taken a piece of toast for breakfast and another for luncheon! I hope there may be reason to believe that the worst is behind us!"

As Elizabeth exclaimed over the good news, all the anxiety of the last weeks seemed to descend upon Jane in a rush, and she could do nothing but hold her beloved sister and weep.

CHAPTER THREE

As spring became summer and the city emptied of those wealthy enough to flee, Jane and Elizabeth continued at Gracechurch Street. Quiet and steady Jane spent most of her time with her aunt, who had slowly improved and begun to put on weight again, though she remained very ill most mornings and could tolerate only small, plain meals. Lively Elizabeth contrived to distract the young Gardiners, who had been used to the regular attention of their mother.

The letters they received regularly from Mary, Kitty, and their mother indicated that the reform of the Bennet family continued. Mary and Kitty were in raptures over the weekly visits of the music and drawing masters, while Mrs Bennet's correspondence contained fewer exclamations and more sense than ever before. She would never be an intelligent woman, or a sedate one, but when properly supported, it seemed she was quite capable of basic good sense and reason. In one letter, she astonished her eldest daughters by writing that she blamed herself for Lydia's intractability, admitting that she had failed to instruct her youngest as she ought.

Jane and Elizabeth both wrote to all their family often— even to their father, who rarely replied, and Lydia, who never did—for as the weeks marched on, they became ever more conscious of how long they had been from home. Delighting in every letter they received in return, they were often to be found just before retiring for the night, sitting upon their beds and looking over their correspondence again.

Mr Gardiner had resumed his usual business activities, although he worked from his study at home at least two days a week. He employed a boy to run messages between his office, his warehouses, and his home on those days, for he could well afford the expense and preferred to remain close to his wife as much as possible.

One sweltering morning in early July, Mr Gardiner was interrupted in his work by young Danny, whose flushed face and panting breaths indicated that he had sprinted the full six blocks from the offices of Gardiner Drapery & Woollens. He handed Mr Gardiner a card and gasped that a 'real swell' had called upon the office and was even now being escorted hence by Mr Sewell, the head clerk.

Mr Gardiner, recognising the name on the card as the owner of an estate which supplied some of his finest wool, was immediately concerned. He had dealt with the estate's steward these seven years but had met neither the former owner, who had died over the winter, nor the son who had then inherited. He bade Danny retire to the kitchens for a rest and some cool water and sat back, racking his memory for any reason such a personage might be visiting without prior notice.

Henry Markham, the earl of Lyfford, gazed out the window upon the unfamiliar sights of Cheapside and resisted the urge to rub his temples. He truly missed his father, gone now these eight months, but if the man were to appear alive before him this instant, Lyfford thought his first reaction would be to shake him for mismanaging his business. And his second, to shake him again for failing to thoroughly educate his son in the running of an estate.

For all the Lyfford family's ancient title and seat in the House of Lords, their hilly lands in Staffordshire produced only two things of value—pottery and sheep. Both, as it transpired, had for the last decade or more been producing the expected quantities but not the expected profit. The stack of account books on the seat beside him testified to these facts, and he now had hopes that the reputed honesty and probity of one E. Jonathan Gardiner would translate into a better price for his fleeces next spring.

His years at Harrow and then Cambridge, where he had taken a first in natural sciences, had not prepared him for this new role. In his youth, Lyfford had been taught to manage tenant concerns and crop rotation in the relatively few fields farmed by the estate. After Cambridge, he had received an education in the political and social concerns of his family. His instruction in the tedious business of making the money which supported it all had been deferred under the mistaken assumption that there was a great deal of time yet available for the endeavour, for the previous Lord Lyfford had been a seemingly hale fellow of one and fifty when a winter ague settled into his lungs and carried him away in under a fortnight.

Lyfford had spent the remnant of winter grieving and the spring trying to comprehend all the information in the accounts. After endless weeks of poring over those ledgers and the market prices listed in the trade papers, he had thrown up his hands and taken his books and his questions fifteen miles across the county and into Derbyshire, to his old friend Fitzwilliam Darcy, who had been running his own large estate for five years with every appearance of success.

It was impossible not to envy the Pemberley estate, which was as large as Lyfford but sat in a verdant, fertile valley, well supplied with streams and woods and vistas both profitable and pleasing. The current master had taken its reins at the age of two and twenty upon the unexpected demise of George Darcy, and if he had ever stumbled in the execution of his duties since that time, Lyfford had not heard of it.

Everywhere he looked as his carriage rolled along the western edge of the estate to the road which would take him to the house, he had seen fields lush with crops or plump live-stock, prosperous tenants and their labourers going capably about the business of coaxing a living from the earth. Lyfford was not a man afflicted with a lack of self-confidence, but he knew that he could not have stepped so ably into his own father's shoes hardly a year after university, and he applauded his friend for meeting that challenge so very well.

Darcy, even more grim and sober now than when they had last crossed paths, generously spent several days explaining the entries. According to the other man, Lyfford's rents were too low, his servants' wages too high, and his fleeces and pottery sold for too little. Lyfford was left with a great deal of work to do and a profound gratitude that two of his three sisters were well settled in marriage and his brother in a captaincy with the Horse Guards. He had only his youngest sister and a widowed aunt to care for and could devote much of his attention to restoring his income.

He was not, as Darcy had hastened to point out, in anything like dire straits. His father's investments were sound, if conservative, and the estate's production could not be faulted. The problem was years of poor bargains with merchants and excessive generosity with servants and tenants. Lyfford wished to be a liberal master, but he had now learnt the difference between liberality and foolhardiness. Correcting his rents could not be done until the leases were renewed, and the question of wages would require very delicate handling indeed, so he elected to proceed directly from Pemberley to London to consult with his solicitors and investigate his heretofore unknown buyers, in hopes that one thing, at least, might be resolved quickly.

Three different concerns purchased from his pottery-works, and he found that two had good reputations; with these, he was willing to renegotiate. The third was not well regarded and would be dropped. The vast majority of his wool went to Mr Gardiner, whose sterling reputation gave Lyfford hope that this part of the business would proceed rapidly and to his satisfaction.

The carriage pulled up before a modern, elegant home that would not have appeared out of place in the newer parts of Mayfair. The clerk disembarked behind him and escorted him through the house and into a well-appointed study. Mr Gardiner was a surprise to Lyfford, who had been expecting a plump, contented old tradesman but was greeted instead by a lean, keen-eyed fellow in his mid-thirties whose speech and dress would not have been amiss at White's.

"Lord Lyfford," he said after Mr Sewell performed the

introductions. "It is a pleasure to meet you. I apologise for not being in the office when you called. My wife has been ill, and I have taken to working here when I might, to be closer to her." Though his words expressed apology, there was none in his tone. This was a man who was not abashed by his care for his wife, and Lyfford respected him for it.

"I am sorry to hear of Mrs Gardiner's poor health," he replied as they took their seats. "I hope she will soon be restored."

"Thank you, my lord. I share that hope. Now, if I may ask, what brings you to see me?"

"I have been looking over my father's books, and to come straight to the point, I am hoping to come to an agreement that next spring, I might sell my wool to you at market rates."

Mr Gardiner cocked his head curiously. "You...wish that I should pay you less, my lord?" he asked dubiously.

"No, sir, I wish you to pay me more. Either my father or his steward accepted a rate somewhat below the worth of the wool, and I intend to correct that going forward. Your reputation is such that I would prefer to continue our business relationship, but only if I receive a fair price."

Mr Gardiner shook his head. "There has been some misunderstanding, I must assume. My lord, the wool your estate produces is among the finest I buy, and I pay a premium for much of it." He turned to his clerk. "Mr Sewell, please return to the office and bring us the Lyfford account ledger and the general wool ledgers for the last three years." He returned his gaze to Lyfford. "Let us compare our accounts, my lord, and get to the bottom of this."

Lyfford agreed and Mr Gardiner called for lemonade and sandwiches while they waited. The clerk returned and Mr Gardiner opened his books while Lyfford found the relevant entries in his. They soon discovered that their accounting systems were wildly divergent—Lyfford's books contained a single line for each annual sale, consisting of the date, poundage and price received. Mr Gardiner's classified the wool by quality, noting the weight of each fleece and payment per ounce. His general ledgers described his offered prices on different breeds and quality of wool, along with the going market rates.

"This will take hours to reconcile," Mr Sewell pronounced. "My lord, if you will allow me to copy out the relevant entries in your books, I will work as quickly as possible, and we shall contact you tomorrow or the next day to discuss the results."

Lyfford agreed, but a thoughtful Mr Gardiner said, "There may be a way to resolve this more quickly, my lord. One of my nieces has a most remarkable head for numbers—she can look at multiple entries and figure them almost instantly. She happens to be in residence with us, assisting my wife during her illness."

"You want your niece to look at my accounts?" Lyfford asked, unsure whether to be horrified or amused.

Mr Gardiner turned a serious gaze upon Lyfford. "It sounds outlandish, I know, but she truly is a wonder at figuring. Her father is a gentleman, and she has been in control of his estate books and her mother's household accounts since she was twelve. I assure you she is not a gossip and will hold your business in confidence."

Though Lyfford had the sense that events were spinning still further beyond his control, he reflected that if the girl was not the prodigy her doting uncle believed, he would lose no more than a bit of time. "Very well," he sighed. "She may attempt it, and if she fails, Mr Sewell will make his copies and we shall meet again another day."

Mr Gardiner rang for a servant to fetch his niece. A few minutes later the door to the study opened, and through it came the loveliest creature Lyfford had ever beheld. He might perhaps have seen a more beautiful face, or more golden hair, or eyes of a deeper blue, but never united and certainly never in company with such a sweet, serene expression.

"You wished to see me, Uncle?"

Her voice was pitched a bit deeper than he would have expected; she would sing the alto part rather than soprano. Her affection for her uncle was clear as she addressed him, and if she was curious about the stranger in the room, she concealed it.

"Come in, my dear Jane. We have a problem with some accounts that we hoped you could solve more quickly than we poor men might." Mr Gardiner brought her forward and introduced her to the young earl. She accepted being introduced to a lord with no more than a blink of surprise. She curtseyed, he bowed, they both expressed pleasure in the acquaintance, and Mr Gardiner immediately launched into an explanation of the problem, pointing out the most recent records in Lyfford's books and his own. He guided her into his own seat behind the desk, with the books laid out before her.

"May I consult previous entries as well, my lord?" She looked directly at him, and he nodded dumbly before his mind had fully registered the question. Good Lord, she was beautiful.

There was silence in the office as she flipped through the books, eyes moving quickly from entry to entry while her serene expression never altered. After a few minutes she paused, ran a fingertip quickly down a column of numbers in her uncle's general ledger, and sat back with a small sigh.

"Assuming my uncle's accounts are correct, and I believe they are, there can be only one conclusion." She looked directly at Lyfford again. "Someone is stealing from you, my lord."

Mr Gardiner looked as though he had suspected as much, Mr Sewell appeared scandalised, and Lyfford was quite simply staggered. Miss Bennet continued, "My uncle has paid market rate for your ordinary fleeces, and three to five percent above market for the more desirable ones. The totals in your books, my lord, are between ten and fifteen percent below what my uncle paid out. In the last three years you have lost twelve hundred and fifty-six pounds, nine shillings, tuppence."

"I had calculated the difference at about four hundred pounds," Lyfford managed to say, astonished by her conclusions as well as the speed of her calculations and the certainty with which she voiced them.

Miss Bennet thought for a moment. "At market rate, for mostly ordinary fleeces...yes. About four hundred pounds. But your flocks must be excellent, my lord, for my uncle classified over seventy percent of your fleeces as fine or exceptional and paid more to get them."

Lyfford could only shake his head in wonder. "Miss Bennet, you are extraordinary."

The lady blushed and demurred, but Mr Gardiner and Mr Sewell both added their voices to Lyfford's praise, and she was forced to accept their fervent thanks before she was released to return to her aunt.

CHAPTER FOUR

J ane returned to her aunt's room to find her awake,
listening as Elizabeth read from a volume of Coleridge.
Both questioned Jane over her summons to Mr
Gardiner's office, but she would say only that she had
performed some few calculations to assist a young gentleman
in understanding his estate's business with her uncle. This did
not entirely satisfy either lady's curiosity, but they knew that
any attempt to breach Jane's discretion was doomed to failure.

As the sisters readied for sleep in their shared room that
evening, Elizabeth took the opportunity to enquire after Jane's
impression of the visitor.

"We spoke very little, but he was polite and seemed somewhat careworn. I dare say he has struggled, inheriting an
estate so young. He appears dedicated to understanding his

situation, which anyone must find admirable. That is all I can say."

"Then I am glad you were able to assist him, and I dare say you have eased his troubles thereby."

"I do hope so, Lizzy."

Lyfford's troubles had, in fact, mounted now that what he had taken for incompetence appeared rather more sinister. Once the shock of the notion had worn off, he was quick to apprehend that this thievery might not be confined to his dealings in wool.

Upon returning that afternoon to Markham House, his London home, he quickly dispatched notes to his pottery buyers, requesting meetings at their earliest convenience. He also sent a man back to Lyfford Hall to retrieve the last five years of ledgers from the housekeeper and the pottery-works. Finally, he sent for the housekeeper of Markham House and requested the accounts for that establishment.

He began to laboriously add up sums from the many entries in the previous year's household accounts to compare to the more condensed records in the estate books. As he wondered whether nine shillings sixpence for scullery candles ought to be accounted a general expense or assigned to the kitchens, he thought longingly of Jane Bennet's easy facility with reckoning and presumably greater knowledge of such homely details.

Later, eating his dinner alone at the family table, he thought longingly of her low, soothing voice and sweet smile. He wondered what they might be speaking of if she were here. *The results of her perusal of the books,* he concluded wryly. Perhaps she would explain to him how the scullery candles ought to be accounted for and whether gratuities to the butcher's boy should be included in the cost of meat or marked down elsewhere. He might then mention how he could not look forward to taking his seat in the House of Lords at the next session; his father's old cronies would expect him to join their party, but he intended to declare for the Whigs.

Lyfford laughed at himself as he finished the strawberry trifle, spinning such a vivid daydream from one brief meeting. Perhaps he ought to visit his club and discover if any of his friends were in town, for he had obviously spent too much time at his labours.

Several afternoons later, a baffled and defeated Lyfford was shown into Mr Gardiner's offices. The tradesman stood to greet him.

"Lord Lyfford, please come in." He gestured the younger man towards a comfortable chair. "To what do I owe the pleasure?"

Lyfford sat and smiled wryly. "The last time we met, you produced a miracle for me. I have come in the faint hope you might do so yet again."

Mr Gardiner returned to his seat behind the desk. "Tell me more."

"It has been in my mind that I ought to hire a secretary before Parliament opens, but now that I am awash in conflicting financial records, I find the need has become urgent. I am overwhelmed and cannot set this business to rights on my own. I thought to ask if you might personally recommend someone before I throw myself on the mercy of the agencies."

"You have discovered trouble in your other dealings, I take it?"

"Yes, and I believe there is more to be found. If I wish to pursue a legal case against the thief, I will need to understand the full extent of these crimes and have them well documented. And if I should decide against exposing my troubles to the world in that way, I would at least wish to know what my income ought to be in future, so that I may plan accordingly."

Mr Gardiner nodded. "Sensible." He steepled his fingers beneath his chin and thought for a moment. "I fear I do not have that miracle for you, my lord, but I know a man who may. An old friend of my father's owns an employment agency, and he has more than a few clients from your sphere. If anyone can produce a fine secretary on short notice, I should think it would be Archibald Morrison. I would be happy to accompany you to his place of business and ask that he handle your case personally."

"If it will not cause you any difficulties, sir, I should appreciate that very much."

"I must thank you for your assistance, sir," Lyfford commented as they travelled back to Mr Gardiner's office after consulting Mr Morrison. "I feel as though I have imposed on your good nature, and you have been all graciousness. I hope that when my aunt escorts my sister to town next month, we might have you and your wife to dine. I have no hostess at present, unfortunately."

"If my wife is well enough to attend, we should be pleased to do so, thank you, my lord."

"And of course, if your nieces are yet in town they are included in the invitation," Lyfford added. "I must say, the more I work with these accounts, the more astounded I am by Miss Bennet's abilities. It takes me hours to go through a comparison between two sets of records, and she was reviewing three simultaneously. I hope you will convey to her my appreciation for her assistance."

Mr Gardiner nodded amiably. "I should be happy to. Although...might you care to join us for dinner? You could then offer your thanks in person."

"I should not wish to impose, sir."

"I dare say my nieces would appreciate some company that is not my own, and our cook is quite accustomed to last-minute additions to our party, for I often invite my associates 'round. But if you prefer the quiet of your own home, I shall not be offended."

"In truth, I should like some company very well myself, sir. I am the only one in residence at the moment and find the evenings do drag on," Lyfford admitted.

"Then please come. We do not dress for dinner when I have been at the warehouse, so we might go there directly, and I shall have an hour with my wife before we dine, if you do not mind being entertained by my nieces."

Lyfford laughed and opined that no one of sense could be opposed to such a scheme, and so Mr Gardiner redirected his driver to Gracechurch Street. They soon arrived and Mr Gardiner waited with him in the parlour, discussing the trials and tribulations of summer in London, while a servant fetched the ladies and informed them of the arrival of a dinner guest.

The Bennet sisters arrived in the parlour arm in arm,

and Mr Gardiner hastened to make the introduction between Lyfford and his younger niece. He saw them safely embarked upon a conversation about the theatre before excusing himself to spend the time before dinner with his wife.

Lyfford was surprised after only a short time in Miss Elizabeth's company by how different the sisters were in both appearance and temperament, yet the bond of affection between them was apparent and pleasing to behold. Both were well read, he learnt as the conversation ranged over a number of topics. Miss Elizabeth was unusually knowledgeable on the subject of literature, both modern and classical, while Miss Bennet was equally as informed with regards to history; each was conversant on current events. Lyfford thought he should never be dull given either of them to speak with; both together provided an intellectual stimulus he had rarely known since university.

Mr Gardiner re-joined the party shortly before the meal, bearing a good report of his wife's health and spirits. Conversation over the meal was even livelier for the addition of their host, whose well-informed mind was paired with a sly wit. As he and his younger niece energetically debated some obscure point of Shakespeare over the fish course, Miss Bennet took the opportunity to murmur to Lyfford, "I hope your trouble with the wool sales has been resolved to your satisfaction, my lord."

"Unfortunately not," he replied quietly. "Your discovery led me to review my other accounts, and there is some evidence of discrepancies in several of them. Mr Gardiner was kind enough to assist me this afternoon in my search for a secretary, for I have realised it is simply too great a task for me alone."

"Oh, dear. I had so hoped the trouble was confined to that

one area of your affairs, my lord," Miss Bennet replied with a sympathetic look. "Were you able to hire a secretary?"

"Your uncle recommended Mr Morrison to me, and he produced what seems to be an ideal candidate—educated and familiar with my social sphere, as well as estate and political matters. I shall interview him in the morning."

"How fortunate that there is such a man available, just when you have need." Her smile of honest pleasure on his behalf nearly stopped his heart.

"He, ah..." Lyfford shook his head a little to clear it. "Pardon me. I lost the thread for a moment. I am told that Mr Boyle is some months returned from the Peninsula, where he served with distinction. He has encountered difficulty finding a position because he has sustained visible injuries. For myself, if he is half as competent as his references indicate, I should be happy to hire him even were he the ugliest fellow in creation."

"The poor man," she murmured, her sympathies caught. "For his sake and yours, I hope that he is exactly what you seek. And if I might assist you in sorting out your accounts, I should be delighted."

"I could not ask such a thing of you, Miss Bennet. It is very dull work."

"I never find numbers dull. They are so clean and rational. One always knows what to expect of them." She sipped her wine, a faint shadow passing through her expression, and he wondered at it.

"If you are certain that it would be no imposition on you or your family?"

Miss Bennet smiled and turned to her relations. "Uncle, Lizzy, might you spare me for an hour or two in the afternoons for a time? I should like to help Lord Lyfford with some maths."

Miss Elizabeth laughed and made a gesture of mock surrender. "Never let it be said I kept Jane from her calculations!" She reached over and patted her sister's hand. "Aunt is much better, and the children have settled into their new routine. I shall manage very well."

"If you are willing to bring your work here, my lord, I have no objection," Mr Gardiner said. "You may use the library, and I will assign a maid to keep propriety for my niece."

An hour was settled upon for the day after next, and the conversation soon turned to matters of general interest. At the end of the evening, the Miss Bennets entertained the gentlemen with several songs. Miss Elizabeth played and both Bennets sang, and Lyfford discovered that Miss Bennet sang quite as well as she spoke, her rich alto blending beautifully with her sister's fine soprano. In his own home later that evening, he thought that he could not recall a more enjoyable occasion, and he went to bed humming the Scottish air with which they had concluded their performance.

> Green grow the rushes, O,
> Green grow the rushes, O,
> The sweetest hours that e'er I spent
> Were spent among the lasses, O.
>
> — ROBERT BURNS

CHAPTER FIVE

L yfford was shown into a well-appointed room when he arrived at Morrison's Employment Agency the next morning. A pot of tea and a plate of biscuits were delivered, followed shortly by Mr Morrison himself, escorting Mr Boyle.

Lyfford's eyes first went to the empty left sleeve pinned to Mr Boyle's jacket, then to the rather livid scar across his cheek on the same side. The fellow's eyes were sharp and clear, however, and his posture erect; his reddish-brown hair was neatly cut and combed, and his suit, though several years out of fashion, was clean and pressed. Mr Morrison conducted the introductions and soon made himself scarce.

He knew that Mr Boyle was three years his junior but, weathered by the Peninsular sun and drawn by recent suffering, the man appeared somewhat older. He was able to demonstrate a fair understanding of the current political climate and a comprehension nearly as thorough as Lyfford's own of the public and private demands of a titled gentleman's life. Before they had even drained the teapot, Lyfford felt comfortable offering him the position. Mr Boyle was satisfied with the terms and soon they were shaking hands on it.

Lyfford arranged for a wagon and two footmen to assist his new secretary in removing from his lodgings for a room in Markham House, where he was installed before dinner. During the meal and over port afterwards he began to acquaint the young man with his business.

In the morning, he sent a note to the Gardiner home, asking if he might bring Mr Boyle with him the next day in order to share the details of his financial affairs with both his secretary and Miss Bennet at once. An affirmative reply was soon received, and the following afternoon they arrived at Gracechurch Street with a stack of ledgers and papers. Miss Bennet received them in the library, and through the whole of their visit the only hint she displayed that she had noticed Mr Boyle's disfigurements was a brief, hard look directed at the maid, whose air of disgust was thereafter carefully concealed.

It was now the secretary's turn to be amazed by Miss Bennet's facility with numbers, as she sorted out several years' worth of Lyfford Hall's household accounts in little more than an hour. In the process, she was able to determine which entries in the housekeeper's detailed accounts corresponded with which in the steward's summaries, and that the two varied by nearly three hundred pounds per annum.

Two days later, after reconciling the three pottery accounts, losses approaching eighteen hundred pounds over three years had been uncovered. Their next visit turned up an annual deficit of over two hundred pounds from Markham House. His father's investments, in a much-needed bit of good news, proved to have been excluded from the rampant thievery.

"If I may be so bold, my lord," Mr Boyle commented as they rode towards Markham House at the conclusion of the investments review, "there is only one person who had the opportunity to seize all those funds and falsify your records."

"Indeed," Lyfford sighed. "Mr Watts, my father's steward these twenty years. God alone knows how much he has bled from us in that time. Over four thousand pounds in the last three years alone. When I think of the improvements and investments that might have been made with such a sum..." He thumped the carriage wall with the side of his fist in frustration.

"Have you any notion what action you shall take?"

"I hardly know. I hesitate to expose my family's business for the titillation of society, but the thought of that man getting away with no penalty save a lost position is galling."

Lyfford turned his steps towards Gracechurch Street on a variety of trifling pretexts over the next fortnight—showing Miss Bennet the beginnings Mr Boyle and his London housekeeper had made in keeping his books in the manner she suggested, querying as to the proper allocation of this or that expense, and the like. During that time, he came no closer to a decision as to how to resolve the situation, though he wrestled with the problem daily. Thus, it felt natural that he should visit her once more.

Over tea, Lyfford laid bare before her his steward's perfidy and his own doubts as to how best he ought to proceed. "What is your opinion, Miss Bennet? You are not so connected to this business as I. I feel you shall see it with clearer eyes."

She considered the question seriously. "In general, I am of the opinion that society is bettered when criminals are held accountable for their crimes. And yet I could not condemn anyone who protected their own privacy by refusing to prosecute a crime which affects only themselves. It is a conundrum, my lord."

"If you were in my place, what would you do?"

She laughed softly. "I would fret a great deal, to begin with, but if such a thing happened to my family, I should like to think I would be willing to endure the embarrassment of exposure to prevent the thief from going on to swindle another. But it would not be easy, and I could not censure a different choice."

Lyfford chewed a bite of orange scone thoughtfully as he absorbed her remarks. "You are perfectly correct, as always, Miss Bennet. I have been so enwrapt in my own concerns that I had not even considered that I may have a moral obligation to ensure he cannot repeat his crimes. It is now clear to me how I must act. I thank you for your counsel."

She blushed and demurred, so he attempted to put her at ease by turning the conversation to the innocuous subject of family. After Miss Bennet spoke of her relations, he found himself affectionately describing his own: his elder sister, Lady Cynthia, married to the heir to a neighbouring estate; his brother, Edward, a captain with the Royal Horse Guards, currently stationed near London training new recruits while he recovered from a wound sustained on the Peninsula; and Lady Julia, married less than two years to a rather ambitious clergyman currently tending a flock near Canterbury. His youngest sister was Lady Ellen, only fourteen years old, a bright and cheerful girl of whom he was particularly fond. His only other close relation was his mother's sister, who had made her home with the Lyffords since being widowed. Mrs Swindon was a clever, sensible woman whose assistance in raising Lady Ellen was the subject of his fervent gratitude.

"I hope you shall have the opportunity to meet Ellen and my aunt in a few weeks, Miss Bennet, when they come to town to prepare my sister for her return to school." This civility was amply rewarded with one of Miss Bennet's luminous smiles.

Elizabeth sat across the room ostensibly reading a novel and was pleased to see her sister so well entertained. *What a disparate group these young men from the north are*, she thought. They had met four in less than a year: three amiable, three honourable, one of the latter very haughty, and one of the former entirely unprincipled.

She still thought Mr Bingley a good man, though she could no longer believe him deserving of her dearest sister. Upon Mr Wickham, she cared not to think at all. Lord Lyfford and Mr Darcy, however, were subjects of fascination to Elizabeth.

Mr Darcy had slighted and offended Elizabeth and, indeed, almost everyone of her acquaintance, so proud of his name and station that he had not even allowed his proposal of marriage to pass without commenting on the disparity between them, in terms as warm as his avowals of love had been. Yet for all his poor manners, he had proved himself a man of honour and of feeling who was valued by his friends and relations, and who had conquered that pride so far as to offer his hand to a young lady of a lower sphere.

But here in her aunt's parlour in Cheapside sat Lord Lyfford, a man of similar age and greater station, paying what Elizabeth began to suspect were more than friendly attentions to a mere Miss Bennet of Longbourn. He was more circumspect in his admiration than Mr Bingley had been, and there was no telling if it would come to anything, but his willingness to befriend the Bennets and the Gardiners had earned her respect and approbation.

These musings were disrupted by the sound of laughter without the house, and she glanced out the open window to see a group of young women, not much younger than her, strolling along the sun-washed street, their parasols waving with their merriment. She stifled a sigh of envy. How she wished she might go for a long ramble in the shade of the trees overhanging Longbourn Brook and hear the birds singing and the cattle lowing in the fields. Even a turn about a park would be some relief, though it could never compare to the countryside.

She did not begrudge her uncle and aunt this time—not at all! But to be confined to a city home in the heat of the summer was a difficult thing for a country lady accustomed to a great deal of freedom. She hid her restlessness from her relations diligently, for she judged it rather selfish to be pining for a walk when her aunt was so weak and her uncle and cousins so worried, but at times it swept over her, and she felt she could almost weep with frustration and longing.

Lyfford spent the next several days in conference with his attorneys, though he did find time to speak with Mr Morrison and request that a discreet search for a new steward be launched. An advertisement was shortly sent to the major papers across England.

As he made the final preparations to return to Lyfford Hall and bring his case before a local magistrate, he sent a note to Mr Gardiner announcing his departure and requesting an opportunity to farewell the family. He was promptly invited to tea the following afternoon, and he accepted with pleasure.

Mr Gardiner and his nieces greeted Lyfford warmly and enquired after his plans. He explained that he would travel to his estate, present evidence to the nearest magistrate who was not a relation, and—God willing—see his steward arrested for years of theft against his estate and family. He hoped to return to London with his sister and aunt in about three weeks.

He soon departed but realised as he was about to board his carriage that he had left his gloves behind. He returned to the house, explained his errand to the footman, and was allowed to return to the parlour. Just shy of the door, he stopped, his stride arrested by the mention of his own title.

"How many calculations has your Lord Lyfford put before you today?" Miss Elizabeth asked laughingly.

"Hush, Lizzy. It was only a question about management of household accounts. The poor man has no one other than his housekeepers to attend to such things. It is natural that he should not apprehend every detail. And he is not *my* Lord Lyfford."

"He very well might be, if he continues to visit so frequently," her sister teased.

"Your wishes are proof of your sisterly loyalty, but do be practical. If my connexions were too low for Mr Bingley, how must they appear to Lord Lyfford? He is an excellent gentleman whom I am happy to know, but I can have no expectations beyond a pleasant acquaintance."

Bingley? Lyfford was somewhat acquainted with a Charles Bingley, an amiable fellow of some fortune but little status.

"Jane, you do not still...?"

"Oh, no. I am quite over my little infatuation, I assure you. I know now that he could not have made me happy. Not for long."

"He might have, had not his awful sisters and top-lofty Mr Darcy poisoned him against the notion!" Miss Elizabeth rejoined with asperity.

Mr Darcy! Lyfford's jaw dropped. There could not be in the whole of England another Mr Darcy who might influence a Mr Bingley away from a lady. He wondered briefly if his old friend had lost his mind, for who could possibly object to Miss Jane Bennet as a potential match to the son of a tradesman, connexions or no?

"I am grateful to them, Lizzy, for though they acted wrongly in telling Mr Bingley that I held no affection for him and in conspiring to keep my presence in London from his knowledge, the pain and embarrassment I endured have taught me to understand myself. If I am to be happy in marriage, I must have a gentleman of firm character, one who will not be repulsed by our family—who I admit can be very silly—or turned aside by others who may wish a more fortunate alliance for him. I should not wish to live as my husband's great regret."

"No alliance could be more fortunate than one with you, my dear Jane! You are everything wonderful. But do you not think Lord Lyfford is that sort of man?"

Miss Bennet laughed. "I thank you, dearest sister, but most men cannot afford to take a wife with such a paltry dowry as ours, and most who could would rather not. As for Lord Lyfford, he is a most pleasant gentleman, and I am glad to count him among my friends."

"He is very amiable and strikes me as a clever sort of fellow. He seems quite perfect for you, but if you are certain that it cannot be, then I only hope you are guarding your feelings."

"I know my own strength now, Lizzy, and shall not so easily open my heart again. You need not be concerned for me."

Lyfford quietly backed up to the head of the stairs and then resumed his trek towards the parlour, stepping rather more firmly than was his wont, ashamed of himself for listening as long as he had. He put on a sheepish smile as he entered. "Your pardon, ladies, I forgot my gloves. Forgive me for intruding." He did not fail to note the blush spreading across the cheeks of both women but affected to see nothing amiss and, having reacquired the errant garments, he made them a brief farewell and went on his way.

CHAPTER SIX

During the three days' travel necessary to reach his country home from London, Lyfford found ample time to marvel at and ponder the events he had pieced together, beginning with that overheard conversation. Darcy had mentioned something about spending the previous autumn with Bingley at a leased estate in Hertfordshire. Knowing that county to be the home of the Bennets, it was no great leap to conclude that the Bennet estate and the Bingley lease must lie in some proximity.

He had met the Bingley sisters only briefly, but this was sufficient to reveal them as ambitious upstarts, eager to claim any acquaintance that might advance them socially. He could easily picture them acting without consideration or remorse to separate Bingley from a lady not well dowered or well connected enough for their tastes. But what might have prompted Darcy to involve himself in such a scheme? He should understand that any gentleman's daughter would be a step up in the world for the son of a tradesman, more so for one with no estate of his own. Furthermore, a beautiful, intelligent, and gracious gentlewoman on his arm would do more for Bingley's social prospects than any dowry. That Darcy would not only wish to separate his friend from such a woman, but would also engage in underhanded tactics to accomplish it, was beyond Lyfford's comprehension. The man was a pillar of moral rectitude and honest to the point of incivility.

Then again, Darcy could be terribly superior, and he seemed to have a particular suspicion of women. He had been chased for his fortune and name from the age of sixteen—with this, Lyfford could sympathise, for he had endured the same—but Darcy's resentful temper had not allowed him to shrug it off as the unavoidable price of being young and rich and master of his own fate. Upon consideration, he thought it entirely possible that Darcy had beheld a woman without means gaining the attention of his wealthy friend and had not looked beyond the disparity of fortune to see the affection she had for him.

Bingley, too, had played a less than laudable part in events. Lyfford had liked the man on the few occasions they had met, but to throw over a woman like Jane Bennet on the urging of others, even relations and good friends, struck him as weak and foolish. Miss Bennet deserved better.

His sister and aunt welcomed him home with every fond effusion a doting brother and nephew could wish. In a private conference before dinner, he revealed the crimes of Mr Watts and assured them that the family's finances were sound despite these depredations and would soon be restored. Over dinner, he described Mr Gardiner and the Bennet sisters and his hope that his relations might meet his new acquaintances soon after they returned to town. Ellen expressed delight at the possibility of finding a friend in one or both of the ladies and Mrs Swindon, always fond of good conversation, was happy to agree to plan a dinner when Lyfford made the suggestion.

"And you, my dear, shall help me," she said to Ellen, "for it is only three or four years until your coming out, and time you began to learn how a dinner for guests is arranged."

Ellen made a face but agreed readily enough to satisfy her elders. "Brother, did Miss Bennet really calculate three years' worth of accounts in her head in less than a quarter hour, or were you having us on?"

"On my honour!" Lyfford exclaimed, laughing. "It was the most remarkable thing I have ever seen."

Lyfford set to his business immediately on his first full day in Staffordshire. It was the work of a day to determine the name and location of the nearest impartial magistrate and acquaint that good man—one Sir Malcolm—with the evidence that Mr Watts, who had vanished into the night scant days before Lyfford's return, ought to be found and arrested. Sir Malcolm took up the case with vigour, and by nightfall Lyfford had little more to occupy him than the usual business of an estate after the master has been away.

Mr Boyle was settled into a room at Lyfford and acquainted with the household there. He joined his employer on tours of the tenant farms, the flocks, the shearing barns, and the pottery-works and was introduced to those dependents of Lyfford in whose concerns he would henceforth be involved. At first, Lyfford felt himself required to remind a few of these people that his secretary's service to king and country was deserving of respect rather than scorn or repulsion for his injuries, but when one farmer spoke to Mr Boyle as though he were addled the former soldier acted before Lyfford could; he gave the fellow a haughty look and pronounced in clipped, educated accents, "Sir, I have lost my arm, not my wits." Lyfford laughed at the tenant's red face and resolved that, as his secretary was obviously capable of enforcing his own place in the estate hierarchy, he would interfere no longer unless asked.

In the increasingly common quiet moments of those long summer days, his thoughts turned with surprising frequency to Jane Bennet. Lyfford knew himself to be dazzled by her beauty, and easily acknowledged that he found her company pleasant. He had not been gone from London a week, however, before he was forced to admit to himself that he missed her with a painful intensity. Although he would never be foolish enough to refuse a glimpse of her person, he found that what he most longed for were her gentle presence and intelligent conversation.

With every day that passed and each piece of information uncovered by the canny Sir Malcolm, it seemed less and less likely that anything of his losses might be recovered. It was not, as he had assured his aunt and his sister, a tragedy, or even much more than an inconvenience, but it was mightily frustrating. His family had been robbed by someone they had not only trusted but had, in fact, paid quite well to see to their interests. It was not merely theft; it was betrayal. He wondered what Miss Bennet would have to say on the matter. No doubt, she would be able to talk him around to feeling more at ease with what could not be changed.

His aunt found him pondering these and other matters

some few days before their scheduled departure for London. She had entered his study and seated herself in the chair opposite before she, with a delicate clearing of the throat, managed to catch his attention.

"I beg your pardon," Lyfford said, startled. "I was quite a thousand miles away."

She waved a hand. "I am not offended. You have had much on your mind of late. But I have recently come to suspect that your increased responsibilities and this awful situation with your former steward are perhaps not the only issues which occupy you. If there is anything you would like to discuss, I hope you know that you may rely upon my discretion...and my affection for you."

He smiled and came around the desk, availing himself of the other chair there and taking her hand in both of his. "Dear Aunt," he said. "You know me too well. I have indeed been preoccupied with another matter and would very much like to tell you everything and hear your thoughts. Let me ring for tea, as this may take some time."

In Gracechurch Street, the Bennet sisters continued to tend to their aunt and the household. Mrs Gardiner's recovery proceeded with painful slowness and many setbacks. Sick-room fare of toast, porridge, and watered broth was often all she could manage, and not as much of even those as any of them would wish. She had ceased to lose weight, however, and the bouts of active sickness came farther apart. She began rising from her bed to walk a little about her chambers, and the clarity of her mind had entirely returned.

While the sisters enjoyed the company of their uncle and

aunt as much as ever and delighted in the open, if occasionally sticky, affection of their cousins, a restlessness had settled
in each of them. Elizabeth spent as much time as possible out
of doors, though it was not half as much as she would have
preferred, in the parks with her cousins. She found her
thoughts often turning to her time in Kent; that had been the
last place, she thought wryly, that she had felt entirely herself.
Her confidence had been shaken by the revelation of Mr
Darcy's affections and Mr Wickham's perfidy, and shortly
thereafter her beloved aunt had begun to suffer so dreadfully
from her expectancy. On the subject of the gentlemen, she
considered herself to have been blind, partial, prejudiced, and
absurd, and had not even the comforts of home to soothe her.
Had it not been for the great confidence and dependence
placed upon her and Jane by their relations, Elizabeth would
have been in danger of feeling very sorry for herself, indeed.

Jane, though equally pleased to be of help to her aunt and
uncle, also did not feel as contented as she ought; she went
through the motions of her days with a serene smile and a
faint, persistent ache of loss. When she heard the knocker at
the front door, her pulse leapt before she remembered that it
would not be the visitor to whom she had grown accustomed.
When her aunt at last felt recovered enough to descend the
stairs and take dinner with the family, Jane wished she might
relay that good news to one who would certainly rejoice in it.

She found herself staring out the parlour window of an
evening, her stitchery quite forgotten in her lap, wondering
whether Lord Lyfford's steward had been apprehended and
hoping that what he had stolen might be restored. Scraping
butter across her toast of a morning, she tried to picture a
breakfast room in an unknown house to the north, where her
friend might be doing the same. With such thoughts and
fancies passing so often through her mind, it was not long

before Jane realised that her heart was not nearly so safe as she had supposed.

Having lived one and twenty years without any man touching her heart before Mr Bingley, she had made the mistake of assuming that only a man very like him could. Both were amiable, to be sure, but Mr Bingley was extremely sociable while Lord Lyfford was more quietly affable. Mr Bingley was the more handsome of the two, but with the clarity of distance Jane understood that his blue-eyed fairness was too much a mirror of her own for a lifetime's viewing. Lord Lyfford's dark hair and regular features were by no means unpleasing, and his green eyes were quite arresting.

But the most telling difference was in how they behaved towards her—Mr Bingley had put her upon a pedestal, calling her an angel and showering her with compliments which had quite turned her head. Lord Lyfford, however, had treated her as an intellectual equal, which no man outside her family circle had done before, and his rare compliments had all been in reference to her mind or her character. He had not once mentioned her appearance.

Comforted by the fact that he was not another Mr Bingley and having got through their early acquaintance without a single fluttering in the region of her heart, she had thought herself quite immune. She had not understood that attraction might creep stealthily into a perfectly comfortable friendship and overturn everything.

Her solace in the midst of this distress was the knowledge, lately learned, that attraction did not necessarily become, or remain, love. She had been attracted to her former suitor, but what she had taken for love had been crushed beneath the weight of his abandonment. She was attracted to Lord Lyfford, she could not deny it. Yet he was still a peer, and she was still the near-dowerless daughter of a country squire, and nothing more unlikely than the friendship they already enjoyed could come of it. She must guard her heart with even greater vigour now that she knew herself to be susceptible to him.

One day, perhaps, she might meet the son of a man much like her father in consequence, or a young associate of her uncle's who could afford a wife who came to him with nothing but her charms and would not cavil at her lack of connexions. She must not make herself unhappy over a man she could not have and who, furthermore, had never raised her expectations. She would not be like Lydia, assuming that every gentleman who smiled at her must be considering marriage.

She undertook to turn away thoughts of him immediately as they occurred and was pleased with her success until one afternoon in the parlour with her sister and aunt. A note was delivered for Mrs Gardiner, who read it with a look of genteel astonishment before turning to her nieces with a grin.

"Well, my dears, Lord Lyfford asks if he might call tomorrow and bring his aunt and sister to make our acquaintance. Now there is a compliment one does not receive every day!"

Jane's heart began beating so hard and fast she could not imagine how her relations failed to hear it. She felt Elizabeth's gaze on her, but looked instead at her aunt, who spoke of her anticipation of a pleasant visit.

"Indeed, aunt," Jane murmured, and affected to be most absorbed in her stitching. She would later, in the privacy of her thoughts, blame the state of anxiety raised by Lord Lyfford's note for her reaction to the letter which was brought in with the day's post only minutes later.

A glance at the direction caused her to think it from her

aunt Philips, but upon opening it she soon recalled that another relative wrote with a very similar hand.

> *Jane,*
>
> *You must come home and convince Mama and Papa to let me out of the nursery. They have me locked in here and I will run mad. I have not spoken to anyone but my family in weeks, much less danced, and they say I will not be out again for over a year! How would you have felt if they had sent you back upstairs after you were out for seven months? It is so unfair! They will listen to you, please come right away!*
>
> *Lydia*

She had hardly read the signature before she stood in some agitation and moved to the writing desk, hurriedly pulling out paper, pen, and ink. She did not notice her relations observing her uncharacteristic discomposure with concern as she grimly penned a reply.

> *Lydia,*
>
> *Had I been sent back to the nursery at fifteen, I would have felt relieved. I was not ready to be out at that age and neither, dear sister, are you. I regret that we all were pushed into society too early and that our parents have only now realised their mistake. Be grateful for this additional carefree time that has been granted to you. Enjoy the last year of your childhood as your sisters were not permitted to do.*
>
> *Jane*

"Foolish girl," Jane muttered fiercely as she folded the page. It was not until she had sealed it—pressing the wax with rather more force than was strictly necessary—and sat back with a frustrated sigh that her aunt delicately cleared her throat and Jane recalled that she was not alone. Her cheeks bloomed crimson as she turned to face her sister and aunt.

"Forgive me for prying, my dear Jane," Mrs Gardiner began carefully, while Elizabeth sat with her stitchery frozen before her and her jaw slightly agape. "I could not help but notice that you seem a little upset. I hope there has been no bad news from Longbourn?"

"No," she hastened to answer. "Well...not as such." She picked up Lydia's note and walked it over to Elizabeth, who quickly read it and scowled so fiercely that it only served to further alarm their aunt.

Jane sat. "There have been some...occurrences, with which we did not wish to bother you and Uncle while you were so ill, nor while you have been recovering. But perhaps now is a reasonable time to acquaint you with them?" She glanced uncertainly at her sister, who nodded resolutely.

"Yes, Jane, I do not believe it too shocking for my aunt's health at present," Elizabeth replied. "I suppose it all began while I was in Kent."

Soon they had made Mrs Gardiner aware of the pertinent events which had transpired as a result of Elizabeth's visit to Mrs Collins. Neither Mr Darcy's proposal nor the true reasons behind Mr Bingley's abandonment of Jane were canvassed; rather, they spoke of the perfidy of Mr Wickham, excepting only the identity of the 'very young heiress' who was nearly convinced to elope with him, and of the startling effects the revelation of his character had on the denizens of Longbourn. They ended by having her read the note from Lydia.

"And what have you replied?" she asked Jane.

"I said that we were all out too young and she ought to be grateful for this additional time in which to be a child."

"Now that is a truth which shall do her no harm to hear," Mrs Gardiner opined.

"Although she is unlikely to heed it," grumbled Elizabeth.

"She is your parents' concern," replied Mrs Gardiner firmly. "Just as Lydia ought to be enjoying her childhood before coming out, so the two of you ought to enjoy being young ladies before you are wives and mothers. Send the letter, Jane, and then I wish both of you to put Lydia out of your minds."

CHAPTER SEVEN

I *was mistaken*, Jane thought as their visitors were admitted to the parlour. *He is not in any way less handsome than Mr Bingley.*

Lord Lyfford entered with a lady on each arm—one, a woman in her late middle years with brown hair gone largely to grey and the same vivid green eyes as his lordship, the other a girl with auburn braids, brown eyes, and an eager expression. Mr Gardiner went forward to meet him, and the men shook hands like old friends. The pleasure of an introduction to Mrs Gardiner was requested and happily granted.

"I say, Mrs Gardiner," Lyfford said with a smile when the formalities were concluded, "I am extremely happy to meet you at last. Your family have sung your praises so long and well that if I did not know them to be honest folk, I should have disbelieved half of it!"

Mrs Gardiner was a tall, well-dressed lady approaching her thirtieth year. Though she was pale and still rather hollow-cheeked as a result of her long indisposition, it was clear that she would ordinarily be a handsome woman. His flattery brought a wash of much-needed colour to her cheeks, and she laughed and thanked him prettily, requesting that he make his companions known to them all.

Mrs Swindon and Lady Ellen were introduced around the room, and tea was brought in. The Miss Bennets served to spare their aunt the chore, and while the Gardiners and Mrs Swindon soon fell into a lively discussion of the Regent's latest lavish building project, Lyfford and his sister sat with Jane and Elizabeth.

When asked about her interests, Lady Ellen happily revealed that drawing and painting were her very favourite things, that she liked to read, but only novels and poetry, and that she was a tolerable pianist but sang like a scalded cat. Lyfford laughingly agreed with his sister's assessment of her own accomplishments.

The young lady admired some embroidery of Jane's, exclaiming over the evenness of the stitches and expressing her wish that she might one day produce something so fine. She then turned to Elizabeth and enquired as to her activities, and soon they were embroiled in a lively discussion of the modern poets while Lyfford and Jane, who were less *au courant* with the subject, were left to find their own topic of conversation.

"I hope," Jane ventured, "that the business which took you away has been resolved satisfactorily."

Lyfford looked rueful. "Not entirely. Although the magistrate turned out to be a clever and conscientious fellow, when I arrived in Staffordshire, Mr Watts had fled. It seems my recent requests for all the account books were enough to spur him into action. But he is now a wanted criminal and shall, I hope, turn up some place or another very soon."

"Oh, dear. I had so hoped all would go well for you." Jane was visibly distressed. "Have you at least been able to recover something of what he took?"

He shook his head. "It transpires that the man is a gambler—and a poor one, at that. The funds most likely vanished as soon as he stole them. But please, Miss Bennet, do not be unhappy on our account—we have not been terribly harmed, and his spree is at an end. It might have turned out a great deal worse." He smiled and changed the subject by commenting, "It must be a relief to have your aunt so much recovered."

"A great relief indeed, my lord," she answered with a fond smile at Mrs Gardiner. "From almost the day of their marriage she has been as a second mother to Lizzy and me. I am convinced that her delight in her recovery cannot be greater than ours."

Lyfford agreed that it must be so, and their conversation then veered pleasantly into memories of childhood and the escapades of their sisters and, in his case, brother. When he finally thought to check his watch, he found that their call was straining the limits of a proper visit.

"Mr Gardiner, Mrs Gardiner, as always a visit to your home brings the greatest of enjoyment," he addressed his hosts, "and I thank you for your hospitality. I hope you will allow us to return it by having you and your nieces to dine at Markham House."

When the Gardiners expressed pleasure in the invitation, plans were quickly settled for three evenings hence, and with a last flurry of thanks and good wishes, the visitors exited to their carriage. On the return journey, Ellen bubbled with excitement over the acquaintance of the Bennet ladies and her chatter was happily indulged by her elders. It was only after they entered Markham House and Ellen scampered off to apply herself to her stitchery that Mrs Swindon turned to her nephew.

"Well, my boy, your Miss Bennet and her relations seem to be everything that is intelligent and genteel. Though I should like to know them better, I suspect you have made an excellent choice."

Lyfford grinned. "I am glad you think so, Aunt, for having been in her company again I am resolved to try to win her, and find I am in no mood to delay."

"Then I had best consult with Monsieur Thibault about the menu for Thursday evening. Nothing but the best for the future Lady Lyfford," she declared with a wink.

"I hope that it may be so, Aunt."

"Well, girls," Mrs Gardiner said after the earl's carriage had rolled away and Mr Gardiner returned to his work. "Dinner at the home of an earl! And an exceedingly pleasant one, at that. I liked Mrs Swindon very well. How did you find Lady Ellen?"

"She is a delightful creature, and everything a young lady ought to be, I dare say," ventured Jane. "I should very much like to continue the acquaintance."

"And you, Lizzy? Did your satirical eye find some fault Jane has overlooked?" her aunt asked with a twinkle in her eye that lifted her nieces' hearts.

"Indeed, no!" cried Elizabeth, laughing. "I only wish we

might persuade Lord Lyfford to give her in trade for Lydia, but that would be a very bad bargain for him."

"Lizzy!" Jane remonstrated, but Mrs Gardiner laughed.

"Oh, do not look at me so, Jane," said Elizabeth impudently. "I should never say such a thing in company, but when it is only us, I think we may admit that our youngest sister is excessively silly and that we should all much prefer one like Lady Ellen."

Jane conceded the point with a tilt of her head and Mrs Gardiner took the opportunity to steer the conversation. "Now Jane, Lizzy, it occurs to me that I had several new evening dresses made just before I became ill, and by the time they all fit me again they will be out of fashion. There is one that I believe could be altered to fit my present shape, but I should like to have Tess and Daisy make the others over for you. It should be just possible to have two of them—and my own, of course—ready for our dinner engagement. What do you think?"

Both girls dutifully protested that they could not accept such a gift, though their eyes sparkled with excitement for they knew their aunt had impeccable taste and would have her way in the end. After a bit of half-hearted wrangling, the business was settled to everyone's satisfaction, and the ladies trooped up to Mrs Gardiner's dressing room to view the gowns in question and make their selections for the much-anticipated dinner.

Later that day, when Elizabeth had a chance to speak to her aunt alone, she said, "Aunt, do have the maids work on my dress last. If they should not be able to finish all three, I shall be happy to wear my old gown. But you must celebrate your returning health by looking your best, and Jane must be given every opportunity to dazzle. She will deny it, but I suspect that Lord Lyfford has a preference for her."

"I share your suspicions, my dear, for though I have seen less of him than you, I have lived in the world long enough to know that a single young gentleman of fortune does not often bring his female relations to visit tradespeople for no other reason than gratitude."

CHAPTER EIGHT

Thursday evening arrived far too soon for Jane, who felt a lifetime's composure unravelling at the seams. She hardly recognised herself in the mirror. In her shimmering spring green silk gown with its fine tracery of silver vines, she appeared, suddenly, as a wealthy woman of fashion rather than the country girl she had always been. She looked as though she belonged in an earl's home.

She was scolding herself for the thought when Elizabeth slipped into the room. "Oh, Jane!" she exclaimed breathlessly. "You have never been in better looks!"

She pasted on the serene smile that had served her so well the last twenty years or so. "Thank you, Lizzy. We may never dine at a peer's table again, so we ought to look our best for it. I must say that gown becomes you very well."

The maids had only just finished Elizabeth's gown an hour

before, so there had been some suspense earlier as to whether her old dotted muslin would be worn instead. The golden yellow lustring suited Elizabeth perfectly, and the simple, elegant cut complemented her slim frame.

Elizabeth grinned. "I should not have minded wearing my old gown, but I own I am vastly glad to have this one. I should have felt quite the country cousin next to you, my dear, without it!"

Jane glanced at the clock. "I expect we should go down now. The carriage ought to be ready soon." The sisters descended arm in arm to find their aunt and uncle ready below.

"Oh, my dear girls, how fine you look!" exclaimed their aunt, and their uncle heartily agreed.

"Can these be the same two girls I once dandled on my knees?" he wondered, coming forward to kiss their cheeks. "How the years do fly, eh?" He turned to the footman, who was opening the door for their exit. "Burns, keep a sharp eye out. You may be required to defend these beautiful ladies from lovestruck swains on their way to the carriage!"

Mr Trelawney opened the drawing room door at Markham House and dutifully intoned, "Mr and Mrs Gardiner, Miss Bennet, and Miss Elizabeth Bennet," before stepping aside for the guests. The Gardiners entered and greeted their hosts, expressing again their pleasure in the invitation. Mrs Swindon bore them off to the sideboard for a drink as the Bennet ladies gained the room.

To see Miss Bennet gowned and bejeweled in such elegance and style as he should like to offer her quite robbed

Lyfford of his ability to speak. He did not see the blush which overspread her cheeks any more than he spied the expression of delight on her sister's countenance as she witnessed it all. Ellen saved them from any awkwardness by committing a slight faux pas in speaking before her elders could.

"Oh, Miss Bennet, Miss Elizabeth, I am so glad you have come." She rushed forward and took one of their hands in each of her own but did not forget herself so far as to raise her voice. "And how lovely your gowns are. Did you get them in town?"

"Indeed, we did, Lady Ellen," Miss Elizabeth replied. "Though I cannot name the modiste. You would have to ask my aunt."

Lyfford regained his composure and stepped up beside his sister to welcome their visitors and offer refreshments. The conversation became general, and the acquaintance between the two families progressed delightfully until the bell for dinner.

"I thought we might dine informally, as the room is so large and our party so small," commented Mrs Swindon as she led them into a dining room which could comfortably seat thirty, though there were place settings at only one end of the long table. Lyfford silently blessed his aunt for removing the necessity of being seated by rank, and deftly manoeuvred himself into a pleasing arrangement by offering Miss Bennet a seat and promptly claiming the one next to it.

Conversation flowed easily, for no one present lacked wit or amiability. When it ranged into realms beyond Ellen's ken, Miss Bennet kindly engaged her in a quiet side conversation on stitchery and the best places in London to purchase silk thread and well-made needles. Observing this, Lyfford felt again all the rightness of his inclination to make them sisters.

When the ladies retired to the drawing room after dinner, Lyfford offered tobacco and port to Mr Gardiner, who declined the former and accepted the latter. "I rarely partake in tobacco myself," Lyfford commented as he poured them each a glass.

"I was quite fond of it before I married, but Madeline does not care for the odour, so I seldom indulge any longer." He accepted the glass Lyfford handed to him but waited until his host was seated before taking a sip. "Ah, this is a fine vintage, my lord."

"I am pleased you enjoy it. It was my father's favourite and one of mine, as well."

Mr Gardiner tilted his glass in a small salute to the departed, and they enjoyed their port in silence for a moment.

Lyfford set his glass down on the side table and gazed seriously at the other man. "Are you authorised to act on Mr Bennet's behalf while your nieces reside with you, sir?"

"I am," Mr Gardiner replied with a curious expression.

"If Miss Jane Bennet is agreeable, I should like to call upon her. And then, if we suit as well as I suspect we shall, I intend to make her an offer of marriage."

Mr Gardiner sat back. "I confess to some surprise, Lord Lyfford. Jane is everything gracious and good, but she is not of your circles."

"She is not, but I think she would do very well there. She is, as you say, all that is gracious and good, and she is also intelligent and capable."

Mr Gardiner nodded but pressed his point. "She has no dowry to speak of, and connexions only to minor gentry and trade. Many would look down upon her."

"As to dowry, I have no concerns." Lyfford sipped his port. "I am not unaware of the difficulties we would face in society, sir. I have considered the matter carefully and have discussed it with my aunt, who is as sensible a lady as could be found anywhere. The very highest sticklers will initially shun her and think me a fool, there can be no debate on that point. But most of society, I think, will not. Some may snicker at my choice, but I think few would cut us. Most of those I would call true friends are untitled, gentlemen who ought not sneer at a gentleman's daughter. My family is old and respected and those who benefit, or desire to, by a connexion with the Markham name or Lyfford earldom will be required to respect my wife or lose my notice."

Mr Gardiner looked thoughtful, and Lyfford continued, "You may be concerned that I would wish to separate her from her family, to guard my standing by allowing her origins to be quickly forgot. I can only assure you that I would not, even if the reaction of society were much worse than I antici-pate. I would be unworthy of Miss Bennet if I could disregard her love for her family, not to mention the respect I ought and do feel for you, sir, in light of all the assistance you have so generously rendered to me."

Mr Gardiner allowed himself a small smile at this reassur-ance. "And your family, my lord? Will they approve?"

"I believe so," Lyfford answered comfortably. "The only difficulty might be my sister Julia. Her husband is ambitious, and she is very conscious of the benefit of our family's standing to his prospects in the Church. But I shall know how to handle Julia, should it come to that." He leaned forward, elbows on his knees and hands clasped before him. "And only think, sir, how as my wife, Miss Bennet would have the scope to truly exercise all of her many abilities. Two households to manage, with the attendant concerns of tenants and servants, as well as the duties of both a political and a social hostess. What better outlets for her natural intelligence, kindness, and graciousness?"

Mr Gardiner smiled. "You have convinced me, Lord Lyfford. If Jane allows you to call upon her, I shall not oppose it."

Lyfford smiled with relief. "Please, sir, call me Lyfford. It is my hope that we shall be related before many months have passed."

"With pleasure, Lyfford, and do call me Gardiner." He looked shrewdly at Lyfford. "If you are anything like I was in the days of my courtship with Mrs Gardiner, you are now wishing I would quickly dispose of this fine port, that we might re-join the ladies."

Lyfford had indeed been wishing just that, but he said, "I would by no means rush you. Enjoy your drink. I dare say I shall manage to contain my eagerness."

"Hm." Mr Gardiner tossed back the rest of his port in one tip of the glass. "Excellent stuff. I shall savour it next time."

Lyfford laughed and similarly drained his own glass. "I shall bring you a bottle when next I call, sir."

CHAPTER NINE

Upon their arrival in Gracechurch Street, Mrs Gardiner immediately retired. Mr Gardiner paused only to tell his nieces how proud he was of their ability to please in any society before he followed his wife, anxious for her comfort. Jane and Lizzy repaired to Jane's room to share their impressions of the evening.

"Oh, Jane," Elizabeth said with a wide smile once the maid was dismissed and the door shut. "Surely you can no longer deny that Lord Lyfford admires you? He was most attentive."

"Lizzy, please...leave this subject. I like him so very well that I cannot—I will not—allow myself to hope unless he speaks." She sighed and began to pull the pins from her hair. Her sister, contrite, rushed to assist.

"I am sorry, my dear. I do not mean to tease. Of course you must protect your heart. I shall say no more about it."

Privately, Elizabeth thought the man was a great fool if he did not speak, but Mr Bingley had been just such a fool and reason forced her to concede that nothing was certain. When the last of the pins were out, she began to tenderly massage her sister's head. "Lady Ellen is very sweet, and I was glad to see her again."

"Oh, yes," Jane answered with an eagerness borne equally from the sincerity of her agreement and her delight in having the subject changed. "And she is so charmingly excited to have friends who are not still in the schoolroom. I look forward to calling on her and Mrs Swindon soon. I dare say we shall not have many more opportunities to visit with her before she leaves for the school term."

"I expect we shall also hear of her from time to time through my aunt, who seems to be forming a firm friendship with Mrs Swindon."

Jane brightened a bit at that. "And perhaps we might all meet again when next we visit my aunt and uncle."

Though she had enjoyed the outing immensely, Mrs Gardiner declared herself exhausted by the unaccustomed exertion. She and her nieces therefore spent the next day quietly at home. On Saturday, they did themselves the honour of calling at Markham House, where they were greeted with pleasure by the ladies in residence.

Lady Ellen was encouraged to act as hostess and served the tea creditably for one so young. The door opened just as she was pouring herself a cup, and she smiled to see her brother there.

"I hope I am not intruding?" he asked, and was unanimously reassured that it could not be so. He accepted a cup of tea and listened contentedly as the ladies resumed their conversation.

After a few moments listening in, he asked, "Should you like a tour of the rose garden, Miss Bennet? It is at its best just now."

"I should like that very much, my lord, if it is no trouble."

"None at all," he claimed, and turned to the others. "Shall we make a party of it?"

Just as he had hoped, Mrs Gardiner declined and Miss Elizabeth said she had rather stay with her aunt, while his own aunt offered that she too would prefer to remain inside on such a warm day. Ellen echoed Mrs Swindon.

"Do go, Jane," Mrs Gardiner urged when her eldest niece seemed as though she were about to change her mind. "It shall be entirely proper, for you will be visible from the house and the street. I know how you love flowers. Do not let this opportunity pass."

Jane agreed and departed the parlour on Lord Lyfford's arm. Downstairs, she donned her bonnet and gloves and accepted her parasol from a maid. She glanced shyly up at Lyfford, who offered his arm and escorted her out and down the stairs towards the rose garden. There they met with Mr Farley, the gardener hired by the late Lady Lyfford, who was removing the browned remains of the early blossoms and inspecting the bushes for any signs of aphids or disease. He happily escorted his master and the young lady through the garden, describing the different varieties present and pointing out the expansion installed by Lord Lyfford's grandmother, the dowager Countess Lyfford.

"These," he declared, turning a corner to arrive before a cluster of three tall, dense rosebushes twined about a sturdy trellis at a dead end in the path, "are the jewel of this garden." He paused while they admired the large coral blossoms which appeared in great profusion and spilled their sweet, rich scent into the late summer air.

"They are lovely," Miss Bennet said, "and so fragrant!"

"They not very useful for arrangements," Mr Farley admitted, "for their stems are quite short and their scent will overpower any other flowers. But they are wonderful here in their natural state, and you will never find a finer rosewater or rose oil than that made from this variety. Indeed, you are fortunate to have come now, Miss Bennet, for most of the open blooms will be gathered for that purpose the day after tomorrow."

"Very fortunate indeed," she agreed, brushing her fingertips across the petals of a particularly spectacular rose. Their tour then concluded, and the gardener returned to his duties with their thanks.

They took another turn about the gardens and walked even more slowly on their return, pausing often to examine this bloom or that. When they had nearly completed their second tour, drawing abreast of a long row of pretty but rather common red roses, Lord Lyfford began the conversation he knew he must have before the one he hoped to have.

"Miss Bennet," he said, "I must make a confession to you, and I fear you shall be very angry with me."

"I cannot imagine how it could be so," she answered with some surprise.

He smiled ruefully. "When I visited you just before my trip to Lyfford Hall, I overheard part of a conversation which was not meant for my ears...on the subject of Mr Bingley. I ought not to have listened. It was ungentlemanly, and I am very sorry."

Jane looked at him as a blush overspread her cheeks, for she knew very well to which conversation he referred. His contrite expression dampened the resentment which rose in her, however, and she took a deep breath before answering.

"It was very gentlemanly of you to admit it, though, for if you had not, I should never have known, and you would not have risked my censure. I wonder why you did," she concluded with a curious glance.

"Simply this—I do not wish for there to be any form of deceit between us." He placed his free hand lightly over the one of hers which was on his arm. "I could not account for my own actions at first. I am not the sort of man who listens at doors. But I soon came to understand that my uncharacteristic behaviour could be attributed to only one thing: a deep and personal interest in the state of your heart."

He stopped walking at that moment, which was fortunate, as Jane suddenly felt herself rooted to the spot. "Miss Bennet," he continued, turning to face her, "you said then that you do not love Mr Bingley. I would very much like to know if you think you might be able to love me. Formal courtships are out of fashion, of course, but as I do not wish for anyone to mistake or doubt my intentions, I spoke with your uncle the other night and have his permission to call upon you if you find the notion agreeable."

She looked into his eyes, finally allowing herself to see all the steady affection she had heretofore denied, and in that instant her guarded heart cracked open and joy flooded in.

"Oh, that does sound agreeable, my lord," she said with a sincerity that could not but reassure and delight an anxious suitor. "It sounds very agreeable indeed."

He smiled at her then such a smile as she had never received, not even from the man who had been so in love with her as to write her a rather bad poem when she was just fifteen. "You have made me very happy, Miss Bennet," he said, lifting her hand from his arm and placing a kiss on the skin of her wrist just above the cuff of her lace summer gloves. She bit her lip to prevent a gasp from escaping, for the action sent a sensation through her which was somehow warm and shivery all at once. "I hope that I shall make you happy, too," he concluded, placing her hand back where it had been and covering it again with his own.

"I dare say you already have, sir," she admitted shyly, and they turned their steps slowly back towards the house. "I can hardly account, though," she said in a rush after a silent moment, "for your wish to call upon me. I have neither fortune nor connexions."

"So your uncle has informed me," he answered comfortably, "though I had already apprehended as much. My income is perfectly sufficient for us both, as well as my aunt and sister...and your mother and sisters, should it come to that. I have connexions of my own, and do not require more. If we marry, I shall repine only the slights you would doubtless endure as a result of the disparity in our situations, for though you are a gentlewoman, we cannot be said to come from the same sphere." He paused, and added reluctantly, "Indeed, that is something you ought to consider—a union between us would, in some ways, cause more difficulties for you than for me."

"You might think so, but you have yet to meet my youngest sister," she said, so soberly that it was a moment before he comprehended the joke and laughed. She laughed along with him, though privately she resolved to, at some later time, do as he suggested and consider the likely pitfalls awaiting her in society.

Today, however, was for happiness—a happiness which could not be concealed from their relations. When they regained the parlour, none there could fail to note the increased ease between them, or the smiling way in which they regarded each other. They would each be quizzed thoroughly after the ending of the call, and their own delight was only magnified when shared with those they loved the most.

CHAPTER TEN

Summer was reluctant to loosen her grip on the south of England that year. One morning, as Elizabeth and Jane awaited Lord Lyfford's call, they read their letters. Elizabeth chuckled over some witticism in the opening lines of a letter from Charlotte, and Jane opened one from Mary.

Jane,

Please forgive the lateness of my reply, but life at Long-bourn has been rather unsettled.

I do not know what you wrote to Lydia, but when she read it, she screamed and flung it into the fireplace. This was rather a futile gesture, as the day was warm and the fire not lit. Kitty laughed and Lydia shoved her so hard that poor Kitty went over backward in her chair and hit her head. Mama marched Lydia up to the nursery while Hill and I took Kitty to her room for a rest.

When I came back down, Mama and Papa were both in the parlour. Mama was crying and Papa was folding up a page that I believe was your letter and looking very grim. Papa enquired after Kitty, and I was able to report that she had a headache but was otherwise unharmed. Mama then asked me the strangest thing—she wanted to know if I felt that I had come out too young. I said I thought I had, and she began to weep again. Papa put an arm about her and led her to the sofa and said that I ought to go, and he would tend to my mother.

Kitty had a tray in her room that night, for her head still ached, and after dinner I went up to keep her company and read her some of the romantic poetry of which she is so fond. I must admit that some of it is rather nice, really, although if I ever feel as though my heart has taken wing, I shall suspect apoplexy before love.

Papa came in later and asked Kitty if she felt well enough for a little conversation. When she said that she did, he apologised to both of us for permitting us to be brought out at fifteen, and said he now wished he had allowed us a full span of childhood instead. He then said that we should no longer be obliged to attend every assembly and dinner party, though for the credit of our family we must not offend our neighbours with constant refusals, and that Mama has agreed to this.

Kitty begs to be allowed to relate what has happened since —she says she will tell it better than I—so I shall now close and hope that you and our London relations are all well and happy.

Mary

"Oh, I ought not to have written in anger!" Jane exclaimed

tearfully, handing Mary's letter to her startled sister. "Only look what has happened! Poor Kitty! And poor Mama and Papa—I had no idea of their ever reading it, Lizzy."

Elizabeth draped a comforting arm about Jane's shoulders as she read. When she was finished, she set the letter down and waited until Jane ceased dabbing at her eyes.

"Jane," she said seriously, "we were all out too young. Our parents were in error, and for my part I do not think it wrong that they should feel it. No real harm has been done—Kitty only had a headache, and in return she and Mary have received an apology that was long overdue and a concession that Mary, at least, shall enjoy."

"It can do no good for them to feel badly over decisions which cannot be changed," Jane said, twisting the handkerchief. "The four of us are too old to be sent back to the nursery as Lydia has been."

"It can do a great deal of good," Elizabeth insisted. "A consciousness of their mistakes with us may make them even more careful with Lydia, who I continue to hope is not yet entirely beyond the reach of amendment."

Jane considered this carefully, and finally nodded. Elizabeth patted her hand. "Now, Jane, what has Kitty to say?"

"Oh, goodness, I have not even opened it." She retrieved the letter and unfolded it, holding it so that they might read together.

> *Jane,*
>
> *If you have not yet read Mary's letter, which ought to have arrived with this one, please put this down immediately and read hers first.*
>
> *Since the events which Mary related, we have gathered from Lydia that she wrote to you requesting some relief of her present situation, and that whatever your answer was, it*

marks you as the most wretched, selfish, and stupid sister who ever lived. (I do not think she grasps the irony of that statement, do you?)

This and many other things were said—or rather, yelled— by her in the days following her outburst in the parlour. And then it stopped. One morning she came down for breakfast and proceeded to behave with perfect propriety and good cheer all day. This continued for nearly a week, and poor Mama was so very happy, for she became convinced that her dear Lydia had finally learnt her lesson. You may apprehend that Mary and Papa and I were rather less sanguine about this sudden reversal.

Our suspicions were confirmed last night, when she tried to run away again and blackened poor Josie's eye in the attempt. Papa gave Josie a crown for her trouble, and fortunately for our family, she seems well satisfied with the bargain. I doubt he would easily find another strong girl to watch our sister at night.

Mama was made very unhappy by these events and wept until she gave herself a megrim. She went to her rooms to rest for a while, and then she came down and said, 'Mr Bennet, I think it is time you sought a school for our youngest.' He said, 'I believe you are right, Mrs Bennet,' and it was settled quick as anything.

So, Lydia is to be sent away just as soon as Papa can find a place she cannot escape from and that will not reduce us to poverty. What do you think of that?

Jane, you will no doubt recall that I was used to follow Lydia in everything. I now look upon my previous behaviour with abhorrence. I wish to apologise for all the times I laughed at you and Lizzy when you tried to teach me better. I ought to have listened. I am very sorry, and I promise to be a much better sister when we are all together again. Please tell Lizzy.

Your remorseful sister,

Kitty

P.S. Papa asks me to add that you and Lizzy are not to think of coming home now, for our aunt needs you, but that if you happen to hear of a school which might be equipped to reform Lydia, he would be interested to know the fees.

Mary and I agree that our pin-money could be forsaken to no better cause, should they be steep.

"Well," Elizabeth said after a moment, "that is a turn I did not expect."

"I am very proud of our mother," Jane said quietly.

"I am astonished by her, but I spoke of Kitty's apology. I think we may hereafter boast of having only one very silly sister."

One morning, as Lyfford and Mr Boyle worked their way through his correspondence, Trelawney entered and handed him a calling card. He glanced at it and told his butler to show his guest to the parlour and order some coffee, and he would be there shortly. After making a few quick decisions on invitations, he left his secretary to pen his replies and went quickly upstairs.

"Darcy! I did not even know you were in town!" he exclaimed with pleasure upon entering, crossing the room to his old friend and shaking his hand. He was pleased to see that Darcy was not so dreadfully grim as he had been in the early summer when Lyfford visited Pemberley. Solemn he was, solemn he had been even in the earliest years of their shared youth, and solemn he likely would always be, but at their last meeting he had felt Darcy was actively troubled, though the man flatly denied it when asked.

Darcy nodded and returned the greeting. "I only arrived two days ago, and as I passed on business yesterday, I saw that your knocker was up, so I thought to call in person instead of sending a note." Just then a maid arrived with the coffee service, and the men busied themselves with preparing their cups.

"How have you been, Darcy?"

"Tolerably well," Darcy replied with a note of irony that struck Lyfford as slightly odd, but he continued with a change of subject. "I heard some tittle-tattle at my club last night that you had set the law on a thieving steward."

"Indeed, I have. Watts was doing us out of nearly fifteen hundred pounds a year, and I found I could not allow him to go forth and perhaps do the same to someone less able to absorb the loss."

"I hope you know what you are about, exposing your business to the gossips in such a manner. When it was mentioned to me, I pointed out that the man was your father's steward, and you had discovered and ended the problem shortly after your inheritance. That will make the rounds, too, I hope, but there are always some who take any opportunity to speak with mockery."

"I thank you for that. As for the gossips..." Lyfford shrugged. "Let them talk. Something far more titillating shall no doubt occur soon, and Mr Watts shall be forgot. I have already hired his replacement and were he only to be captured, I should soon forget him myself. I now have more pleasant matters to dwell upon."

"Oh?" Darcy said, raising an eyebrow.

"I have met the lady I hope to make my wife. I hope to have very happy news soon, for she is everything I have ever wished for and more, and I believe she holds me in some affection."

"My congratulations, then. Who is the lucky lady?"

Lyfford looked thoughtful. "I recollect that you have some slight acquaintance with her, actually. She is Miss Jane Bennet of Longbourn, in Hertfordshire."

Darcy choked on his coffee.

Lyfford smirked. "Indeed, I believe I have you to thank for her single state. Your interference in her relationship with Charles Bingley was badly done, old friend, and yet I cannot find it within myself to censure you too harshly—it has been very much to my benefit, after all. But I shall take this opportunity to warn you against trying such a thing with me."

"How do you know all of this?" Darcy asked, bewildered.

"An overheard conversation between Miss Bennet and her sister, and later conversations of my own with Miss Bennet."

There was silence for a long moment, and then a question from Darcy which sounded as though it were being dragged from him under torture. "Which sister?"

"Miss Elizabeth." Lyfford watched curiously as his friend's countenance paled. Darcy seemed frozen for a time, then with a groan he slowly bent, folding his arms across the table before him in a most inelegant pose and lowering his head to the wooden surface, against which he proceeded to softly knock his forehead several times.

Lyfford waited for a moment before commenting, "I sense that there is part of the story of which I am yet ignorant."

Darcy slowly sat up and resumed a more dignified posture. He fixed Lyfford with an assessing gaze for a long moment and then, with the air of a man unburdening himself of a terrible weight, he gave Lyfford to understand the whole of his strange history with Jane's beloved sister. From a careless insult at a country assembly to a proposal scorned, he entrusted the other man with the secrets he had carried since April.

"Miss Elizabeth Bennet, eh?" Lyfford's astonishment was patent. "Well, she certainly does not approve of your work to separate her sister from your friend, but from what little I heard I did not get the sense that she hates you, either."

"Until she corrected me—no, until I was reasonable enough to give credence to her correction—I did not know myself. And I am heartily ashamed of the man I have become."

Lyfford blinked in surprise and felt himself unequal to comforting his generally stoic friend, but gamely made the attempt. "Darcy, you are one of the best men I know. Your manners are occasionally lacking," he admitted, "but in essentials you are a fine and worthy gentleman."

"A fine and worthy gentleman," replied Darcy with bitter derision, "cultivates his manners so as to make those around him comfortable. He does not stand against the wall at an assembly where ladies go in want of a partner. He does not assume that anyone lower than he in consequence is also lower in worth. He does not arrogantly meddle in affairs which are not his own. And he most certainly does not display such overweening vanity and pride as to convince the finest lady he has ever known that he is the last man in the world she could ever be prevailed upon to marry!" His fierce expression collapsed into despondency.

Lyfford moved to the sideboard and poured a finger of brandy, setting the glass in front of Darcy before resuming his seat. "I confess, I am surprised. Though I could envision you setting aside considerations of fortune for love, I would not have thought you would discard those of class as well."

"I would not have, for any other lady," Darcy admitted. "Elizabeth Bennet is the most excellent woman of my acquaintance. She is kind and clever, well read and able to slyly tease without malice as none other. The tender attention she gave to her sister's care at Netherfield while neatly countering the withering comments of Miss Bingley...she is remarkable. Love was my only consideration." He gave Lyfford a curious look across the table. "I would have thought you, too, would adhere to social expectations, yet you are doing as much and more for Miss Bennet."

"Well, as I think you have learnt, when you meet an extraordinary woman, you may be required to sacrifice something to win her. If she were Mr Gardiner's daughter rather than Mr Bennet's, I would still pursue her, and society be damned."

Darcy's eyebrows raised. "I will grant you that she is very beautiful, but is that really worth the sort of censure you would face if she were a tradesman's daughter?"

Lyfford sighed. "Did you ever bother to converse with Miss Bennet beyond the usual pleasantries? Or did you take one look at her pretty face and assume there was nothing behind it?"

The blush which overspread Darcy's cheeks was answer enough, and Lyfford continued. "You praise her sister's intelligence, but Miss Bennet is similarly astute. She is a great reader of histories and better informed on current events than many parliamentarians I have met. She and her sister take the newspapers daily, and if you wish to have a serious discussion on the Peninsular campaign, or the Corn Laws, or the state of the workhouses, I suggest you take yourself to Gracechurch Street rather than White's. She has an incredible facility with numbers and can reconcile several years of accounts in her head. And in addition to all of that, she is gracious and kind, and yes, beautiful."

"Has she any flaws at all?"

Lyfford narrowed his eyes at his old friend. "I know you well enough to apprehend that you are irritated because I have made plain to you your mistake in dismissing her. But I shall answer you nonetheless—yes, she does have flaws. She wants so very much to believe the best of everyone that she will ignore their failings and foibles until they harm her or her loved ones...and even then, she may try to explain them away. Sarcasm and spite generally escape her, for she takes the words of others as given and does not seem to catch their tone or intent as you or I might. Her mind is of a very literal bent, which is why she cares little for novels and for poetry not at all. She has, I think, something of a horror of chaos and disorder which she hides behind a mask of serenity."

He took in Darcy's stunned expression and concluded, "I have not wasted my time whispering compliments in her ear. I have made it my business to know the woman I hope to marry."

They sat in silence for a moment before Darcy grudgingly offered, "Then you have employed your time much better than I have done, and now reap the rewards."

Lyfford sat back and sipped his coffee, eying his old friend as his clever mind assembled the pieces before him—Darcy's surprising tale, his intense reaction to the mere mention of Miss Elizabeth Bennet, and his clear despondency over her rejection even these many months after the event. When he was satisfied that he was not greatly in error to suppose that the gentleman still held the lady in much esteem, he spoke.

"The Miss Bennets are acquaintances of yours, and now that you are aware of their presence in town, the polite thing to do would be to call upon them. You may join me one of these days—in my carriage if you fear to have your own seen in Cheapside," he concluded with a teasing smirk.

Darcy appeared by turns startled, hopeful, then resigned. He shook his head. "I doubt that I would be welcomed there."

"Knowing them as I now do, I feel confident that you would be received cordially. As to whether or not you would find yourself welcome, well...that is information I should wish to have, in your position." He smiled and stood, clapping Darcy on the shoulder. "Come, do not overthink this. Let us go there directly, for Miss Bennet expects me at some time or other, and I shall be your support as you attempt to repair relations with Miss Elizabeth."

CHAPTER ELEVEN

Darcy soon found himself borne away towards Cheapside against all his better judgment. They stopped for luncheon at White's on the way, so as not to impose on the Gardiners for the meal. During the second leg of the journey, he was largely silent as he girded himself for the encounters to come, while Lyfford eyed him speculatively but left him in peace.

If he had thought his lessons in humility began and ended with Miss Elizabeth Bennet's harsh rejection of his proposal, he was proved wrong that day. The Gardiner home was a model of elegance and good taste both within and without, far from the gilded ostentation he would have expected in a wealthy tradesman's dwelling. Mrs Gardiner's dress and manner were the equal of any he had met with in the Countess of Matlock's parlour, and superior to some. She was alone when they first entered but greeted them in all civility and pleasantly brushed off Lyfford's apologies for bringing an additional guest with no advance notice. She then sent for her nieces, who soon arrived.

As they greeted one another, Darcy examined Miss Bennet closely for any symptom of resentment and found none, save that her politeness towards him was perhaps a touch cool. Her reception of Lyfford was everything proper, and the smiles she directed at him were neither ingratiating nor too delighted. But it was all there in her eyes, Darcy soon realised, for they fairly glowed when her gaze lit upon her suitor, and he was honest enough to acknowledge there had been something of that in the way she had looked at Bingley almost a year ago.

Then his reprieve was over. He turned to the younger Bennet sister and bowed. "Miss Elizabeth, it is a very great pleasure to see you again." He felt his face grow warm and noted the blush on her cheeks as she curtseyed.

"I thank you, Mr Darcy. Have you been in town long?" They made stilted conversation for a few moments before the tea tray arrived, when they thankfully settled into their chairs and soothed their agitated sensibilities with the familiar rituals of tea service.

Another caller arrived only a few minutes after them. Mrs Burgess was known to all present save for Darcy, for she was an intimate of Mrs Gardiner's. A witty, rather cynical lady of some forty years, Mrs Burgess's accents were less educated than her friend's but, as Darcy soon discovered, her mind was not.

The topic of the afternoon was the recent news of a slave rebellion in the West Indies, in which several British plantation owners had been killed. Darcy had merely skimmed the stories in his morning papers, finding the subject distasteful. Lyfford deplored the example set by Britain's use of slaves in its colonies when the practice had long been outlawed in the homeland, and he received a sharp, though not unkind, retort from Mrs Burgess that the empire's failure of morality and humanity was far worse than mere hypocrisy.

Miss Bennet ventured that never, to her knowledge, had any system of indenture ended save by its victims making the practice too costly to its perpetrators, citing several historical examples. Miss Elizabeth then wondered aloud how many more lives, both citizen and slave, must be lost before the government would ban slavery from all its holdings, and if there was any way in which the common people might agitate for swift action on the subject. From there the conversation ranged broadly across the origins of the slave trade: Britain's culpability in bringing it to the newly independent American colonies, where it now flourished; the potential economic effects of an abrupt end to the practice, both in Britain and America; and the morality of consuming the fruits of slavery, such as sugar and cotton.

These were not ladies who remained deliberately ignorant of the world under the guise of feminine delicacy, nor were they subject to men who would keep them so ignorant on those grounds. They were intelligent, quick-witted women who gloried in the exercise of those talents, and Darcy began to wish that he had not so diligently protected his sister from distressing truths. Perhaps she would not have been so vulnerable to Wickham, had she a realistic idea of the wrongs and evils in the world.

He also, for the first time, came to understand the closeness between the sisters, for while he had a very good notion of the attractions Miss Elizabeth held for quieter, less social people, he had been unable to account for that lady's extreme attachment to her elder sister, who he had previously thought rather dull. Here, among friends and relations, and free of the stifling conventions of a small market town, Miss Jane Bennet showed herself to be the equal of her sister in intellect. Indeed, they complemented each other very well, Miss Bennet's thoughtful and resolutely factual commentary both informing and enlivened by Miss Elizabeth's more subtle and emotional way of thinking.

"Perhaps when you are in Parliament, Lord Lyfford, you might canvass the subject with your party," Mrs Burgess suggested, shocking Darcy with her boldness.

"Indeed I shall, ma'am," Lyfford answered affably. "And though I shall not be in a position to submit my own bills for a few years, if there are any in waiting, you can be certain I will support them." He clapped his hands together and looked about the group. "After such a serious discussion, I feel the need for some fresh air. Perhaps we might take a turn about the park just down the street?"

All of the young people were for the excursion, while Mrs Gardiner and Mrs Burgess declined. Parasols, bonnets, hats, and gloves were fetched, and soon the foursome was making its way down the street, exclaiming over the beauty of the day and the profusions of flowers in the front gardens of the homes they passed, when at this time of year they would usually be dying back. The gentlemen commented with satisfaction on the extended growing season and the expectation of an excellent harvest.

When they reached the park, Lyfford offered Miss Bennet his arm. Darcy did the same for Miss Elizabeth, and though they began closely grouped, the former couple quickened their steps to seize a bit of private conversation.

Mr Darcy and Elizabeth walked in awkward silence for some minutes. The park was familiar to Elizabeth, so she watched Jane and her suitor, who had a rather furtive exchange and then seemed to settle into a more relaxed conversation. Mr Darcy, for his part, looked about the small but pretty park, before he finally looked at Elizabeth and followed her gaze to the couple before them. They were laughing at some shared joke, looking into each other's eyes and quite oblivious to all else.

"Your sister seems very happy," he commented, though he knew he trod on dangerous ground with that subject.

"Yes, I do believe she is, and there can be no one more deserving," Elizabeth agreed with a smile.

"I...I expect to see Bingley while I am in town and had planned to make a confession to him and ascertain whether his interest still lay in that direction, but now I think perhaps I had better not."

"A few months ago, I would have been delighted by the notion, but no longer. I dare say it has worked out for the best. Mr Bingley was all amiability and pretty compliments, but Lord Lyfford is a man of substance—I mean that by reference to character, not wealth. I have come to believe, through observing them together, that Jane need never doubt the constancy of his affections. She has bestowed her love on a more worthy object this time."

"He is truly an excellent fellow. We have been acquainted from the cradle. He is only a year my junior, our mothers were good friends, and our estates lie not twenty miles apart. We even attended the same schools, though we drifted into different circles at Cambridge. I know him well—he will not break your sister's heart."

"I had very little worry on that score, but it is reassuring to have my impressions confirmed."

She watched as Mr Darcy took a breath and wondered whether he would dare to broach what remained uneasy between them. "Miss Elizabeth, I feel I must apologise to you, for...well, for the whole of our acquaintance, in truth. But most particularly for the conceited and insulting manner in which I declared my wishes to you last April."

She was silent for a moment, and then replied quietly, "My own manners were wanting for much of our acquaintance, and that evening in particular. In hindsight, it was hypocritical of me to censure yours."

"I cannot concede that your manners were in any way at fault. My behaviour merited the severest reproof, and yet you did not deliver one until it could hardly be avoided. That my vanity took your tolerance for affection was my mistake alone. Your behaviour towards me was better than I deserved. Indeed, I can scarcely credit your present forbearance, for I must be the last person with whom you would wish to be taking a walk."

Elizabeth was much struck by this humility and self-deprecation from him—he, who had been always so proud, so confident. There was no satisfaction in knowing herself to be the cause.

"Let us not quarrel for the greater share of blame annexed to our many misunderstandings," she said gently. "The conduct of neither, if strictly examined, will be irreproachable, but since then, we have both, I hope, improved in civility. For my part, sir, all is forgiven. The information you provided in your letter has resulted in such astonishing and beneficial changes in my family that I find myself entirely incapable of holding a grudge."

"You shared the letter with your family?" he asked, clearly shocked and dismayed.

She was quick to reassure him. "No, I have shewn it to no

one, though I did relate all its information to Jane, who is the model of discretion. Between us we agreed that the ladies of Meryton and Longbourn must be guarded from the depravity of Mr Wickham, and to that end I told my father all his history, save for the identity of the lady who was nearly convinced to elope with him. I described her as a very young heiress who is the daughter of a gentleman well known to you. It is not untrue, after all." She looked at him, hoping he would approve of her explanation.

"Entirely true, and yet perfectly obfuscatory," he agreed with an admiring glance. "And your father, did he act upon the information?"

"He was persuaded to do so in the end, and Sir William Lucas was a great help in the business as well. But surprisingly, it was my mother who emerged as the heroine of succeeding events," Elizabeth said, and then related to an astonished Mr Darcy a summary of the upheaval caused at Longbourn by the revelation of Mr Wickham's character, and the reformation which followed. She glossed over or omitted the most embarrassing details when possible, being all too well aware of the gentleman's opinion of her family and wishing to impress upon him the good which had come about as a direct result of his information.

"I still cannot account for Lydia's stubbornness in his defence, however," she concluded. "Mama, Mary, and Kitty all believed it upon the instant, probably because it came from Papa, who never gossips."

Mr Darcy shook his head. "Wickham. He causes trouble even when he is prevented from causing trouble. I dare say he had her thoroughly beguiled. He has faults enough, but a lack of charm is not among them. That, I fear, is mine to claim."

"Charm," Elizabeth sighed. "It is like a trifle filched before dinner—it gives a momentary pleasure but offers no real nourishment."

They walked on quietly for a few moments, and then Mr Darcy spoke. "I must commend your parents for their actions in service of your family and of the people of Meryton. I have lately learnt how difficult it can be to overcome the habits of many years, how blind we can be to our own failings until events conspire to open our eyes, and how tempting it is to simply retreat into that state and pretend that we have not failed at all. That Mr and Mrs Bennet have so zealously committed themselves to the betterment of their children, I can only find admirable, and I hope that Miss Lydia shall be greatly improved by it."

"She is to school," Elizabeth said quietly, "if one can be found capable of handling her rebellious spirit without cruelty, and which my father can afford. She will not heed our parents, but it is hoped that the authority of teachers and the censure other girls might direct her thoughts in more fruitful directions."

He considered for a moment. "There is a school in Warwickshire, Mrs Madsen's Academy for Young Ladies, of which I know because several friends have had sisters or cousins attend, to good effect. It is a place where a family might send an incorrigible daughter. I understand that their curriculum is one of firm discipline, abundant exercise, and real academic study as well as more traditional feminine pursuits. You might mention it to your father."

Elizabeth brightened, pleased to have Mr Darcy offer such generous advice. "I shall do so, sir, I thank you. But I have not asked—how does your sister? Is she awaiting your return at Pemberley?"

"No, she is here with me, for my business shall take at least a fortnight and she cannot resist the opportunity to scour the shops for new music sheets and pretty fans," he said indulgently, then looked down at her with a rather tentative air. "Will you allow me, or do I ask too much, to introduce my sister to your acquaintance during our stay in London?"

"I should be delighted to meet Miss Darcy," she answered in all sincerity, which raised such a smile in him as to bring a blush to her cheeks.

"I am sorry, Lizzy," Jane said later, after they had seen the gentlemen off and their aunt to her chambers for a rest, "that you were so unexpectedly faced with Mr Darcy. It would have been better had they at least sent a note round first."

Although her heart was still pounding from the unexpected encounter, Elizabeth made a dismissive gesture. "Do you know, I believe it was best this way. There was no time to become anxious, or to revisit in my mind scenes best forgot. It was, in some ways, like meeting with a stranger."

"Lord Lyfford said he had had the story of your acquaintance from Mr Darcy, and thought a great deal was left unresolved. He hoped you would use the opportunity to speak privately, but I feared you would merely have a rather uncomfortable walk. I was concerned for you. Was there any pleasure to be had in the conversation?"

Elizabeth patted her sister's hand in assurance. "Less pleasure than necessity," she prevaricated. "We each apologised for our failures in judgment and behaviour, and I thanked him for the information which has been the cause of our little family revolution. He then said that he admires our parents for their actions—can you believe it?—and has given me the name of a school which may be able to reform our Lydia. Do not let me forget to write Papa tonight. Oh, and he shall be bringing Miss Darcy to meet us some time or another."

"To meet you, I should say," Jane countered, and her sister blushed. "But naturally I shall be happy to know her as well. It was kind of him to mention the school. I only hope it, or some other, may be found within the reach of our father's purse."

"As do I. It will do Lydia good, I think, to leave our family circle and understand her own insignificance. I fear the disgrace which must await her if she does not. But perhaps," she continued, her voice taking on a teasing note, "we shall not long be quite so insignificant, if our sister becomes Lady Lyfford."

It was now Jane's turn to blush. "Oh, I do hope it might be so. Not for his title and position, but for himself. I believe I could be quite happy living over a shop if it were with him. I might even prefer that, for it is rather daunting to think of the circles in which he moves and how they might receive me." She sent a worried glance at her sister. "You do not think—?" she began, then bit her lip, shook her head, and said no more.

Elizabeth moved close to her sister and clasped her hands. "What is it, my dear?"

In a very small voice, Jane asked, "Do you think that Mr Darcy will speak against me to Lord Lyfford as he did to Mr Bingley?"

"Oh, my poor Jane," Elizabeth sighed, enfolding her sister in an embrace. "I ought never have told you about that. And no, he shall not do any such thing, I am sure of it. Mr Darcy has learnt his lesson about meddling in the affairs of his friends. Even had he not, your Lord Lyfford is fully cognisant of earlier events and would greet any such attempt with the suspicion it deserved. You need have no fears on that score."

"I love him, Lizzy. I had no notion how much I could feel

for a man until I came to know him. It is frightening to be so much in the power of another."

Elizabeth could not then help but recall the power that *she* had unknowingly wielded over another. She had long regretted the harshness of her speech to him and her misjudgment of his character, but it was in that moment that she truly came to feel remorse for the broken heart Mr Darcy must have suffered at her hands.

CHAPTER TWELVE

The following morning over the breakfast table, Mr Darcy turned to his sister. "Georgie, do you recall my mentioning the Bennets to you in my letters from Hertfordshire last autumn?"

"Oh, yes, and then you met with Miss Elizabeth Bennet in Kent this spring." Georgiana smiled. "But I do not believe you have mentioned them since."

"Well, Miss Elizabeth and her eldest sister are in town, and I called upon them only yesterday. I wonder if you might care to meet them? Miss Bennet is being courted by Lord Lyfford, so she may be our neighbour soon. I think you would like both her and Miss Elizabeth very much."

"I should be happy to meet anyone of whom you approve," she answered quietly, her innate shyness and desire to please her brother warring within her. "Will you tell me a little more about them, please?"

"They are the daughters of a country gentleman and have not the airs displayed by so many in the *ton*. Miss Bennet reminds me a little of you at times. She is often quiet and always kind. When she is comfortable, however, it becomes clear that she has a fine mind and is not afraid to think and speak on any subject. Miss Elizabeth is livelier and more gregarious, but like her sister she is both amiable and intelligent. She will sharpen her wit on anything which offers itself up as a stone, but it is done in fun and without malice. Their aunt with whom they stay, Mrs Gardiner, I have met with only once, but she seemed to me to be very like her nieces—perhaps more like Miss Elizabeth than Miss Bennet. I have yet to meet Mr Gardiner."

"Are we to call upon them?"

"If you agree, yes. I will not force the acquaintance upon you if you do not wish it."

"Oh, no, as I said, I am happy to meet them. It is only that I am nervous around strangers, as you are aware." She smiled ruefully.

"I know, dearest." He looked at her for a long moment as she sipped her tea, the morning sun glinting across the blonde braid draped over her shoulder. She had requested and received permission to put her hair up upon leaving school, but since Ramsgate she had returned to wearing it as a girl. He would keep her a child all her life if he were able, but that could not be. Her hair would be put up again, sooner than either of them would like, and she would be required to face society and all the perils of suitors and courtship. Perhaps the transition would be eased somewhat if he began now to treat her more as an adult.

"There was a time," he began slowly, marshalling his

thoughts even as he spoke them, "when I planned that Miss Elizabeth would soon become your sister." Georgiana's startled gaze flew to him, but he was looking out the window, remembering those sunny April days when his hopes ran high. "But my manners were not what they ought to have been, and my performance before her and all her family and friends in Hertfordshire gave her a disgust of me. This, I learnt in Kent, when I made her an offer which she roundly and rightly refused." He looked up to find his sister staring at him, open-mouthed.

"Brother, I cannot believe you would ever act in such a manner as to give a decent woman a disgust of you!" she exclaimed. "There must be something very lacking in her judgment!"

"If only you could have seen me then, you would be shocked by how I behaved. Lady Catherine herself could not have made a more disgraceful display of misplaced pride. Meryton is a little market town and boasts only a handful of men who might by the most generous measure be called gentlemen. The Bennets are the first family of the area, though Longbourn is not a fifth of Pemberley. I felt myself very much above my company there and did not scruple to conceal it. I assumed that any overture towards myself was made to gratify their own ambitions. It never occurred to me that some, at least, were merely being friendly to a stranger in their midst, and I rewarded their courtesy with contempt. When I made my offer to Miss Elizabeth, I disparaged her family to her face and called her connexions a degradation to my own. I thought she would be flattered to hear of the great tribulations I was willing to endure for the sake of love. Lord, what a boor I am." He shook his head.

Georgiana sat with wide eyes and a hand over her mouth

and did not speak for some moments. "I...I find I am now surprised that she is willing to speak with you at all."

He smiled ruefully. "Lyfford's courtship of her elder sister no doubt influenced her to show me more courtesy than I deserved. However, we were able to have some private conversation yesterday while walking in the park, during which I apologised to her, and she has said that all is forgiven. That she has now allowed me back into her acquaintance and is willing to meet you is proof of her generous heart."

She drew a deep breath and squared her shoulders. "Well then, Brother, I shall do my best to be her friend—but only if you shall do the same. Let her see the Fitzwilliam Darcy that I know, for I could not bear to have a friend who thinks ill of you."

"We are in accord, then, for I cannot bear to have Miss Elizabeth think ill of me, either."

Darcy had been greatly tempted to ask to be allowed to accompany Lyfford to visit the Gardiner home again, but recalling the jest his old friend had made—'if you fear to have your own carriage seen in Cheapside'—which had been less a joke, perhaps, than Lyfford knew, he determined to escort his sister there alone. Georgiana, for her part, looked more eagerly at the scenery than she customarily would, no doubt to distract herself from those formidable introductions which were soon to take place. When they ventured beyond her knowledge of the city, she asked where the Gardiners resided and heard for the first time the word 'Cheapside.' It was then explained that Mr Gardiner, uncle to the Miss Bennets by way of their mother, was in trade and lived within a mile of his warehouses. This was startling to a young lady who, in her sixteen years of life, had known naught of London but Mayfair, Bond Street, and Hyde Park, yet such was her trust in her brother that she immediately began to view her afternoon as a grand adventure and peered out her window more eagerly still.

There was nothing in the tasteful prosperity of the Gardiner home to give her unease, nor in the welcome they received there. Mrs Gardiner seemed to Georgiana little different in dress and manner than other ladies of her acquaintance, and the Miss Bennets were just as her brother had described them. She was a little intimidated by Mr Gardiner, who had been working in his study and was summoned to meet their guests, but seeing the real affection with which his wife and nieces greeted him and his own display of happy manners, she was soon able to relax enough to speak several words together in response to a question of his.

Mr Darcy was more surprised by Mr Gardiner than he had been by Mrs Gardiner; here was no uncouth, vulgar mushroom, but a man of sense and education who welcomed Darcy and his sister into his home without fawning or obsequiousness. It was the work of a very few minutes' conversation to make Darcy again feel deeply ashamed of the meanness with which he had formerly thought of these people, without having known them.

The two Bennet sisters were at pains to make Miss Darcy comfortable, for both had quickly apprehended her shyness and began to speak with her of music, knowing from a certain former acquaintance of Miss Darcy's passion for the subject. Their solicitude served them all well, and a lively debate on the merits of modern composers was soon underway.

Content to see his sister so happily engaged with the other

young ladies, Darcy bent himself to the task of pleasing his hosts. Mrs Gardiner soon mentioned her youth in Lambton, and they passed a pleasant time reminiscing over all the excellence of that area.

From her own conversation, Elizabeth spared a part of her attention to observe their gentleman guest with her aunt and uncle. When she was able to catch a glimpse of Mr Darcy, his expression was so far removed from disdain of his companions as to demonstrate that the improvement of his manners which she had recently witnessed had at least outlived that day. Never before had she seen him so little concerned with his own consequence, so unreserved, so desirous to please his company. She had expected since their final encounter at Hunsford that he should hate her for what she said then. His civility the other day had surprised her, but his demeanour now, towards people he had once referred to as a 'degradation,' struck her with all the force of a thunderbolt. She unwillingly recalled the uncomfortable thought that she had, not many months before, broken his heart.

Into that moment of confusion walked Lord Lyfford, and the genial hubbub of greetings which followed gave Elizabeth a moment to blink away the prickling in her eyes and compose her thoughts. He greeted Miss Darcy with pleasure and enquired as to her activities since last they met before claiming the right of a suitor and bearing Jane away for as private a conversation as might be had in a rather full parlour.

"I am told, Miss Darcy," said Elizabeth when the courting couple left them, "that you play the pianoforte very well."

"Oh, no, not very well," the young lady demurred, "but I

do like it above anything. I should be very happy to hear you play, Miss Elizabeth, for when my brother was in Hertfordshire, he wrote to me that he had rarely heard any performance he enjoyed more than yours."

Elizabeth laughed. "He has exaggerated most dreadfully, and if you ever do hear me play you shall be sadly disappointed, I fear. I have had all the usual instruction, of course, but I simply cannot be bothered to practise as much as I ought. Your aunt, Lady Catherine, was most severe upon me on that point."

Miss Darcy covered her mouth as she giggled. "Lady Catherine does not even play!"

"But if she had ever learnt, she would have been a true proficient!" Elizabeth declaimed. "Or so she assured us."

Such a look of mischief came across the girl's face then as to make Elizabeth lean forward in her seat, eager for the response which engendered such an expression. "But she did learn," Miss Darcy whispered. "Of course she did—who ever heard of an earl's daughter who was not instructed in music? My uncle, Lord Matlock, says that she simply has no sense of rhythm. She would play all the right notes in the correct order, but she could not turn them into music no matter how she tried. She went through twelve music masters, and not one of them could improve her!"

Elizabeth's laughter rang over the gathering, drawing the attention of everyone. She waved them away and wiped at her eyes, shaking with mirth. "Well, that puts an entirely different complexion on the business, does it not? I shall be forever grateful to you for that story." Impulsively she laid a hand over her new acquaintance's. "Dear Miss Darcy, I am so very glad to have met you."

The younger girl blushed and ducked her head, but managed to say, "And I you, Miss Elizabeth." Elizabeth sat back and steered the conversation to books, and the young ladies soon found they had very similar tastes in poetry but rather divergent preferences in novels. Miss Darcy was caught up in the recent craze for gothics, while Elizabeth preferred Fanny Burney and the like.

Reluctantly, Mr Darcy disengaged himself from his hosts rather after the time when they ought more properly to have left. He had enjoyed the conversation very much and enjoyed even more the glimpses he caught of his sister enjoying herself with Miss Elizabeth. He expressed his pleasure and gratitude to them so warmly as to raise a slight blush in Mrs Gardiner. Elizabeth delivered his sister to him and went to stand by her aunt.

Mrs Gardiner murmured something to Elizabeth, who answered with a nod. She turned to the Darcys. "We are having a special dinner on Tuesday in celebration of Elizabeth's birth. We should be delighted if you and your sister would join us. It will be only our family and Lord Lyfford's, and you, should you accept."

Mr Darcy nearly forgot to check with his sister, so clearly eager was he to acquiesce, but one look at her shining face made obvious her answer, and the engagement was confirmed with alacrity. They left then, in the company of Lord Lyfford, and Mr Gardiner returned to his work. When Elizabeth and her aunt returned to their seats, Jane remained standing, her hands clasped before her and her colour high.

"Oh, Aunt! Oh, Lizzy!" she exclaimed. "Lord Lyfford has asked if he might speak privately with me tomorrow morning, on a very particular subject."

CHAPTER THIRTEEN

As the heat of summer waned, a certain segment of society had returned to town, and with them came gossip—some of it about the Lyfford family. Lyfford tried to ignore it, preferring instead to focus on his business and his courtship, but he had soon found it necessary to accept a few invitations, largely to show society that he was not cowed by the talk of his financial losses.

That evening, however, found him out for another purpose —a ball was put on by Mrs Norton-Howell, the wife of a highly influential member of the Commons and rising leader of the Whigs. Having done his duty by the wallflowers, Lyfford had just acquired a glass of punch and begun to look about for his host when he heard a somewhat familiar and rather grating voice off to his left.

"Where is he, Charles? You said Mr Darcy would be here."

"I said he might be here," a man sighed, somewhat impatiently. "I am not his social secretary, you know."

"I am quite sure you said that he would be here," the lady retorted. "You are so absent-minded, I despair of you at times. Oh, there is Lord Lyfford! I am sure he will know where Mr Darcy is."

"Caroline, I really do not think—" the man protested, and then Lyfford was confronted by a vision of ostentation in the form of Miss Bingley, whose voice he now was able to place, too late. Her brother, looking rather embarrassed, hurried to catch up with her.

"Lord Lyfford," she cooed, showing far too many teeth. "What a great pleasure it is to see you again."

"Miss Bingley," he answered with a shallow bow. He then nodded to her brother. "Mr Bingley."

"How d'you do, Lord Lyfford?" Bingley asked amiably.

"Very well, I thank you, and you?" They made tepid conversation for a few minutes before Miss Bingley claimed that her brother had been looking for Mr Darcy, and it had occurred to her that Lord Lyfford might have seen him.

"I believe he decided not to attend," he replied.

"Oh, that is too bad," Miss Bingley remarked with feigned unconcern. "But how fortunate that we should have met with you! I hope this shall be the first of many such pleasant encounters between us this autumn."

"I am surprised that you would say so," he remarked, "for it is my understanding that you disapprove of the lady I am courting."

Miss Bingley sputtered. "I-I would never, my lord! I was not even aware you were courting anyone. There has undoubtedly been some misunderstanding."

Lyfford watched as she looked about frantically, clearly trying to guess which of the ladies she had lately disparaged might have somehow caught his eye.

Her brother's manners were more equal to the moment, and he stepped in before she could ramble further. "Allow me to wish you success in your courtship, sir, and every happiness to you and your lady thereafter."

"Thank you, Mr Bingley." He smiled and sipped his punch. "I shall be certain to convey your kind wishes to Miss Bennet."

Both Bingleys went pale and silent for a long moment. Miss Bingley eventually recovered enough to ask, in rather strangled tones, "Do you refer to Miss Jane Bennet, of Longbourn?"

"The very same."

"I was not aware you frequented Hertfordshire," she said curiously, with a faint sneer of distaste.

"I do not. We met here in town. One has a great deal of business when one inherits an estate, you know...or perhaps you would not. At any rate, some of my business was with her uncle. We became acquainted through him."

Bingley, less eager to continue the conversation than to prevent his sister from saying something unwise, recovered himself and spoke. "You are a lucky man. She is a most excellent lady and, if I may be so bold as to say it, more than equal to the position of Lady Lyfford."

Lyfford inclined his head. "That she is, indeed."

"Now, her uncle here in town, that would be Mr Gardiner, would it not?" Bingley asked.

"Yes. He buys a great deal of the wool my estate produces, but...well, I assume you have heard about my former steward?" Bingley nodded with an air of embarrassment, and Lyfford continued, "I am sure there are few in town who have not. Mr Watts had been recording incorrect totals in the books to disguise his crimes, so when I first met with Mr Gardiner, I thought he had been paying too little. He was gracious about the misunderstanding, and indeed extremely helpful in discovering the truth of the matter."

Miss Bingley, who liked hearing praise of Miss Bennet's relations in trade almost as little as she liked hearing praise of the lady herself, interjected. "And I am sure he was quick to introduce you to his pretty niece, was he not?" She moved closer and placed a hand on his arm, affecting a concern which failed to reach her flinty eyes. "I feel I must warn you, Lord Lyfford. We have known the Bennets for a year, and they are artful, scheming people. You will not have met the rest of the family, but they are dreadfully vulgar." She drew out the words with relish. "The mother is constantly plotting to make matches for the daughters, who in their turn fling themselves at any man of means who crosses their path."

Her brother was urgently whispering her name and even went so far as to tug on her arm, but Miss Bingley would not be stopped.

"Jane Bennet can be very sweet, I grant you, but you have not known her as long as I have. Her sole object is to trade her beauty for wealth. Why, she nearly got her claws into my brother when we were in the neighbourhood! That would have been terrible, but it would be even worse for you, what with her vulgar relations. I am only glad we met and I was able to warn you before it was too late to disentangle yourself."

She drew breath to continue, but Lyfford held up a hand and the gesture, combined with his outraged expression, was sufficient to quiet her.

He leaned in and lowered his voice, for he had no desire to draw the attention of others to their conversation. "Am I to understand, Miss Bingley, that my judgment of character and my understanding of the social order are being questioned by the daughter of a tradesman?" Miss Bingley blanched, but he continued relentlessly. "Your brother is very nearly a gentleman, but you—you are grasping and overambitious, and all of society knows it."

Miss Bingley paled even further and swayed as though on the verge of a faint. Her brother quickly wound his arm about hers, and she leaned on him heavily.

Lyfford turned his eyes to Bingley, who was now red faced and speechless. "Take control of your household, sir," he advised impatiently, "before your sister besmirches your family's good name." With that, he made the shallowest of bows and turned on his heel, losing himself in the mingling crowd.

The next morning Jane donned her best day dress, a fairly new muslin sprigged in blue and yellow. Her hair was done by her aunt's maid. Lizzy pressed her own opal necklace upon her sister for the occasion, and when she was fully dressed, coiffed, and bedecked, Lizzy kissed her cheek and said, "You will be very happy, Jane."

Jane smiled tremulously. "I keep imagining that he will not come or that he comes to break off his courtship."

"It cannot be so. The man is most thoroughly smitten, and anyone who has seen you together will say the same."

"I know I am probably being silly, but I shall not feel easy until the words have been spoken."

Elizabeth threaded her arm through her sister's and declared, "I dare say he shall do a creditable job of it. I rely on you to tell me all, you know, for I think I shall otherwise go through life without knowing what a proposal ought to be like!" This made Jane laugh, as intended, and they proceeded to the breakfast room in good humour. She was cajoled by her relations into taking some toast and jam with her tea, though she rather felt as if her stomach were full of bees.

Mr Gardiner retired to his study after the meal, and the ladies to the parlour. Mrs Gardiner wisely asked Jane to read to her and Elizabeth while they attended to their stitchery, and the activity proved a far better distraction than her own work basket would have been. Three quarters of an hour passed in this quiet manner, until the knocker was heard and Jane dropped the book. She only just managed to reclaim the volume and her place in it when the servant announced Lord Lyfford and showed him into the room.

Lyfford bowed to the ladies as they stood to greet him. "Mrs Gardiner, Miss Bennet, Miss Elizabeth, good morning to you all."

Mrs Gardiner curtseyed, as did her nieces. "A very good morning, I think, my lord."

"I hope it may prove so. Miss Bennet has informed you that I wished for a private word?"

"She has. Lizzy and I will leave you now. My husband has allowed that you may have ten minutes alone, but the door shall remain ajar." She smiled and beckoned her younger niece. Jane stood before the settee, the light of the morning sun spilling over her head and shoulders, looking very nearly as nervous as she felt.

He moved to stand before her, opened his mouth to speak, then smiled ruefully and shook his head. "I had a pretty little speech prepared, but I fear it is entirely forgot." He gathered her hands into his. "To meet you thus, privately, your beauty crowned in sunlight—I am robbed of all sense, all reason, even my very breath."

Jane caught her own breath at that. Her imaginings had not prepared her for his fervent words or the passion darkening his green eyes, equal parts thrilling and frightening to her sheltered soul.

"When first we met, I was drawn to you. When I began to court you, I was captivated. But now that I know you as I know my dearest friend, now that you *are* my dearest friend, my only wish and hope is to spend all the days of my life with you. My precious, brilliant Jane, will you marry me?"

She dropped her gaze to their joined hands. The sight was pleasing beyond anything she had ever known before. "Yes," she whispered. "Yes, my lord, if you truly want me."

He extracted one of his hands and tilted her chin up so that he might see her face again. He bent towards her and expressed his opinion on that score as warmly as a man in love might be expected to do.

"Can you doubt it?" he asked an endless moment later.

Quite breathless from a first kiss which had more than answered all her girlish dreams, Jane could only shake her head.

He touched his forehead to hers. "I love you, Jane Bennet."

"And I love you. So very much."

In unspoken accord they moved onto the settee, hands still joined. "I have come up with a plan which I hope you shall like," he said.

"I dare say I shall, unless it requires us to separate," she answered with a brilliant smile.

He laughed. "That is precisely what I hope to prevent. I must leave for Lyfford Hall next week. I cannot send my new steward to supervise the harvest alone. I had thought to stop at Longbourn on the way and apply for your father's blessing on our betrothal. If you were to travel with us, my aunt would be sufficient chaperone for the short journey from town, and then if one of your parents or sisters is willing to come to Staffordshire with us, you would have a chance to become familiar with your new home."

"Yes, my lord, I should very much like to go with you, if it can be arranged."

He brought her hand to his lips briefly. "Let me be Henry to you when we are private, my dear. I have longed to hear my name on your lips almost as much as I have longed for the right to call you Jane—my Jane."

She blushed and assented readily. "Oh, if only Lizzy could come, but we cannot both leave my aunt. She is near her time and rather more easily fatigued than any of us should like. How long shall we be away?"

"A month, or very nearly, between travel and the harvest. And with your permission I should like to host a dinner or two, that you might begin to meet our neighbours."

She found the idea agreeable, and they happily discussed the details of the proposed journey and visit until they were interrupted by the entrance of Mr Gardiner. They hastily let go of each other's hands, to the amusement of the older gentleman.

"I take it she has not refused you, then," he commented.

Lyfford rose and approached him, hand outstretched. "You may congratulate me, Gardiner, I am the most fortunate of men."

They shook hands warmly as Mrs Gardiner and Elizabeth appeared in the doorway. They were voluble in their approval of the engagement, welcoming Lyfford to the family with great cheer. He remained at Gracechurch Street for several hours more, departing only shortly before dinner to inform his aunt of the good news and begin writing to his family. Later that evening, Jane took up her pen to similar purpose.

Dear Mary,

I beg your indulgence and ask that you gather the family before reading to them the following pages. I ask you because you are the steadiest of us all. Make certain that Mama is seated. Be assured, this letter contains no ill news.

Jane

Dearest Mama, Papa, Mary, Kitty, and Lydia,

I hope you will all forgive me for this surprise. I have said nothing before now in case it all came to naught. Near midsummer I met a young gentleman who later began to call upon me. Today he has made me the happiest young lady in the world by asking for my hand in marriage, and I have consented, for I love him more than I can express. Were he a shopkeeper, I should have accepted him happily, but he is a gentleman and more: he is Henry Markham, the earl of Lyfford.

We shall depart with his aunt, Mrs Swindon, a respectable widowed lady, for Longbourn on Wednesday morning, and I hope you will all make him and his aunt welcome. If one of you will accompany us, we shall the next day or the one following proceed to Lyfford Hall in Staffordshire, where he shall oversee the harvest and I may become acquainted with my future home.

Papa, although I am of age, he intends to ask for your blessing and I hope you will not give him much trouble over it. He is truly the best of men and I know you shall come to love him as a son, as will my dear Mama.

Mary, Kitty, Lydia, I bring to you an elder brother well versed in the position, for he has two younger sisters and a younger brother of his own.

You cannot know with what eager anticipation I look forward to seeing you all in a few days and making my betrothed known to you.

Your most fortunate daughter and sister,

Jane

CHAPTER FOURTEEN

T he following day, Elizabeth and Jane returned Miss Darcy's call, passing a pleasant hour with their new friend. Her brother was out on business, and as there were no other callers present, they set about getting to know each other, Elizabeth and Georgiana in particular. Jane gently encouraged this, saying little of herself beyond what was necessary to answer a direct question, then smoothly deflecting attention to one of the other two.

Elizabeth was entirely delighted by her new acquaintance. Miss Darcy was a sweet girl, not deficient in understanding, well educated and well mannered, lacking only self-confidence to make her a truly exceptional young lady. To think that Mr Wickham had described her as 'very, very proud'! Had he told her no other untruths, she would have to despise him for that alone.

The butler entered three quarters of an hour after their arrival, bearing a silver tray with two cards upon it. Miss Darcy glanced at them and blanched. "I am not at home," she told the butler, who nodded and departed. She looked at her guests and blushed. "You must think me terribly rude, but there are...certain visitors who are used to call here that my brother allows me to refuse if he is not available. I know I must learn to be more comfortable in company, but there are some among my acquaintance who are, well...difficult."

Elizabeth smiled. "I understand completely, and it is your right as hostess to decide whom you do and do not wish to receive. When your brother is home, that right is his. I do not think you rude at all."

Jane agreed, and thus reassured, Miss Darcy was able to resume their conversation with a light heart. When they took their own leave, Elizabeth practically dragged Jane from the front door to the carriage and burst out laughing as soon as they were seated within and underway.

"Oh, Jane! I saw the tray on the sideboard by the door— the visitors Miss Darcy refused were Mrs Hurst and Miss Bingley!" And though Jane would later feel rather ashamed of herself, she too laughed heartily.

The amusement was shared with their aunt when they returned, and that lady enjoyed the joke, for though she had met its subjects only briefly, their treatment of her nieces was enough for her to have formed a firm opinion of their characters.

"And how did you find Darcy House?" she asked, looking at Elizabeth.

"It was lovely, Aunt, though somewhat outdated inside. It struck me that if you had been decorating a house twenty years ago it would have been very like. I assume it was their mother's design, and she has been gone these fifteen years or more."

Mrs Gardiner smiled. "No doubt the future Mrs Darcy will enjoy refurbishing it all."

Jane wondered if that task would fall to her sister but wisely remained silent, only smiling to herself as Elizabeth began to describe the exceptionally fine tea service with its design of heather and ferns.

When Lyfford called upon Jane two days after their engagement, with him came a lean and rather tanned young man in a fine blue military coat. "My dear Jane," he said, "you will never guess who appeared at my doorstep just as I was leaving. Please allow me to introduce my brother, Captain Edward Markham of the Royal Horse Guards."

"I am delighted to meet you, Miss Bennet, and I can see that my brother's description of you was not exaggerated," he said with a crisp bow.

"I am delighted to meet you, as well. Lyfford speaks of you often."

"You must only believe half of it," he declared with a sly look at his brother.

"Which half?" she wondered with a slight smile.

Captain Markham laughed. "Why, the good half, of course!"

"But he has never spoken any ill of you," Jane replied.

"Then you may believe it all," he chuckled. He was introduced to Mrs Gardiner and Elizabeth, as well as to Mrs Burgess, who was also visiting.

"I understand that you are at present training new offi-cers," Jane ventured once they were all seated with cups of tea. "How do you find it?"

Captain Markham ran a hand through his sun-streaked dark hair and shrugged rather helplessly. "Some of these boys —for boys they are, with commissions newly purchased—sit their mounts like sacks of potatoes. I ask you—why would a lad who can hardly manage a canter join the Horse Guards?"

"I have seen your company on parade, Captain, and they are very dashing," Mrs Burgess commented. "I dare say that might turn a young man's head as easily as a young lady's!"

"We shan't be so dashing with those lunkheads in our ranks!" The younger brother laughed, then sobered. "These lads and I are for the Peninsula in the new year. They have a great deal to learn these next months."

Lyfford turned to his brother, startled. "You have your orders, then?"

"I have been found able to return to active duty, and my assignment is to finish training these recruits, then accom-pany them to join the rest of the regiment on the Continent. We sail on the fourth of January, seas permitting."

Lyfford rubbed a hand across his mouth and fell silent. Jane asked the captain how he occupied himself during his free time in London. It transpired that an officer in command, such as he was, had very little time to spare with a war going on. Those scattered hours he tried to spend with his brother and his few civilian friends in town.

Elizabeth asked him his thoughts on the progress of the war since Salamanca, where he had been wounded, and soon a rapid, vigorous discussion of the subject was underway. The brothers had a brief and civil debate over the question of how much longer the conflict might last.

Some while later as the visitors were beginning to take their leave, Lyfford pulled Jane aside. "My dear, the decision is entirely yours, but I hope you will give some thought to the notion of being married before Edward ships out. I should very much like to have him there."

Jane smiled and pressed his hand. "I have no objection to the idea and require no further time to consider. Let us speak with my family when we are at Longbourn. We may set the date and arrange for the banns."

He closed his eyes and let out a soft breath of relief, then bent over her hand and placed a soft kiss on the back. "Thank you, dearest Jane. You cannot know how much that means to me."

"Oh, I rather think I do know," she said sympathetically. "I have only to imagine that Lizzy might not be at our wedding, and I find that I understand your wishes very well."

Tuesday evening found Jane and Elizabeth in the dresses they had worn to dinner at Markham House, though they did their hair more simply and eschewed jewellery. Jane had earlier presented her sister a posy of late blooms to commemorate the day, and Elizabeth pinned a little spray of lavender, vervain, and tiny white asters from it onto her bodice.

The Darcys were the first to arrive. After greeting their hosts, they approached the sisters and offered Elizabeth felicitations on the anniversary of her birth. Miss Darcy had put her hair up for the occasion, and after Elizabeth commented on how becoming the style was, she enquired if she should be coming out the following year.

"Oh, I do not know," she replied. "I think I had rather wait until I am eighteen, if my brother will allow it."

"It is better to delay a year if you are not ready," Elizabeth agreed, then cast a teasing look at Mr Darcy. "If your brother objects, you must send him to me and I shall quarrel with him until he relents, if only to have peace!"

The Darcys and Jane all laughed at that, and Mr Darcy said, "Indeed, I am in no hurry to relinquish my sister to some undeserving fellow—and they are all undeserving, you understand. No, dearest," he patted his sister's hand, "it shall be as you wish."

"There, you see, your brother is easily brought around to a right way of thinking when faced with a disputatious female," Elizabeth said to Miss Darcy. "Only become one yourself, and everything shall always be exactly as you like it."

She giggled. "Do you give lessons, Miss Elizabeth?" Darcy, who had never known his sister to tease anyone, much less a recent acquaintance, appeared torn between shock and pleasure.

"Perhaps I ought!" Elizabeth said, laughing. "Is there a great demand, do you think?"

Lord Lyfford and Mrs Swindon were then announced, and now that the entire party were assembled the conversation became more general. Drury Lane Theatre had recently announced a limited run of *Twelfth Night*, with a famous American actress in the role of Viola, to commence early in the new year. Everyone present was determined to see it if they might. A plan was quickly formed to make use of the Darcy box for the occasion, and it remained only to settle the precise date.

Excitement over this future occasion and a lively debate on the merits of other productions of Shakespeare they had seen carried the company into dinner and through the second course. From there, the discourse touched upon opera (several of those present did not care for it, and the subject was quickly abandoned), literature, and music. Lord Lyfford described becoming enthralled with the folk music of Prague on a trip there with his father before the war, telling the others of wandering the streets of that old city and feeling that around every corner there would be another man with a fiddle, or perhaps a small band of players, spilling the vibrant strains of their music into the summer air in return for whatever coin passers-by dropt into their hat or instrument case. "I should very much like to return," he concluded, "when travel to the Continent is eased by the end of the present conflict."

Mr Gardiner and Mrs Swindon had also been to the Continent before the war—he on business, she on her wedding trip —and the remainder of the meal passed happily as they and Lyfford recounted sights seen and experiences had, while the rest of the party asked questions and speculated as to where they might like to travel at some future time. Elizabeth joked that she should like to go to France in search of novels which had not been made available in England and then to Switzerland that she might indulge in their famous chocolates while reading her new French novels. Mr Darcy expressed an interest in Italy for its art and culture, while his sister wanted nothing more than to visit Germany for the music. Jane wished to see Italy and Greece, for their historical significance, and Mrs Gardiner declared that she had been a poor sailor, indeed, even on the brief crossing to Ireland, and that Scotland was now her idea of the ideal destination for a tour.

Mrs Swindon, having seen as much of Europe as she wished in her youth, now wished that she might visit India and the Orient, and return home with many trunks filled with their vibrant fabrics. Mr Gardiner raised his glass to her and said that she might save herself a great deal of time and trouble by coming to his warehouse in February, when he expected a shipment of fabrics from those very places. It was a moment before she comprehended the sincerity of his offer, and arrangements were soon made that she should be notified when the awaited goods arrived.

As the ladies made their way to the drawing room after the meal, Mrs Swindon laughingly praised Mrs Gardiner's good sense in attaching herself to a man who was not only an excellent fellow, but who could also offer her an endless supply of dress-lengths.

"Why, my dear Mrs Swindon," that lady exclaimed, "it was my ambition from the time I sewed my first petticoat to marry a draper! And here you see how successful I have been."

As the gentlemen settled into their chairs and Mr Gardiner readied the port, Darcy drew Lyfford aside for a moment. "Bingley called upon me yesterday. He told me of your meeting at the Norton-Howell ball."

Lyfford grimaced. "I rather lost my temper with his sister, but damnation, the chit is aggravating. I suppose I ought to call upon him and apologise."

Darcy's eyebrows rose at the word 'chit,' though he silently agreed it fit Miss Bingley. "Bingley has said he means to thank you for it. It seems you have opened his eyes to the very material damage Miss Bingley's pretensions might cause his family. He has invited their great-aunt Bingley—a right Tartar, by all reports—to stay with them in hopes that she will be able to teach Miss Bingley better manners."

Lyfford looked startled. "I had no notion of my words being taken so seriously."

"It is well that they were, I think. He has needed to do something about her, and if he does not feel himself capable of exerting his authority, then let the aunt try for a time while Bingley rearranges his ideas. He also understands that he has been lenient with her for too long to expect her instant obedience now."

"Well, I cannot say that I am sorry for either of them. She was positively vicious on the subject of Jane and all her family, and he did no more than whisper at her to stop."

"It is 'Jane' now, is it?"

Lyfford grinned. "There will be no formal announcement until we have her father's blessing, but we are betrothed. We go to Longbourn tomorrow, then on to Lyfford. When do you go to Pemberley for the harvest?"

Darcy turned his glass absently. "I have determined to remain in town. My steward is more than capable, and I have recently discovered some long overdue business here."

"Ah," said Lyfford and sipped his port. "May I wish you all success in your business, then?"

Darcy blushed. "There is very little chance of it, I fear, but I find I must make the attempt."

The gentlemen did not spend above half an hour over their port and entered the drawing room to find the three youngest ladies clustered about the pianoforte, Miss Elizabeth and Georgiana playing a duet while Miss Bennet sang. They stayed by the door until the performance ended, then announced themselves with loud applause. Miss Elizabeth stayed at the instrument, playing several light and cheerful airs while the others conversed. Mrs Gardiner was well entertained, flanked as she was by her beloved husband and her new friend, Mrs Swindon. Lyfford and Miss Bennet took the opportunity to canvass a few final details of their trip on the morrow before joining the Darcys.

"I hope, Miss Darcy," Miss Bennet said after she and Lyfford had acquainted the young lady with their travel plans, "that you might visit my sister once or twice while I am away."

"I can think of nothing I should like better," came the young lady's reply, "and if your aunt's health allows, I shall also invite her to visit me."

"I thank you. Although I very much look forward to the trip, I have been reluctant to leave my sister alone. I am very happy to know she shall have your excellent company."

Georgiana blushed and smiled at Miss Bennet's sincere gratitude and approval. "I will look forward to hearing your impressions of Lyfford Hall when you return. I have always thought it lovely."

"That is very much at odds with Lord Lyfford's description of 'a draughty old pile of stones,'" Miss Bennet said with an arch look at her betrothed, who laughed. Darcy chuckled as well, and Miss Darcy hid a smirk behind her hand.

"I shall go relieve Miss Elizabeth," she said. "She ought to have a greater share in the conversation at her own party!"

Darcy looked startled as his sister made her way across the room. "I do believe that is the first time she has ever volunteered to play outside of her family circle."

"Perhaps she is beginning to outgrow some of her shyness," Lyfford commented.

"Or perhaps she has been influenced for the better by her new friends," Darcy answered, with a nod of the head to Jane and then to Elizabeth, who was just approaching.

"Of what am I being accused now?" Elizabeth asked with a laugh as she took a seat with the others.

"Of influencing Miss Darcy to perform in the company of people who are not her relations," her sister said.

"Oh, I must acknowledge my guilt, then! Whatever shall my punishment be?"

"You shall be burdened with my gratitude and approbation," said Darcy solemnly.

"A great weight indeed!" she laughed, her cheeks turning a becoming pink.

The party broke up soon thereafter, in deference to the early departure planned for the morning. Georgiana arranged with Miss Elizabeth to call on Friday, while her brother wished Lyfford, his aunt, and Miss Bennet fair weather and good roads.

CHAPTER FIFTEEN

The farewells exchanged at Gracechurch Street the next morning were nearly as tearful as they were joyous. There was much pleasure to be had in the knowledge of Jane's future happiness, but everyone in the house would miss her, and none more so than her sister.

Mr Gardiner had, several days prior, pressed upon his eldest niece a purse containing an amount she could not imagine spending in three months, much less one. She protested, but he would not be gainsaid and told her that he would vastly prefer that she have ample funds available to her and not need them than find herself in need and not have them. He also said that he would not accept the remainder upon her return, so she might as well enjoy herself with it while she was away.

"Perhaps," he suggested, "you might wish to go shopping

in the nearest village once or twice, to signal to the populace that the future mistress of Lyfford Hall is not too proud to buy their wares, and they need not fear a loss of custom with your advent."

Such things had not occurred to her before, but she immediately saw the wisdom in her uncle's suggestion. "I suppose I must demonstrate what sort of mistress I intend to be, from the moment I set foot on the grounds," she mused. "I must be, as you said, the future Lady Lyfford rather than plain Jane Bennet."

Later that same day, Jane and Elizabeth had a serious conversation about their aunt's health and their fear that she might lack the strength to deliver the child she carried. Jane extracted a promise from her sister that an express would be sent with the news—whatever it proved to be—should Mrs Gardiner be brought to childbed while Jane was in Staffordshire.

As Jane embraced her sister before stepping into the carriage, she whispered, "Take care of my aunt and write to me as often as you may."

"You may depend upon it." Elizabeth stepped back, took the hands of her cousins, and encouraged them to wave goodbye.

The journey to Longbourn was very pleasant, for the three travellers were each eager to please and be pleased by their company. They stopped at an inn for refreshment near the midpoint of their journey, and Jane found such an enterprise to be very different when emerging from a carriage with a crest on the door and entering the establishment on the arm of a lord. They were shown to a private parlour and served a tea which was far better than that which she had been served in the main room when last she stopped there with her father. The innkeeper himself popped in to enquire as to their comfort and satisfaction, and Jane wondered if she would ever be entirely comfortable with such deference.

During the last stage of the short journey, her thoughts remained on how her life would soon change. Though she had every expectation of felicity in her marriage, she felt a natural anxiety at the prospect of stepping from the small country society of her upbringing into that of the peerage. As was her wont, she worried more for Lyfford than for herself— would he be ridiculed by his peers for choosing her? Would her lack of sophistication become an embarrassment to him? She felt that she could not really blame his acquaintance if they did not accept her, for she was not what they must expect for him, but neither could she look forward to the demonstration of such feelings.

She wished very much to have her dear Lizzy nearby as she settled into her new life, both in Staffordshire and London. She wondered if Mr Darcy would renew his proposals, the acceptance of which would place her sister within twenty miles of Lyfford and in the same echelon of society in town. If he did not, or if she refused him again, Jane hoped that she would be allowed to bring Elizabeth to live with them for much of the year.

As they passed through Meryton, Jane began to point out sites of interest, both general and personal, and Mrs Swindon remarked that the village nearest Lyfford Hall, Ardgale-on-Trent, was rather larger but not otherwise dissimilar. "You shall feel quite at home there in no time," she predicted.

"Yes," Jane replied, recalling her uncle's advice that purchasing from local shops would signal that the mistress of Lyfford Hall was not too proud to buy their wares.

I suppose I must demonstrate what sort of mistress I intend to be, from the moment I set foot on the grounds. I must be Lady Lyfford rather than plain Jane Bennet.

Soon the carriage pulled into Longbourn's drive, and someone must have been watching for their approach, as the Bennets had filed out of the house before the equipage came to a halt.

Mrs Bennet fluttered up to them as soon as they disembarked, embracing her eldest child. "Oh Jane! My Jane! You have been gone so long! Welcome home!"

"Oh, Mama, how I have missed you!" She returned the embrace with a fervour that surprised her mother. "How I have missed you all!"

Mrs Bennet kissed her daughter's cheek and held her at arm's length for a quick survey. "You are blooming, my love. Now, you must introduce us to your young man." She beckoned Mr Bennet to join them and, with a faint, ironic smile, he complied.

Once introductions were made, Mrs Bennet announced, somewhat nervously, that rooms were prepared at Longbourn for the visitors. "I hope you will find them comfortable. Our servants' quarters are very small, I fear, but if you will tell me how many you have brought, we shall contrive."

"I sent a man ahead yesterday to bespeak rooms at the inn for my secretary and steward. If you would accommodate my valet, my aunt's maid, and the maid Mr Gardiner has sent for Miss Bennet within the house, my coachman and grooms can make do in the stables." Lyfford glanced briefly at the servants' carriage, just now pulling in behind. "The other driver will stay at the inn's stables with that coach."

"That is easily accomplished," Mrs Bennet said with some relief.

"Perhaps Lord Lyfford would like to meet the rest of the family?" Mr Bennet murmured to his wife, not unkindly.

"Oh, indeed!" Mrs Bennet exclaimed. "Jane, you must do the honours." Having got through the immense event of meeting a lord who wished to marry her daughter, she felt herself entitled to a few moments in which to calm her racing heart. As her eldest led their guests towards her sisters, Mrs Bennet smiled up at her husband, and he smiled down at her and offered his arm.

"There, you see, my dear, she has not brought home a young man who will look down upon us," he murmured.

"I should not blame him if he did," she replied quietly, taking the offered arm. "But I would wonder if he were right for our Jane." Mr Bennet patted her hand and they followed along behind the other party.

Jane, Lyfford, and Mrs Swindon had by then reached the other Miss Bennets, but all of Jane's intentions of genteel introductions were stolen by her surprise. "Mary!" she exclaimed. "You have changed your hair! It is quite flattering."

Mary blushed and fingered a curl that hung by her cheek. "Kitty suggested the style."

"You did well to listen to her," Jane commented. "She has the best eye of any of us."

Kitty grinned at her elder sisters. "There was an assembly last weekend, and Mary danced all but three sets, though gentlemen were scarce, as they always are!" Mary's blush deepened.

"I think we may dispense with the formalities, as we are soon to be family, do not you, my dear?" Lyfford said to Jane, who could not but agree. He turned to the two young ladies. "I apprehend that you are Miss Mary and Miss Catherine," he said, looking to each of them in turn, and then bowed while they curtseyed. "I have heard so much of you from your eldest sisters that I feel I know you already."

"We have not had Jane here to tell us much about you, but I am very happy to meet any one with the good sense to love her," said Kitty with a smile. Mary seemed happy to allow

Kitty to speak for both of them and only nodded her agreement.

He turned to the last remaining sister, who stood fidgeting on Kitty's other side. "And you must be Miss Lydia. Good day," he said with a bow.

She stepped forward and said boldly, "You ought to marry me instead. I'm much more fun than dull old Jane."

A horrified gasp of "Lydia!" came from every other Bennet in unison, but Lyfford threw his head back and laughed. "My dear, you did not tell me that your youngest sister was such a jokester. She is very amusing."

Lydia stomped her foot, blushing with mortification. "I am not joking! You will be bored with Jane in a month. She doesn't like to do anything but read dreary books, play the silly harp, and stitch. I like parties and balls and dancing, and I'm very jolly, all the soldiers said so."

Mr Bennet hurried to Lydia, taking her by the arm and all but dragging her to the house, whispering angrily in her ear. Mary watched with narrowed eyes for a moment, then dropped a curtsey to her future brother. "Forgive me, but I think I ought to go help Papa." She turned and hurried after her father, disappearing into Longbourn.

Inside the house, Mr Bennet was addressing his youngest in the hall. "What can you have been thinking, Lydia? How could you be so very rude to Lord Lyfford?"

"I was trying to save him from a future of unending dullness," Lydia replied peevishly. "And get myself out of this prison. He's not the sort of man I really want, but he'd do."

"He'd do? A peer of the realm would do? By God, Lydia, you are the stupidest girl in Christendom!" Mr Bennet cried.

Mary stepped forward and spoke with a calm more deadly than rage. "The soldiers did often say you are jolly, Sister. Do you know what else they said, when you were not listening? They said you were ripe for the plucking and plotted to entice you into deeds no young lady should commit outside of marriage. There were wagers—wagers, Lydia!—on who would have you first."

"That is not true! You are just jealous of all the attention they paid me!"

"I am not and have never been jealous of you, Lydia," Mary replied implacably. "But only think for a moment. People do not notice me at parties and balls—you have commented on it often enough yourself. They say things near me that they ought not, for they do not realise I am there. I heard the officers talking about you more than once. They did not flock to you because you are charming or pretty or special in some way—they came to you in hopes of being granted liberties that no other girl in the room would even consider without the blessing of the church given beforehand."

Lydia had gone red as a beet, while her father was pale as parchment. "Is this true, Mary?" he croaked.

"Every word. I would not be surprised if one of them had succeeded."

"I would never!"

Mary's eyebrows shot up. "Your behaviour indicated to all and sundry that you would, sister...and with very little persuasion."

Lydia gave an inarticulate cry and lunged at Mary, but was brought up short by her father, who stepped behind her, grabbed her by the arms, and half-carried her up the stairs to be locked in the nursery. Mary watched them go, her expression hard but her heart pounding a wild tattoo in her breast. As poorly behaved as Lydia was, Mary would not further shame her by announcing she had instructed Sara to inform her when her youngest sister's courses arrived each month.

Outside, Mrs Bennet, Jane, and Kitty all turned away from the spectacle as the door of Longbourn closed behind Mary and faced their guests in mortification. Mrs Swindon affected to be extremely interested in a cluster of dahlias near the drive. Jane spoke first. "Oh, I am so sorry you had to see that. Lydia is..." she trailed away, searching for a word that was both truthful and kind.

"Spoilt. Lydia has been spoilt from infancy," Mrs Bennet said softly. "When she was born, the midwife said there could be no more. So, I indulged her dreadfully, because she was my last, and I was no longer thinking of the son who would surely come next. I am sorry for how she has behaved today. Please do not blame Jane for my errors."

"Mrs Bennet," Lyfford said gently, stepping forward and taking one of her hands between his. "Many a family has spoilt their youngest, and we all have relations for whom we must blush. Think no more on it, I beg you."

Mrs Bennet smiled tremulously up at him. "I thank you for your forbearance, my lord."

He offered her his arm. "I believe a stroll about the garden is just the thing to revive the spirits after a family tiff, do not you, ma'am?" She smiled and nodded and took his arm, while Jane, Kitty, and Mrs Swindon fell into step behind them. They moved along the path on the side of the house, and he continued,

"Allow me to tell you of my uncle Reginald Markham. He is my father's younger brother—by a quarter of an hour. Nothing will convince him that they were not, at some point in their infancy, switched. He is certain he is the elder and speaks of it wherever he goes. I tell you truly, ma'am, there is nothing quite so mortifying as finding myself at a dinner party with him..."

Mary joined them a few minutes later, and when Mr Bennet eventually left the house, having given his youngest daughter a thorough tongue-lashing and himself a more silent but no less comprehensive scolding, he found his family and his guests wandering the garden in good spirits. He attempted to apologise to Lord Lyfford for the scene his daughter had caused but was told that his wife had already done so and the incident was now to be forgot. Lyfford requested the favour of a private word with Mr Bennet if it was convenient, and the two gentlemen retired to the study while the ladies made for the parlour.

"Oh, Jane," Mrs Bennet sighed happily as they returned to the house. "You have found yourself such a very nice young man, and so handsome! You shall be very happy, I am sure. Tell me, do you think his brother might like one of your sisters?"

Half an hour after the two men repaired to the study, Jane was summoned to join them. She entered the room and closed the door behind her. "You wished to see me, Papa?"

"First, my dear girl, let me tell you that I have given this betrothal my blessing. Your young man has convinced me that he shall take excellent care of you."

Jane beamed and hurried across the room to embrace her father. "Thank you."

"Well, well," he said awkwardly, patting her back. "I hope you will be very happy."

"Oh, I shall," she said with such certainty that he felt just a little more reconciled to the idea of losing her. She stood back and beamed at him briefly before turning the full force of that delighted expression upon her betrothed, who caught his breath.

"If it is all the same to you, sir, I should like to put the betrothal announcement in the London papers immediately," he said.

"Of course, of course," Mr Bennet said with a wave of his hand. "Now, Jane, Lord Lyfford wishes that you understand all the details of your settlement." He gestured to the pages spread out before him.

"Oh, I am certain all is proper," she protested.

Lyfford said, "It is for your own protection, my dear. I feel very strongly that a woman should know what has been settled upon her, and how various events might change her circumstances. And if there is within anything to which you object, I should like to know before your father and I sign it."

"Very well," Jane agreed, and took the seat that was offered to her.

The two men went through the document with Jane, ensuring her firm understanding of the arrangements which had been made. Lyfford's income was revealed to be well over eight thousand pounds per annum, and Jane suddenly understood how the family had continued quite comfortably without the funds Mr Watts had been stealing.

Jane found nothing to object to in her settlement, save that her betrothed had been over-generous. But he would not be moved, and in the end, she was forced to agree with many thanks for his care and concern. The papers were then duly signed, both Lyfford's copy and Mr Bennet's, and they left the study to re-join the others in the parlour.

"Well, my dears," Mr Bennet began when all were assembled, "I have given Lord Lyfford my blessing to take our Jane away from us. We have gone over the marriage settlements he had drawn up, and I have signed them." He looked over his spectacles at his eldest daughter, eyes twinkling. "There is no getting out of it now, Jane."

The other Bennets came and offered their congratulations and best wishes to the couple. When everyone had said their piece, Mrs Bennet could not remain sedate any longer. "Oh Jane! I knew you could not be so beautiful for nothing!"

"Mama..." Jane sighed.

"When will you be married? We must begin planning!"

"We have not decided on a date, but Lyfford's brother leaves for the Peninsula on the fourth of January, and we both wish that he shall attend. I had thought, perhaps..." She glanced at her betrothed. "...the week before Christmas?"

Lyfford's smile was pure delight, but Mrs Bennet was less sanguine. "Why, that is less than three months away! And you shall be gone for a nearly a month! Oh, I meant to tell you— your father and I cannot leave Lydia just now. One of your sisters shall have to travel with you. But when would there be time for you to have a trousseau made? Mrs Wilkins is not as quick as she once was, and I would not trust her assistant's seams for a kingdom." She drew breath to continue, but Mrs Swindon interrupted.

"Mrs Bennet, you shall not be alone in this. Our dear Jane wishes to return to London after our trip, to see how Mrs Gardiner does. What better place than town to order her trousseau? I shall accompany her and ensure she has everything she will need for married life, while you arrange the wedding here. When every needful thing has been ordered, Jane may return to you, and I am certain the modiste can send a capable seamstress here to attend to the final adjustments when all is otherwise complete. And of course, if there is anything needed for the wedding or the breakfast that cannot be acquired in Meryton, you have only to write to me."

"Oh." Mrs Bennet visibly relaxed. "Oh, you are a treasure. Yes, if I need not concern myself with the trousseau, it will just be possible to plan the wedding and breakfast your nephew deserves in that amount of time."

Lyfford grinned. "I beg you will not impoverish Mr Bennet on my account, ma'am. Give my Jane the wedding she wants, and I shall be vastly contented."

"I should prefer something simple," Jane said.

"Oh, but..." Mrs Bennet trailed off, looking from Jane to Lord Lyfford and back. Jane's wishes, though gently proffered, were firm, and her betrothed would take her part in any disagreement on the matter. She drew a breath and nodded. "Of course. Of course, my dear Jane, it is your day, after all."

Jane smiled softly and squeezed her mother's hand. "Yes, it is, Mama. But I leave the breakfast entirely in your hands, for no one sets a better table than you."

Mrs Bennet dimpled at that compliment and was satisfied.

CHAPTER SIXTEEN

J ane requested her middle sister's company for a walk in the garden before dinner, and there she asked if Mary would accompany her to Staffordshire. Mary was silent for a long moment, then turned to her eldest sister and spoke earnestly.

"Kitty should go with you. Do not think that I should not like to see your new home, Jane—I should, and I depend upon you inviting me after you are married. But the changes in our household have been more trying for Kitty than for me. She has done so very well, I think she ought to have this treat, and she shall enjoy having new scenery to sketch."

Jane embraced her sister. "It is very generous of you to concede the trip to Kitty, and perhaps you are correct that she deserves it. But if you will not come now, I shall insist upon a very long visit later. You must not make any commitments for the summer until we have settled the dates of your stay with us."

Mary smiled. "I shall happily agree to that and will look forward to seeing you and to knowing my new brother better. On short acquaintance, he seems everything a young man ought to be."

"I may perhaps be biased, but I do not believe you will have cause to change that opinion," Jane said with a blush. They walked on for several minutes before Jane said, "You are greatly altered, Mary, and I do not only refer to your very becoming coiffure. You seem more tranquil and happier than I have seen you in many years."

"You may thank Papa for that. Though having a quieter home and our parents taking an interest in Kitty and me has contributed greatly to my happiness, I do not believe I really began to change until Papa took my education in hand a few months ago. He took away all my books and tracts, handed me a copy of *Evelina*, and said I might read that or nothing. Of course, I believed that the reading of novels would set me on a path to sin and debauchery," she continued wryly, "so I was very angry, and resisted for nearly a month. But you know how difficult it is for me to go even a day without a book, and I was quite miserable. Eventually, I gave in. Much to my shock, I enjoyed it, and I found myself no more inclined to vice than I had been before. Papa and I discussed the story at some length, and we were surprised to find that our opinions were in accord more often than not. He then gave me *The Mysteries of Udolpho* and advised me to read it as satire. I found it extremely funny. Papa has since been selecting all of my reading. My mind and understanding have been greatly broadened by the exercise, and my opinions softened, which I believe was his intent."

To say Jane was shocked would not be overstating the

case. That her indolent father should have taken the time to personally oversee Mary's further education was far beyond anything she would have expected. "I am very happy that you and Papa have found a subject to entertain you both," she finally managed to say. "If you should care to discuss your reading with another, I am sure Lizzy would be pleased to correspond with you on the subject until she returns to Longbourn."

Mary was very much struck with this idea and eagerly adopted it.

Jane soon sought Kitty out in her chamber and put to her the question of joining them on their trip to Lyfford. Kitty's expression lit with delight, which quickly shifted to consideration, then resignation. She shook her head and said, "No, Mary ought to go. It is her right as the elder, and really, I do not know what I should have done without her these last months. There were times I think I might have run mad without her calm good sense."

Jane laughed. "Well, here is a fine conundrum! You see, my dear Kitty, I have asked Mary, and she said you should go." She took her younger sister's hand. "I do not think she will be moved—you know how stubborn she can be—so if you do not oblige me, I shall not be able to go either!"

Kitty's jaw dropped. "She did? But why?"

Jane explained Mary's reasoning, bringing a flush of pleasure to Kitty's cheeks at this second-hand praise. Seeing this, Jane realised how unaccustomed Kitty was to any sort of approbation and felt greatly ashamed.

"Oh, Kitty, I am sorry I did not take more of an interest in you and Mary when we were all together."

"I should not have liked for you to do so," Kitty replied frankly. "Until recently, I cared only for Mama's opinion and

Lydia's. But let us speak of happier things—for instance, when do we leave?"

Jane laughed and sketched out their plans, and helped Kitty look through her dresses with a view to what she ought to bring with her. She sent for Mary, who arrived to Kitty's effusive thanks for the opportunity to travel.

Dinner that evening was a lively, pleasant affair, with Lydia confined upstairs and Mrs Bennet's carefully planned dishes covering the table. The subject swiftly turned to that nearest Mrs Bennet's heart—the wedding. After some discussion the date was settled for Tuesday, the fifteenth of December. Mr Bennet was tasked with visiting the local vicar, Mr Rudolph, in the next few days to arrange for the reading of the banns.

Lyfford was reminded of a matter he had wished to discuss with Jane and her parents. "I wonder if I might ask my godfather to conduct the ceremony. I cannot say that he would be able to attend, but I should like to make the request. I should of course be delighted to have your Mr Rudolph perform the rites if my godfather cannot make the trip."

Jane instantly answered that she had no objection, and they looked to Mr Bennet for a final answer.

"Well, well, I see no reason why not. Mr Rudolph is a good sort of clergyman, but he is no one's godfather here. Unless yours is the Archbishop of Canterbury—I think that might be a bit too much excitement for our little village," he chuckled.

Lyfford blushed slightly and said, "No, indeed, he is not the Archbishop of Canterbury." He took a sip of his wine, shot Jane an apologetic glance, and added, "He is the Archbishop of York."

There was a bit of a commotion as Mrs Bennet nearly fainted and had to be revived with a whiff of her vinaigrette. She spent the next five minutes waving her handkerchief before her flushed face and muttering, "Bless me! An archbishop for my Jane's wedding! Oh my!"

CHAPTER SEVENTEEN

Despite all the fond farewells Mrs Bennet felt necessary to express, the travellers departed Long-bourn the next morning only half an hour later than planned. Kitty was almost giddy with excitement, for though she had been to London several times to visit her aunt and uncle, she had never in the whole of her life ventured further north than Stevenage. Nearly the whole of the voyage would be new to her, and hers was a character which thrived on novelty.

Lyfford and Mrs Swindon, being both well travelled and familiar with this route in particular, were able to offer the Miss Bennets information regarding many of the areas through which they passed. That night they stayed at an inn where Lyfford was well known. Rooms had been arranged in advance and Jane and Kitty, who had never before stayed at an inn, agreed that the room they would share for both propriety and safety was clean and pleasant, and even the little trundle bed for the maid appeared to lack nothing in the way of comfort.

"Only imagine, Jane," Kitty whispered after they had all retired, "soon this sort of journey will seem very commonplace to you. What a very different life you shall lead!"

"Yes, I expect it shall be very different. I only hope I am up to the task of being a good wife to a man in his position," Jane answered.

"I dare say you will have a great deal to learn in the beginning, but you will have Lord Lyfford and Mrs Swindon and any number of servants to help you along," Kitty replied comfortingly.

"You are right, Kitty. I shall just have to apply myself to learning my role."

Two days later came the day Jane would first see her future home. She looked towards the event with an equal admixture of anticipation and anxiety, though she strove for the sake of her companions to conceal her discomposure. The scenery as they entered and progressed through Staffordshire was a source of delight to all within the carriage—for Jane, a distraction from her worries; for Kitty, who had never before seen such peaks and crags, a simple delight; and for Lyfford and his aunt, the familiar scenes of home.

Passing through a lush river valley in mid-afternoon, they turned off the great road and onto a smaller one which wound its way towards the wooded hills rising in ever-increasing ranks from the eastern edge of the valley. They passed a gatehouse of ancient stone covered in ivy, a thin curl of smoke puffing from the chimney, and continued for a half mile before the carriage turned around a great stone pavilion and came to a halt. Lyfford opened the carriage door. Outside, a groomsman was already lowering the steps. "Come, my dear," Lyfford said, smiling and holding a hand out to Jane, "and see your new home."

She took his hand and allowed him to assist her down, then turned and was struck mute by what lay before her. A wide drive extended arrow-straight a quarter mile up a gentle incline to the courtyard of a vast Elizabethan mansion of pale stone aged to gold: three lofty storeys, plus attics under the peaked slate roof; a dozen chimneys visible and more, no doubt, behind; wide wings to each side jutting out around the centre with its arched double door under a heraldic carving ten feet high. Jane wondered giddily how long it would take Mr Collins to count all the windows in this enormous place.

"Oh, Jane," Kitty breathed, descending from the carriage to stand beside her.

"Will it do, my dear?" he asked.

"You are very fortunate that I am not prone to fainting," Jane scolded.

Lyfford chuckled and Kitty stifled a giggle behind her hand, causing Jane to relent and smile up at him. "I shall become lost on the way to breakfast every morning for a week at least, I am sure of it, but yes...it will do."

They returned to the carriage for the short trip up the drive and found the butler and housekeeper awaiting them with a small army of footmen to take charge of their trunks. Jane was presented to Mr Nevins and Mrs Dumfries as the future Lady Lyfford, whereupon she was greeted with the deepest bow and curtsey she had ever received.

They entered the house, stepping into a square, high-ceilinged entry not much wider than the great doors, panelled in carved wood ten feet high with bright bas-relief plaster above. A great staircase dominated the other end, passages leading off to either side of it. As they proceeded up the stairs,

Mrs Swindon gestured to her left. "In the main, the public and guest rooms are on this side of the house, while the private and family rooms are on the other."

They ascended to the third floor, emerging into a long gallery hung with portraits of Lyffords and Markhams past and present, interspersed with fine landscapes.

"If you look out the windows here, you will see something you may like," Lyfford suggested. The sisters obliged and moved to the nearest casement, through which they spied the vast rear terrace and the expansive lawn and garden beyond it. Further beyond on a wooded elevation, a thick stone tower of medieval design emerged above the treetops.

Kitty gasped. "You have a castle?"

"The tower only. The rest is little more than foundation walls."

Kitty sighed dreamily, staring out the window at the tower. "I should very much like to go there."

"The first fine day that I can be spared from the harvest, we shall take a picnic and explore it," he offered, and the notion was gladly accepted by the ladies.

They proceeded thence down the gallery to the guest rooms, and Lyfford was left behind as Mrs Swindon conducted them into a lovely suite of two chambers with a shared sitting room between them. The sitting room was as large as the bedroom Jane shared with Elizabeth at Long-bourn, and both bedrooms rather larger. Each had a dressing room, and in each of those was a maid busily unpacking the ladies' trunks.

Jane had been given a room papered in delicate yellow flocked with white and pale blue. The plaster above the paper was stamped with a repeating primrose pattern in the Tudor style, which was reflected in the heavy dark furnishings, brightened by light and cheerful upholstery and bed-hangings. Kitty's room was nearly identical, save that the predominant colour was a pleasant light green with cream and silver accents. The maids were summoned from their labours and Jane was introduced to Maggie, a quietly competent young woman who would be tending to her during her stay, while Kitty would be seen to by Amy, a housemaid who had only recently begun to study under Mrs Swindon's maid and was thrilled to be attending a guest for the first time.

After Mrs Swindon's departure, while Kitty chatted happily with the young maid about her gowns and how she liked her hair done, Jane left Maggie to her work and granted herself the luxury of a silent turn through her room, reflecting with amazement that she, Jane Bennet, daughter of a country squire of absolutely no renown, was to be mistress of this vast home and responsible, jointly with her husband, for the prosperity of all who depended on the estate for their living.

She opened the drawer of the little writing desk under the window and found it stocked with fresh paper, quills, and ink. She considered writing to Lizzy straight away but decided that she had best allow the surprises of the day to settle in her mind before she attempted to put them into words.

Drifting to the window, she found a pleasant view of a vast sunken garden, occupying easily thrice the ground of the house itself. Beyond the garden lay the road, and in the distance, sheep dotted a craggy hillside. Thinking of Lyfford's sheep and the wool that brought her dear Henry into her life, Jane smiled.

CHAPTER EIGHTEEN

A bit after midday the following day, the Monday after Elizabeth Bennet's birthday, just as the Darcy carriage was pulling away from the house on its way to Gracechurch Street, another carriage was coming to a stop before a smaller home a few streets away. From this equipage descended a well-dressed woman in her eighth decade. Her spine was ramrod-straight, her white hair was perfectly coiffed beneath a bonnet of velvet and sarcenet, and the ebony and silver walking stick in her hand was more accessory than aid. She flicked her eyes over the house's façade, pursed her lips long enough to utter a soft grunt and strode briskly up the stairs to the door, waving off the groom who scrambled to assist her.

Ignoring the knocker in favour of rapping the knob of her stick against the door, she presented her card to the footman who opened it. Reading the name thereupon, he swiftly opened the door wide and gestured her in. "Welcome, madam. The ladies are in the parlour. I will escort you."

"No, no. Take me to my nephew. I am here at his behest and will speak with him first," she directed briskly.

"Of course, madam. Right this way." The footman bowed and led her away from the parlour and into the library, where her quarry sat reading his correspondence in an armchair by the window. Upon seeing who had entered, Charles Bingley sprang to his feet, carelessly discarding his letter onto a table as he crossed the room.

"Aunt Bingley! I had not expected you so quickly!"

She tutted and accepted his enthusiastic embrace with more pleasure than she showed. "Your message convinced me that haste was necessary, Charles. If Caroline has insulted a peer, she needs taking in hand immediately. You were entirely correct to send for me."

"And I am very grateful for your coming," he exclaimed. "I fear I need you as much as she does, for she will not heed me. I hope you may teach me, by your example, how to manage her." He escorted his great-aunt to the most comfortable chair in the room—the one he had just been occupying—and saw her settled before he rang for tea.

"Before we discuss Caroline, my boy, why is it you and she are living with the Hursts, when your father left you a fine house on a better street?"

Bingley sighed. "It is let. As far as anyone else knows, that is so I may increase my income until I am married. In truth, it is because I do not wish to live alone with Caroline. She enjoys Louisa's company, so she is not always hounding me."

"Humph." She fixed him with a glance that conveyed her disapproval, and he shrank back in his chair. "You were too young to truly fill the role of head of the family when your parents died, but you are four-and-twenty now, and I expect you to act like it. Put some starch in your neck, boy!"

"I intend to, Aunt," he said seriously.

"Well." She nodded sharply. "We shall return to that subject another day. Now, tell me everything about Caroline's faux pas that was not in your letter."

Bingley candidly related the story of the incident at the Norton-Howell ball, which led to the tale of his autumn in Hertfordshire and acquaintance with the Bennets, particularly the eldest daughter of the house. When he ran out of words, his elderly relation looked thoughtful as she checked the teapot and poured them each a cup.

"Correct me if I have missed any critical points—you courted a young lady last autumn but were persuaded by your sisters and friend to leave her without so much as a farewell. When next you hear of her, she is being courted by Lord Lyfford, and Caroline abuses this young lady's character in conversation with him, which makes him justifiably angry."

Bingley grimaced. "In essence, yes. And to make matters worse for Caroline, Lord Lyfford and Miss Bennet are now betrothed. The announcement appeared in the papers this morning. Caroline was more than displeased when she saw it. She and Louisa have been shut away in the parlour all morning, and I have little doubt as to the subject of their conversation."

She gazed shrewdly at him over her cup as she took a leisurely sip. "And what is your reaction to this news?"

He drummed his fingers on the arm of his chair for a moment before he spoke. "I did care for Miss Bennet, truly. I was more than half in love with her. But my sisters objected and so did Darcy, upon whose counsel I depend...perhaps too much. Yet with the passage of time, I can admit that I would not so easily have been dissuaded were I not also intimidated by her.

"I am not an intellectual man, Aunt, you know this. Though I did earn my degree at Cambridge, it was not a pleasure for me as it was for some, like Darcy. I vastly prefer sport or a ball or even a dinner party to any book. Miss Bennet is very well read and takes such pleasure in deep conversation that I believe I knew, in my heart, that were we to marry she would one day find herself terribly bored with me." He sighed. "My manner of extricating myself was cowardly. I allowed myself to be carried along by my relations and friends because part of me was relieved to be offered such an easy escape."

"It is just as well that your association broke off when it did, I should think, for it does not sound to me as though you and she could have made each other happy. But your leave-taking—or lack thereof—was very badly done indeed, and I shall insist that you apologise to the young lady when next you meet."

He nodded, his expression rather grim. "I have been intending to do just that, Aunt. It will be mortifying, but it must be done if I am ever again to be able to think of myself as a gentleman."

"As it should be," Mrs Bingley declared, levering herself from the plush chair with the aid of her stick. "Get back to your letters, Charles. I believe I shall rid myself of the dust of the road and then see what your sister has to say for herself."

Bingley's brow furrowed into a concerned expression. "You do not wish for my presence?"

"My dear boy, I have had Caroline's measure far longer than you. She will not deceive me, if that is what concerns you."

Bingley had no valid argument against that. "As you wish."

"Things usually are," she commented, and left the library. She was shown to her room, where she found Higgins, her maid, had unpacked her trunks and had warm water waiting. She refreshed herself and changed into a day gown which was not creased from travel. Higgins repaired the little damage her bonnet had done to her coiffure, for Mrs Bingley did not care for matron's caps and was secretly rather vain of her thick, milk-white locks, preferring an ornamental comb among them to any bit of lace and muslin. She then made her way down to the parlour, where she shamelessly eavesdropped by the open door.

"Caroline," Louisa sighed, "we have been discussing this for hours and have been treading the same ground for half that time, at least. Charles has been saved from a match imprudent as to fortune and standing, and I do not see why you cannot simply be satisfied with that."

"Jane Bennet cannot be allowed to marry Lord Lyfford! He is almost as much Mr Darcy's friend as is our brother, and such a union will continually place that conniving Eliza Bennet in Mr Darcy's path! I will not stand for it!"

Out in the hall, Mrs Bingley smirked.

"So you have said," Louisa replied in a tone of great weariness. "And yet there is nothing we might do about it. Even if there were, I would not do it, for I am sick to my bones of the entire subject."

"Louisa!" Caroline cried, outraged.

Mrs Bingley, determining that the moment of dissension was ideal for her purposes, placed herself at the threshold, thumping her cane against the floorboards to draw the astonished attention of her nieces.

"Caroline Horatia Bingley!" she declared sternly. "What is

this I hear about you outraging a peer of the realm? Have you not the sense God gave a flea?"

"Aunt Bingley!" Louisa gasped, while her sister appeared to be trying to breathe underwater. Mrs Bingley moved into the room and sat, uninvited, across from the pair.

"Well, niece? What foul imp of the mind induced you to insult Lord Lyfford's choice of a bride, hmm? Do you not realise what very uncertain ground this family stands upon in society's eyes?"

"I...I..." Caroline stuttered, and Louisa wisely chose the path of utter silence.

"Well?" the elder lady barked.

"I was not thinking of Lord Lyfford at the time!" Caroline burst out in sheer frustration. "I was thinking of Mr Darcy and of keeping him safe from that artful hoyden, Eliza Bennet!"

Mrs Bingley sat back slowly, her stern expression shifting to resigned annoyance. "Is the worth of all the world to be judged solely on whether they aid or hinder your foolish quest to become the mistress of Pemberley?"

Her youngest niece shot her a look of great offence, but before she could speak, Mrs Bingley continued. "I take it that this Miss Eliza is some relation to Lord Lyfford's betrothed...a sister, perhaps?" Caroline nodded sullenly. "Which makes her the daughter of a gentleman—a position to which *you* can never aspire, for your birth is long behind you. Let me be entirely clear, Niece. Mr Darcy of Pemberley is no more likely to wed a tradesman's daughter than to ride down Rotten Row in his nightshirt and slippers. Whomever he marries, this Miss Eliza or some other, she will not be you, and if you were sensible of your own good you would have accepted that years ago and made a respectable marriage. As it is, you are disliked by much of society and very nearly on the shelf."

Caroline gasped with outrage. "I am not!"

"You are three and twenty, of course you are almost on the shelf," Mrs Bingley said dismissively. "Or were you referring to the other bit?" The younger woman purpled with rage and insult but could not seem to put words to her emotions, her jaw flapping in inelegant silence.

Her great-aunt leaned forward, hands clasped over the knob of her stick, a glint of unholy delight in her eyes. "Your brother has called for me to take you in hand, Caroline, and repair the damage you have wrought. Until I have seen real and substantial improvement in your manners, you may consider me your faithful shadow."

CHAPTER NINETEEN

E lizabeth welcomed her callers with genuine pleasure that afternoon, for she was more delighted with Miss Darcy every time they met, and the awkwardness between Elizabeth and Mr Darcy had faded rapidly since their revealing stroll in the park. His manners in her presence had been both faultless and quietly amiable; she, in her consciousness of having dealt him a wound, had taken care to treat him with kindness. This was their third visit since Jane's departure. He had accompanied his sister on her promised call on Friday, remaining only a few minutes himself but leaving Georgiana there for an hour, and they had come again the next day, but he had only greeted her and Mrs Gardiner before going about his business. Today, however, he had reason to linger and was determined to do so.

After they exchanged greetings and sat down, Elizabeth

offered Mrs Gardiner's excuses, for that lady had found herself rather fatigued and left her niece to receive any callers that afternoon. Mr Darcy soon pulled from his coat a piece of newsprint carefully folded so as to fit in his pocket without creasing the notice printed thereupon. He handed it to Elizabeth, saying, "I thought you had likely read the announcement of your sister's engagement in the papers this morning but brought it just in case you had not."

Elizabeth smiled broadly. "Oh, yes, we had the pleasure of seeing it over breakfast. Not that there was any reason to believe that Papa would refuse his blessing, of course. We have saved it for Jane. I thank you for thinking of us when you saw it, and I should very much like to keep this one for my memory box, if you do not mind."

"It is yours," he replied, returning her smile.

"When do you expect to hear from Miss Bennet?" Georgiana asked.

"Oh, not for a week at least, I should think. They hoped to make Lyfford Hall on Saturday, but if they encountered bad weather or trouble with the carriage, they might not arrive until today or tomorrow." She broke off to nod her thanks to the maid who had arrived with the tea tray and set about making a pot for her guests.

"Perhaps," she suggested as she unlocked the tea caddy, "you might tell me something of the house and the estate, to assuage my curiosity while I await word from my sister!"

They were happy to do so and told Elizabeth all they could readily recall of the house and grounds. "Oh, Jane shall be enchanted," Elizabeth said happily when they were done. "Old houses like that, which have kept their original fittings, have such a sense of history. And Jane loves nothing better than a sense of history! May I ask, how old is Pemberley?"

"A little over a century, is that not correct, Brother?" Georgiana asked.

Darcy nodded. "Yes, much newer than Lyfford Hall, and it is the third Darcy family home. The first was in use for many generations before elevation of our family's position in society required a larger, finer dwelling. The second was built—rather stupidly, I must say—on low-lying ground and was decimated by a flood less than five years after it was completed. Pemberley was built in a more rational location thereafter."

A question about Pemberley's grounds and gardens led Mr Darcy to expound happily on the topic of the estate's many woods, flowering trees, and extensive walking paths. Never had Elizabeth seen him so loquacious; his love of his family home rang through with every word. When he paused, seemingly abashed at his own verbosity, she encouraged him to continue.

"Is the original house still in existence?" she asked.

"Indeed, it is. It was extensively renovated after the family left it and is now the dower house."

"How old is Longbourn?" Georgiana wondered.

"Oh, let me think..." Elizabeth considered. "I believe it must be a hundred and fifty years, perhaps rather longer. Papa surely knows, but he does not like to speak of family history, knowing he is the last Bennet who will be master of Longbourn."

Realising that she had led the conversation into gloomy waters, she quickly added, "But having met his heir, Mr Darcy, surely you will agree with me in rejoicing that we do not share a family name, and hardly need claim the connexion at all!"

Mr Darcy laughed, and turned to his sister to explain, "Do you remember my telling you of Mr Collins, whom I met with in Hertfordshire and in Kent? He is Mr Bennet's heir, a cousin of some remove."

"The 'ludicrous parson', as you called him?" Georgiana said and grimaced. "Oh, I should hate to see Pemberley taken by someone like that. You have my sympathy, Elizabeth."

"Never fear, my dear Georgiana!" Elizabeth exclaimed. "My silly cousin had the great good luck to marry a woman of unimpeachable good sense, whom we hope will bear him an intelligent son and prevent him from ruining Longbourn—although I fear he will insist on turning my father's study into a shrine to your aunt." Georgiana giggled at the notion.

"And now, sir, I have some news for you," Elizabeth declared with a grin at Mr Darcy. "I have had a letter from my father—an event at least as unusual as a betrothal, I assure you—and, after debating for a time between several schools, he has selected Mrs Madsen's Academy, which you suggested. He waits only to hear when they may receive my sister."

"I am happy the information was of use to him," Mr Darcy replied seriously.

"Which of your sisters is to school?" Georgiana asked.

"My youngest, Lydia. She has a rather rebellious nature, and our parents hope that the regularity and discipline of a boarding school might improve her where the more informal atmosphere at home has failed," Elizabeth said cheerfully. Mr Darcy, knowing more of the situation than his sister, could only admire her easy reply.

It became clear at Gracechurch Street over the following days that Mr Darcy was courting Miss Elizabeth Bennet. He was earnest in his attentions and pleased to find the lady receptive in kind. He visited daily—the sole exception being Sundays—and was assiduously amiable and gracious to Mrs Gardiner on the increasingly rare occasions she appeared in the parlour, to Mr Gardiner on the increasingly frequent occasions when he did, and to Elizabeth always. Georgiana had her studies to attend, but she did make time to accompany her brother every third or fourth day.

She shared with both of them the highlights of the much-longed-for first letter from Jane in Staffordshire, and with the gentleman, her anxious hopes that Jane would find the neighbourhood as congenial as the house. He was unable to offer her much reassurance, having ventured only rarely into the area since childhood, except to say that Lyfford and his aunt enjoyed many of their neighbours and that must be a mark in favour of the place.

Darcy, endeavouring to be more open with her, asked her opinion on a dispute between tenants that his steward had written of, which had lately escalated to threats of violence. It seemed that one man's cow had broken the other's fence in its quest for the succulent grasses on the other side. The cow's owner said the fence was shoddy and ill-maintained to begin with, while the fence's owner disagreed and demanded recompense. Darcy allowed that the fence was not the best to be found on the estate, but it was not nearly so rickety as the other man claimed. After considering several solutions, they agreed that the two men ought to be equally responsible for the materials the repair would require, but the cow's owner should perform the restoration, as he had such strong opinions on what constituted a good fence.

So marked was Darcy's interest that when he arrived one afternoon with his sister during the second week of his daily calls, Mr Gardiner requested that the young gentleman join him in his study for a time. Georgiana was sent to the parlour to see her friend while her brother, with masterfully concealed trepidation, obeyed what both men understood was a command cloaked in civility.

When they had taken their seats and Darcy declined a brandy, Mr Gardiner did him the favour of coming directly to the point. "You visit my niece every day that my house is open to callers, sir. I must enquire as to your intentions."

"I have only one intention, Mr Gardiner, and that is marriage," Darcy replied promptly. "I hope, by constant display of my improved mind and manners, to show Miss Elizabeth that I have attended to the reproofs she voiced when she refused my first offer, that she may perhaps be inclined to accept my next."

This recital took Mr Gardiner rather by surprise though, canny man of business that he was, his only outward reaction was a slight narrowing of his eyes. "You have already proposed?" he said after a silent moment.

"She did not tell you." Darcy, pleased by Elizabeth's discretion, fidgeted with his cuffs. "Yes, I made her a proposal this past April when we both stayed in Kent. She very rightly refused—my manners and my conceited view of myself had given her a disgust of me, and she had little hesitation in informing me so."

"So, you proposed to her and were answered with a long list of your faults in her eyes. Yet you come back for more."

Darcy shrugged. "I love her, and she was generally correct as to my faults—I could not deny it once my anger had cooled and I had looked back upon our acquaintance through her eyes. I had not thought to ever see her again, but I tried to amend my failings, both because it was simply the right thing to do and to honour my memories of the lady who had ripped the blindfold from my eyes."

Mr Gardiner could hardly believe what he was hearing, and still his guest had more to say.

"And then I learnt that my old friend Lyfford was courting Miss Elizabeth's sister. I came, that first time, to apologise if the opportunity arose. But having been in her presence once more, I found I could not stay away, and resolved to try again —to truly try, for the first time—to win her."

"That is quite a story, sir. I know Elizabeth's value better than most, I dare say, but I have always expected that she would attract a man from my sphere rather than yours— among my acquaintance, intelligence in a woman is not sneered at, as I believe it may be in 'higher' circles. A clever wife can be of great benefit to a man in trade, as I have cause to know."

Darcy inclined his head. "It is as you say, but I care little for society and their ever-changing mores. I participate only to maintain my true friendships, and for the sake of my sister and the children I hope one day to have. Miss Elizabeth's wit and humour are what first drew my attention and captured my heart. And surely you would not argue that a clever wife would not be of benefit to a gentleman, too, so long as he did not fear her intelligence?"

Mr Gardiner sat back and eyed the other man shrewdly. "You'll do. You may continue to call upon my niece so long as she welcomes your company and all the proprieties are observed. But there will be no stolen intimacies, however trifling, with my niece while she is under my care, do you understand me, sir?"

Mr Darcy nodded sharply. "I will treat Miss Elizabeth as I would have a suitor treat my sister, you have my word upon it. I respect her too much to attempt any such thing, and I do not doubt that she would have me out on my ear without your assistance if I did."

Gardiner stood and extended a hand to Darcy, who rose from his chair and shook the other man's hand firmly. "I believe we are in accord, Mr Darcy. I thank you for bearing with my inquisition. I stand in place of her father while she resides with me, and I take that responsibility very seriously."

"I do not look forward to the day when young men fill my parlour to moon over my sister, sir. I am glad Miss Elizabeth has such devoted protection as I hope to give Georgiana."

"Go on to my parlour then, sir, and see what progress you can make with my niece. I fancy I should not mind calling you nephew one day if she is agreeable."

CHAPTER TWENTY

Over dinner on their first full day in Staffordshire, Lyfford had reminded them that he would be very much engaged with his steward for the next week or more and would unfortunately be available only in the evenings. With his estate business and Jane's comfort in mind, they had discussed dates on which they might entertain and decided to hold a dinner party on the following Wednesday. Mrs Swindon invited Jane and Kitty to take part in the planning if they wished, and both agreed.

Monday morning after breakfast, Lyfford rode off with Mr Davies, and the ladies convened in the sitting room to compose a guest list. Mrs Swindon briefly described the people she felt Jane ought to become acquainted with first— primarily their nearest neighbours in terms of distance and the highest-ranking locals—and they considered the personalities and positions involved, and made a list which promised a fairly congenial company without offending anyone of importance in the community. Between the three of them, they made quick work of writing and addressing the invitations, and then they sought out Mrs Dumfries to inform her of the event and request that the cook have a suggested menu for their review by Thursday. They parted to their separate amusements for the afternoon, reuniting for dinner and the comfort of an evening in their small party.

The following days in Staffordshire passed in similar manner. While Lyfford saw to the harvest, Jane spent the mornings with the housekeeper touring the house and learning how it was run. Kitty often accompanied her sister and learnt, much to her betterment, that marrying the sort of man who can afford an orangery was not all luxury and amusements. She began to ask her own questions of Mrs Dumfries and to prepare herself for the future she desired.

After dinner on Tuesday evening, Lyfford handed Jane a note that he had received from his elder sister, Mrs Edgerton, who lived not five miles distant, saying that she hoped to meet her future sister on any date convenient for Miss Bennet.

"Oh, yes, we ought certainly to meet before the dinner party, as there will be little chance to get to know each other in that setting. Though she graciously agrees to come any day I name, do you know if there are any particular days she prefers to remain at home to her own callers?"

He thought for a moment. "Mondays, I believe."

Jane nodded. "Perhaps we might invite her for this Thursday or Friday, whichever she prefers?"

"I shall reply with that plan directly," Lyfford agreed with a smile.

Later in the week, the Bennet sisters went to stretch their legs in the sunken garden after their time with the housekeeper. They had not been there long when Kitty mentioned that Mary had been teaching her how to keep Longbourn's household books.

Kitty confessed she had not paid much attention to Mary's lessons, assuming that every home had its own way of going about things and that she would just have to learn a different way when she married.

"I am fortunate to have learnt so much about running a home from Aunt Gardiner and about entertaining from our mother," Jane said. "And yet there is still a great deal for me to learn here. What I know is very general—how to keep accounts, how to plan a dinner, how to resolve quarrels among the servants, how to be attentive to the tenants. But I do not know this household, these servants and tenants, these neighbours. That would be true no matter who I married and is something you will also face in time. There is so much that one cannot know in advance, so it is best to learn everything that one can."

Kitty nodded sombrely. "I shall, to be sure. If I find a gentleman I wish to marry, I should hate to begin by disappointing him with my incompetence!"

Jane sighed. "I hope I shall not disappoint the earl. All of this," she gestured about them, "is simply home to him. He has seen Longbourn, of course, but I do not think he can understand what a great change it shall be for me, not merely to run a home, but one such as this! And there is the house in town, also. I know I shall learn it all in time. I only hope I do not err spectacularly first."

Kitty took her elder sister's arm and laid her head on her shoulder. "At least when I marry and must face these problems, I shall have you to turn to for advice, but you are the first of us to wed. I do not know how to comfort you, except to remind you that you will have a husband who loves you very much and will surely be inclined to forgive any mis-step you make."

Jane smiled softly and tilted her head to rest briefly atop her sister's. "I am glad you are here with me, Kitty. Seeing Lyfford so often in my aunt and uncle's home made it easy for me to forget who and what he is to the world. I have been reminded rather forcefully by being here, and it has made me fretful. But you are correct. He loves me, and he has chosen me to be Lady Lyfford—a position of which he currently understands more than I do. I must trust that he knows what he is about."

On Friday afternoon, Jane and Mrs Swindon awaited their visitor in the family sitting room. They stood as the door opened and a lady of about Mrs Gardiner's age who strongly resembled the younger Markham brother swept in with a cheerful smile, proceeding directly to Jane with her hands held out.

"Miss Bennet! How delighted I am to meet you after all of my brother's letters extolling your virtues." She clasped Jane's hands in hers and beamed, then recalled herself long enough to grin at Mrs Swindon. "Oh, good day, Aunt Bea."

The older lady chuckled. "Welcome, Cynthia. I see you do not require me to make the introductions, but please allow me to perform the office for Miss Bennet. Dear Jane, this is Cynthia Edgerton, my eldest niece."

Mrs Edgerton stepped back and curtseyed, while Jane did likewise. "I am sorry if my informality shocks you, Miss Bennet, but I already consider you quite part of the family, after all my brother has written of you. I hope you will call me Cynthia, and if you are not yet comfortable with that, consider it an open invitation."

Jane could hardly resist such easy charm, and said, "Only if I may be Jane to you."

They sat and took tea and spoke for over two hours. Cynthia's was a large, noisy household of three generations, which sounded to Jane not very unlike Longbourn during her childhood when her grandmother yet lived, save that the Edgertons could boast of more males. Cynthia had four children with another expected in the spring, and two of her husband's brothers were yet at home as well as his father. "I am a managing woman," she said quite frankly at one point, "and I have married into a family which provides me with all the chaos I can tame—and more, at times!"

Jane was pleased to find that this sister who lived so close, and would therefore be often encountered, was so amiable. They traded stories of childhood antics—the Bennet girls', the Markham brood's and the current crop of little Edgertons'— and spoke a little of the upcoming dinner party, at which Jane would meet Mr Edgerton and his father. Jane expressed her eagerness for the acquaintance, and they parted on excellent terms.

Jane let out a long breath and sagged in her seat as the door closed behind Cynthia, and Mrs Swindon looked at her curiously. "Surely you were not nervous, my dear Jane? I am certain my nephew and I have both told you how agreeable Cynthia is."

"I..." Jane looked at her hands. "You did both tell me so, but I confess I was rather nervous. I do so wish for all of his family to like me."

"Well, my dear, there is only Julia—Mrs Carteret—yet to be met with, and the rest of us most definitely do like you," the older woman said with a smile.

Something in the older lady's tone had Jane cocking her head and asking, "Ought I be concerned about my reception by Mrs Carteret, ma'am?"

Mrs Swindon twisted her hand in an equivocal gesture. "Perhaps. Perhaps not. Julia has always been ambitious, but one can never be certain where that ambition will lead her behaviour. I know she does not approve of Lyfford's choice, for she has written to both of us on the subject, but if she is sensible of her own good by way of her husband's, she will be civil...if only civil."

Jane absorbed that information. "Is it my lack of fortune of which she disapproves?"

"Oh, perhaps somewhat, but it is standing for which she truly cares. When she was out in society, she pushed him towards every unattached earl's or duke's daughter to be found, without regard for temperament or inclination. She herself was determined to marry the son of one of those earls or dukes—preferably the eldest—but she lacked both the charm and the beauty to accomplish that feat. After three Seasons, she understood that her ambition would not be gratified in that way, and she accepted the proposal of Mr Carteret, who is a cousin of the Earl of Moyne and quite as ambitious as she. He means to be a bishop at the very least, and Lyfford's close relationship to the Archbishop of York was not the smallest of Julia's attractions in his eyes.

"You bring no connexions which may be of use to Mr Carteret as he rises in the Church, and that is her real objection. If she is wise, she will do nothing to jeopardise the connexion which already exists through her brother. Alas, ambition is not always wise, so I cannot truly predict how she will greet you when you eventually meet."

"I understand. I shall not now be disappointed if she is cold, or even unkind. It is best to be prepared for these things, I think."

"You are a good girl, Jane, and if Julia chooses to be uncivil, my nephew will bring her around to a right way of thinking. Do not trouble yourself about it overmuch."

On Saturday, preparations for the dinner party having largely moved into the sphere of the servants, Jane and Kitty explored the attics with Mrs Dumfries. There they found a number of treasures of which Jane took note in case she might wish to re-do any rooms at a later date, and also a clock and a dressing mirror much more to her own tastes, as well as a very pretty screen painted with roses, which she asked to have placed before the washing stand in her future chamber.

On Sunday morning they took the carriage down to the village to attend services. The church was quite full of people who all seemed to be determined to get a good look at the young earl's betrothed, and at her sister while they were at it. Jane and Kitty both blushed from the notice as they made their—seemingly very long—way to the Lyfford pew in the front. Jane let out a small sigh of relief as they were seated and she no longer had to directly confront all the attention which was directed their way. Lyfford's expression was apologetic as he murmured, "They are good people, by and large, and the novelty of your presence will soon fade."

Jane said quietly, "I do understand, and I expect this is rather how your friend Mr Darcy felt when he first entered the assembly rooms in Meryton." Lyfford chuckled.

When the service ended, a number of people wished to make her acquaintance, although most of those who were willing to elbow their way through the press to succeed in that endeavour seemed to be young ladies or the mothers thereof, come to look Jane over critically and welcome her to the community with the barest civility. She bore them with that placid gentility which had served her so well in other difficult situations, leaving them with little to criticise and all the more frustrated for it. Lyfford remained firmly situated next to his betrothed, occasionally favouring a lady whose minimal politeness slipped for a moment with a stern look. Kitty fixed herself at Jane's other side and slightly behind her, saying little and wearing a pleasantly interested expression behind which she grew increasingly incensed. Mrs Swindon stood on his other side and conversed easily with those who waited for their chance at the newcomers.

When finally they were able to make their way to the church door, they were greeted with sincere pleasure by the parson, whom Lyfford introduced as Mr Phelps. In the churchyard they met with many acquaintances of Lyfford's and Mrs Swindon's who had not cared to engage in the battle to speak with them inside. These were also, in the main, a more welcoming group. Though obviously curious about the future first lady of the neighbourhood, most greeted Jane with real courtesy, and she was glad to know that Lyfford's assessment of the populace had not been far off the mark and she would be able to make friends and pleasant acquaintances here. One young lady, Miss Beaton, was near in age to Jane and rather reminded her of Charlotte Lucas in manner. Her parents also seemed pleasant on such brief acquaintance, and Jane was glad to learn from Mrs Beaton that they would certainly attend the dinner at Lyfford Hall on Wednesday and were very much looking forward to it.

When they were settled in the carriage and away from the church, Kitty could contain herself no longer. "Those horrid ladies who crowded about us after the service! I am very sorry if I am speaking ill of any of your friends," she added to Lyfford and his aunt, "but the way they looked down their noses at Jane! I just wanted to...ooh!" Having no ladylike words to express her ire, she ended with a noise of pure frustration.

"Many of the daughters of the gentry in the area hoped to be the next Lady Lyfford," Mrs Swindon commented. "Or else their mothers hoped it for them. There is always some resentment when a gentleman as eligible as he removes himself from the market, but I thought Jane did very well." She turned to Jane with an approving smile. "They wished to find fault with you, and you thwarted them beautifully." She then addressed Kitty. "Your feelings on your sister's behalf do you credit, Miss Catherine, but those ladies will be Jane's neighbours for many years to come, and most of them will get over their dashed hopes in due course and may even become her friends. Such is the way of things."

CHAPTER TWENTY-ONE

S ubsequent days passed quickly, and the morning of
the dinner party brought some much-welcomed post.
Kitty glanced briefly at Lydia's missive and tossed it
aside with a brief comment to Jane: "More complaints."

Jane opened Ellen's letter, which was dated nearly two
weeks prior, and read.

My dear Jane,

*How happy I was to receive my brother's letter informing
me that we shall soon be sisters! I confess I had long hoped for
this outcome and am so very pleased! I hope you will write to
me and tell me how it came about, for his letter was sadly
short of details, and as soon as you have arranged the date, I
hope you will inform me.*

I am too giddy to write more now, so I trust you will forgive me and know that I am
    Your terribly pleased future sister,
    Ellie

Jane smiled and carefully folded the letter. She opened Elizabeth's letter with a calmer heart and read with delight but little surprise of Mr Darcy's attentions. When she had finished, she told Kitty, "My aunt is well and has not yet delivered, as of Thursday."

"Oh, that is good. Mary says Father has received a letter from the school he wishes Lydia to attend, and they will take her in January."

"That is excellent news. Has Lydia been informed yet?"

"Yes. Mary writes that she shouted that she will be glad to be anywhere other than Longbourn and her departure could not come too soon." Kitty grinned. "And then Mary added her opinion that finally there is a matter upon which we can all agree!"

Jane laughed. "Mary has a lovely dry wit, does she not? I am glad she now chooses to exercise it more often."

Maggie turned Jane's hair into a veritable masterpiece that evening, a braid twinkling with peridots wrapt about her crown like a coronet, curls spilling from its circle. A silver locket engraved with an iris set off the simple cut of the dress, while the more intricate hair-style complemented the gown's embroidery; the combination of simplicity and detail was elegance itself.

Kitty looked every inch the young lady in her new bronze

silk with a pearl pendant and her hair done up in the Grecian style which suited her so well. When they met in their sitting room prior to going downstairs, they talked over each other in a flurry of compliments.

"Kitty," Jane said as they descended the stairs, "thank you again for coming here with me. I am very proud of the young lady you are becoming, and I know my new neighbours will have a most excellent impression of our family through meeting you."

Kitty blushed. "I hope it shall be as you say. I have caused you enough embarrassment in the past to last our lifetime and will never willingly be so ill behaved again."

"I am certain of it, my dear Kitty, and am convinced that Elizabeth was correct when she said, some weeks ago, that we may now boast of having only one silly sister!" Jane declared. They were laughing together over the joke when they entered the drawing room and could not know the lovely picture they presented—two pretty and fashionable ladies, in the bloom of their youth and health, eyes sparkling with laughter and sisterly affection. But Lyfford saw, and his heart swelled with the domestic felicity which was soon to be his. Mrs Swindon also witnessed the scene and thought with satisfaction of the impression these girls would make upon their guests.

"My dear Jane, I have no words. You are enchanting," Lyfford said as he bowed over her hand, before performing a similar service for Kitty. "And can this be our young Catherine, grown into a beautiful lady in an instant?" The younger Bennet blushed anew and thanked him prettily.

The Edgertons arrived first, by Cynthia's design, for she wished a display of the family's approval for all the guests. Next came the Fairchilds, whom Jane and Kitty had not met. The Beatons arrived soon after and were flattered that the Bennets recalled them from their meeting in the churchyard.

Lyfford offered an arm to Jane, and they began to move about the drawing room while Kitty approached the Miss Fairchilds to get to know them better. They paused to speak with Sir Walter and Lady Miller; the gentleman was the village magistrate and a distant cousin of Lyfford's and would be seated to Jane's left at dinner, so she took a little extra interest in him.

"And are there many rogues and brigands to be met with in the area, Sir Walter?" she asked with a smile, and the middle-aged knight laughed.

"No more than in any market town with the river trade, and less than some," he replied jovially. "Avoid the docks and keep hold of your reticule when you visit the shops, and you will find it far safer here than in town, Miss Bennet."

"I understand you hail from Hertfordshire," Lady Miller said. "I have passed through it a number of times on the way to London—a very pretty county."

"I may perhaps be biased, but I can only agree with you," Jane replied. They spoke for a few minutes more before moving on, making polite conversation with their guests until the bell rang.

Lyfford escorted Lady Miller, as the highest-ranking female guest, in to dinner, while her husband offered his arm to Jane. Mr Norman Beaton reached Kitty before his brother could and triumphantly led her into the dining room while Mr Tobias Beaton was left to the indignity of escorting his own sister, who laughed at his scowls.

Mrs Swindon had planned the seating with care, situating Jane between Lyfford and Sir Walter, with Mr Phelps and Miss Beaton across from her. Kitty was between the two Mr Edgertons and across from Miss Fairchild, so both the Bennets were separated during the meal from any possibility of conversation with those ladies who did not approve of their coming. If the congregation of ladies in the drawing room after dinner could not be looked forward to with unadulterated pleasure, at least the meal itself promised nothing but amiable company.

Jane and Kitty had been deeply involved in the planning of the menu and were in some anticipation for each course. The soup was a specialty of Lyfford's cook—a rich, creamy bisque of autumn squashes with thyme and roasted garlic, garnished with pomegranate and toasted pumpkin seeds. The second course was fish: braised cod, seared trout fillets, and eel and onions in oyster gravy. Jane surreptitiously gauged the enjoyment of their guests as she maintained her part in the conversation and was relieved to note that everyone appeared pleased with the selections thus far.

Next came the entrees, and more than one guest gasped softly as the servants entered with platters of food that were very nearly works of art. There was a turkey and lentil ragout, the colours of the vegetables bright against the dark sauce; a roasted ham covered in perfect, round slices of orange pinned to the meat with cloves in clever designs; partridge roasted on a bed of pumpkin and rosemary; and butter-glazed chicken sliced onto a crisp bed of spinach and drizzled with a tart lemon sauce.

"Mrs Swindon has outdone herself," Sir Walter commented to Lyfford, after sampling the ham and the partridge with equal delight.

"I understand that it was not she who planned the menu," Lyfford replied, smiling at Jane, who blushed.

"Well then, Miss Bennet, be assured I shall always accept any invitation of yours," Sir Walter replied appreciatively.

After the entrees was a light remove of nuts and cheeses, including Mrs Bennet's own recipe for candied hazelnuts, which Jane had brought with her. Lyfford and Miss Beaton were both particularly delighted by those, and the latter pressed Jane for the secret. "Instead of adding water to the sugar, cinnamon, and cardamom, use the juice of an orange or two and a bit of melted butter," Jane confided.

When everyone had indulged their taste for sweets, Mrs Swindon rose and signalled to the ladies that it was time to withdraw, leaving the dining room to the gentlemen, their port, and their cigars. Miss Trenton, who had spent much of the meal glowering in Jane's direction, tried to meet up with her in the hall, but Miss Beaton reached Jane first, smoothly slipping her arm through Jane's and speaking brightly of her delight with the pineapple cake. The other young lady turned away with a disgruntled look and took the arm of her mother.

"Miss Trenton has set her cap for Lord Lyfford these five years at least," Miss Beaton murmured quickly as they progressed down the hall in pairs. "And her mother has spoken of the match far longer. She and Mrs Fairchild have a great rivalry on the subject, but Miss Fairchild is a sweet girl with no desire to be a society lady."

"I thank you," Jane whispered back as they reached the drawing room and separated. She only had a moment to mention to Kitty that she would like her to find a few moments during the evening to give her attention to Miss Johnstone, an elderly spinster of more breeding than means, before she was caught by the Trenton ladies and Mrs Fairchild, who commenced an interrogation on the subjects of Jane's family, estate, and education that was less subtle than persistent. They meant to make her uncomfortable and took no pains to hide their motives.

How she wished Elizabeth were with her! But what could not be helped must be endured, so she answered with cheerful brevity, frustrating her audience with her lack of detail and of shame. They would tut amongst themselves for months over the information they drew from her—four sisters and no brothers! A country attorney for an uncle! Not yet presented to the Queen!

After ten minutes of this inquisition, Miss Fairchild, blushing with mortification, drew her mother off on the pretext that she had stepped on her hem and thought it might have ripped in back. After they left the room to assess the damage, Jane excused herself by saying that she must attend to the other guests.

Mrs Swindon pulled her aside for a moment with the offer of a glass of orgeat and quietly asked how Jane was faring. Receiving a positive answer, she smiled approvingly and said, "I have already heard from several people who are impressed with both you and your sister. Now, let us attend to our guests." She bustled off to ensure that everyone was comfortable and to nudge the younger Miss Fairchild, who seemed rather bored with the adult conversations, to play some music for the gathering.

The gentlemen entered soon thereafter, and Jane had to stifle a laugh when Mrs Trenton practically shoved her daughter towards the pianoforte, at which Miss Beaton now sat. The other young lady graciously ceded her place and made her way over to Jane with a twinkle in her eye. "How long do you think it shall be until your betrothed can free himself?" she asked Jane, with a nod of her head towards the door where Lyfford had been accosted by Mrs Fairchild the moment he set foot into the drawing room.

Lyfford answered the question before Jane could, bowing and smiling to Mrs Fairchild before crossing the room to them. Miss Beaton laughed. "Lord Lyfford, whatever did you say to leave her with such a sour look on her face?" she wondered.

Lyfford grinned. "Only that I could not bear to be parted

from my betrothed a moment longer," he replied, bowing over Jane's hand. Mrs Fairchild gave a sniff which could be heard across the room and turned away, joining her sometime-friend Mrs Trenton in whispered conference.

Miss Trenton played very well; there could be no disagreement on that point. She performed a Haydn sonata and a Bach cantata and was greeted with sincere and vigorous applause when she rose from the instrument. Before any other young lady could volunteer, Mrs Trenton commented in a carrying voice, "Perhaps Miss Bennet might favour us with a performance?"

Though her motive was apparent to all—her daughter's performance would be difficult to follow—Jane was not perturbed. After all her time in London, away from her instrument, she had spent many hours of the last week preparing for this moment and said only, "I should be happy to. Miss Beaton, would you be so kind as to turn the pages for me?"

That young lady graciously agreed and followed Jane to the musical corner. A murmur swept through the gathering when she sat not at the pianoforte, but at the great and gleaming harp which had been brought down from the music room that morning. There was already music on the stand and, having been assured by Miss Beaton that she would be able to follow and Jane need not signal for the page turns, Jane flexed her hands a few times and brought them up to the strings.

Lyfford drifted forward as she performed Beethoven's 'Six Variations on a Swiss Song.' His pride and affection were writ plain across his face, and most of the guests smiled to see it. The looks on the faces of the Trenton ladies might have curdled milk, however. Mrs Fairchild's disgruntled expression quickly faded to resignation as she came to the realisation that this was no young man's folly but a sincere attachment.

With hardly a pause, Jane launched into a Petrini sonata, a more challenging song which proceeded at a livelier pace than her first. She got through the piece with only a few small errors, and those detectable only to herself, standing at the song's conclusion to a swell of applause easily as robust as that which greeted Miss Trenton's performance.

"Brava, Miss Bennet," said Mrs Davis, who sat near the instrument. "I predict you will inspire a rage for the harp in town if you continue to perform after your marriage."

Jane blushed and thanked her. Lyfford approached, beaming, and she gratefully took his arm, for she was feeling rather shaky in the aftermath of her success.

The other young ladies were prevailed upon to exhibit, with the varying degrees of success often encountered at a country gathering, and Jane and Lyfford were happy to sit together and listen, conversing with their guests between performances. The gathering broke up slowly, the older guests trickling out first, and it was well past midnight when the door shut behind the Millers and the Edgertons, who were the last to depart.

"I think that came off very well," Mrs Swindon commented as they mounted the stairs, and her nephew was quick to agree.

"What is your impression of our neighbours, my dear?"

"I found most of them very pleasant," Jane replied, "and I think Miss Beaton may become a particular friend."

"Oh, I like her too. And the Miss Fairchilds are very nice. They remind me a bit of Maria Lucas, but with less giggling," Kitty said artlessly, and Jane could only laugh.

"I am happy that you enjoyed yourselves," Lyfford said.

"I let it be known that we wish to enjoy our family party tomorrow," Mrs Swindon told them as they reached the third floor. "But we must expect many of the ladies to call on Friday."

Jane and Kitty acknowledged the information and, after exchanging good-nights with their hosts, returned to their chambers.

When she went to her chambers, Jane found herself unable to sleep. She wished to speak to Elizabeth, knowing how her sister would find amusement in the people and events of the evening. She sat at the writing desk in her room, instead, and wrote to Elizabeth, giving an account of the dinner party and briefly sketching the characters of her future neighbours. She rather dwelt on the unfriendly trio, relating their antics in a wry style she knew would amuse her favourite sister. After concluding her account and enquiring after her London relations, she paused to re-read Lizzy's most recent letter before picking up her pen again.

And now, I hope you will grant me the privilege of an elder sister and allow me to advise you on a matter in which I flatter myself that I have rather more experience. I thought before I left town that Mr Darcy retained an affection for you, and your account of his frequent appearance in my aunt's parlour leads me to believe that you may expect a renewal of his addresses at some time in the future unless you make an effort to dissuade him.

I will urge you, then, out of my love for you and long knowledge of your habits, to be not content to live in the present day but to give serious consideration to the future. That you may receive his proposal seems likely, and I would desire above all that you be prepared for such an event and both certain of and content in your reply. That he is an excellent gentleman who loves you I believe we may both agree, but this means nothing if you do not and cannot love him.

Examine your heart, dearest Lizzy, and be sure you understand it. I should hate to see you regret an ill-considered answer when it might so readily be prevented by a period of reflection now.

I believe I understand better than you how easy it is to mistake attraction for love, and love for friendship. I thought I loved Mr Bingley, but I did not, and then I was hopelessly in love with my dear Lyfford before I even understood that I felt an attraction to him! Love is not the simple thing that novels and poetry speak of. It is by turns subtle and overwhelming, it may slip silently into your heart or strike like a bolt of lightning. Only you can know how far and deep your affection extends, and then, I think, only by careful examination of it.

I hope you will forgive my presumption in writing the above, for I would more than anything wish to see you as happy as I, dearest sister.

Ever yours,

Jane

CHAPTER TWENTY-TWO

When Georgiana Darcy was shown into the parlour on Gracechurch Street, she found Elizabeth composing a letter at the desk by the window.

"Oh, I hope I have not interrupted you," she said.

"Not at all," Elizabeth smilingly replied, wiping her pen and setting it in the holder. "My sister Mary has sent me quite a long letter in which she offers her thoughts on *The Children of the Abbey*, and I have been composing my reply these three days. I shall resume it later."

"My brother has charged me to tell you that he will be unable to call today, for he has had an urgent letter from Pemberley's steward and must do some research before he may answer."

"Oh dear, I hope he shall not be called away."

"I asked the same, and he thinks not. It is a matter of a dispute over the use of a stream which runs through both Pemberley and a neighbouring estate. My brother said something about Pemberley being downstream and having rights to block any use which would pollute the waters, but I confess I do not know what is happening or how it may be resolved. I am not even sure which of our streams is involved."

As *The Children of the Abbey* was a novel Georgiana had also read, it was only natural that they should discuss it while the tea steeped. They found a general confluence of opinion between them, though Elizabeth was less inclined to view certain aspects of the story through the lens of romance than the young and very sheltered Miss Darcy. They were cheerfully debating whether or not the central couple of the tale were truly suited for a lifetime of happiness together when the knocker was heard. A murmur of voices rapidly escalated to the sounds of an argument, until footsteps were heard on the stairs and a voice familiar to both young ladies cried out, "No, I shall not wait! Either she is home, or she is not, and whatever the case I shall not leave until I have had satisfaction!"

"Oh, no..." Georgiana moaned softly, cringing into her chair. Elizabeth stood just as their unwelcome guest appeared in the doorway, the Gardiners' footman looming apologetically behind her.

"Georgiana Darcy!" Lady Catherine de Bourgh cried, spotting her mortified niece. "What do you here?"

"I...I am calling upon my friend, Miss Elizabeth Bennet, whom I believe you know," she answered in a trembling voice.

"I am very disappointed in you, niece," Lady Catherine said, glowering at her relation. "And in your brother for

181

allowing you to pay visits in this part of town. But that is a matter for a family discussion. Indeed, perhaps it is better that you are here," she speculated. "Yes, perhaps it is. You will learn from me how to deal with importunate upstarts." Her gaze swung to Elizabeth and hardened. "You can be at no loss, Miss Bennet, to understand the reason for my journey to this...distasteful part of town. Your own heart, your own conscience, must tell you why I come."

Elizabeth looked on with unaffected astonishment. "Indeed, you are mistaken, madam. I have not been at all able to account for the honour of seeing you here."

"Miss Bennet," replied her ladyship, in an angry tone, "you ought to know that I am not to be trifled with. But however insincere you may choose to be, you shall not find me so. My character has ever been celebrated for its sincerity and frankness, and in a cause of such moment as this, I shall certainly not depart from it. A report of a most alarming nature reached me two days ago. I was told that not only was your sister on the point of being most advantageously married, but that you, that Miss Elizabeth Bennet, have been accepting and encouraging the regular attentions of my nephew, my own nephew, Mr Darcy. Though I know it must be a scandalous falsehood, and though I would not injure him so much as to suppose the truth of it possible, I instantly resolved on setting off for this place that I might make my sentiments known to you."

"If you believed it impossible," said Elizabeth, colouring with astonishment and disdain, "I wonder you took the trouble of coming so far. What could your ladyship propose by it?"

"At once to insist upon having such a report universally contradicted."

"Your coming to Cheapside, setting foot in the home of my uncle, will rather be a confirmation of it if, indeed, such a report is in existence."

"If! Do you then pretend to be ignorant of it? Has it not been industriously circulated by you and your infamous relations?"

"I never heard such a report," Elizabeth replied icily. "And my family would never stoop to such stratagems. They care too much for my happiness to behave so."

"And can you likewise declare that there is no foundation for it?"

"I do not pretend to possess equal frankness with your ladyship. You may ask questions which I shall not choose to answer."

"This is not to be borne. Miss Bennet, I insist on being satisfied. Has he, has my nephew been calling upon you? Has he been courting you?"

"Your ladyship has declared it to be impossible."

"It ought to be so. It must be so, while he retains the use of his reason. But your arts and allurements may, in a moment of infatuation, have made him forget what he owes to himself and to all his family. You may have drawn him in. Certainly, you have learnt at your mother's knee how to captivate a man of higher station than your own! She married from trade to gentry, and now your sister marries from gentry to peerage! I see how you and your sisters have been instructed in those wiles which turn men's heads!"

"You will not insult my sister!" Elizabeth lashed out so fiercely that the older woman flinched. "Or my mother, for that matter. The one is everything that is honest and true in this world, and the other loves us without restraint. You may say what you wish of me, your ladyship, and I will bear it with all the patience I possess, for the sake of your better-mannered relations. But you will be silent on the subject of my own family if you would have me hear you any further."

Silence hung heavy over the parlour for a long moment before the great lady gathered herself to reply. "Very well. I came here to discover one thing, and I will have my answer. Tell me for once and for all, are you engaged to my nephew?"

Reluctant though she was to oblige Lady Catherine with an answer which could only give her pleasure, she could not and would not be dishonest in the case. "I am not."

Lady Catherine was indeed pleased. "And will you promise me never to enter into such an engagement?"

"I will make no promise of the kind."

"Unfeeling, selfish girl! I am ashamed of you!" She drew breath to continue her harangue but was interrupted by a sharp, authoritative declaration.

"Madam. You will leave. Now." Mrs Gardiner stood in the doorway, her face pale with exertion and anger, the footman and the Gardiners' man of all work behind her.

Their visitor whirled. "Who are you to speak to me in such a manner? Do you not know who I am?"

Mrs Gardiner was unimpressed. "I am the mistress of this house, and you are an unwelcome intruder who has come into it uninvited and insulted my niece. I do not care what name or title you fling at my head, for this is my home, and you will leave it immediately or my servants shall carry you hence."

Lady Catherine's face purpled with shock. "I am not accustomed to being spoken to in such a manner!"

"I find that very surprising," Elizabeth's aunt commented, then gestured to the men. "Wilkins, Moore, please remove this woman from the house."

"I will go," the great lady replied resentfully. "But do not think you have carried the day, Miss Bennet. I shall know how to act." She lifted her nose into the air and swept from the room, trailed by the servants.

"Are you well, Lizzy?" Mrs Gardiner asked.

"Oh, yes, Aunt. I thank you for coming to my rescue, but I am quite well." She went to her aunt and said, "Come, take my arm and I shall help you back to your chambers. You ought to be resting."

"Thank you, Lizzy. I think that may be best." Elizabeth looked over her shoulder and mouthed a silent apology to Georgiana as they left the room. Georgiana topped up both of their cups of tea while she waited for Elizabeth's return, adding rather more sugar than she usually took to her own, for she was feeling rather shocked.

Her friend returned, dropped heavily into her chair, and gratefully accepted the refreshed cup that Georgiana offered. They sat in silence for a moment, until Georgiana offered in a tone of wonder, "Your aunt is magnificent."

Elizabeth laughed softly. "She is, is she not? I hope to one day be half so remarkable."

"But you were!" Georgiana cried. "You stood up to my aunt in a way I have never seen nor imagined! You were so brave and imperturbable!"

"Perhaps in the moment I put on a fine show, but inside I was quaking, I assure you." She set down her cup and held out her hands, which trembled. "I have never before been spoken to in such a way, with such venom and inconsideration united. I find I am rather upset by it," she said, and as she finished, tears began to spill from her eyes.

"Oh, my dear Elizabeth!" Georgiana cried, rushing to kneel before her friend's chair and proffer her handkerchief before taking Elizabeth's free hand between her own. "I am mortified to be related to that woman. It ought to be she who apologises, but please, allow me to say how very sorry I am that a relation of mine has treated you so infamously!"

Fitzwilliam Darcy was in the midst of composing a lengthy express to his steward at Pemberley when a soft knock sounded on the study door. "Enter," he called.

Dunleavy opened the door just enough to slip inside and quickly closed it again, sagging against the portal in patent relief for a heartbeat before resuming the usual dignity of his post as Darcy House butler. His neckcloth was slightly askew, and his breeches had lost a button at the left knee; it was the first time in his fifteen years of service that Darcy had seen the man less than immaculate.

"Sir," Dunleavy began, sounding rather breathless. "Lady Catherine de Bourgh is here and insists upon seeing you." A rather uncertain look flickered across the man's face before he squared his shoulders. "I attempted to convince her to wait in the parlour while we fetched you, but she refused. She was determined to seek you out at once, and though Johnson and I tried to block the doorway, she pushed past us. Since we dared not lay hands upon her without your order, I fear she is now roaming the house in search of you."

"Good God!" Darcy exclaimed. "Has she lost her senses? I thank you for the information, Dunleavy. Please remain close by until this is resolved." He hurried from the study and made his way towards the commotion he could dimly hear once he reached the hall. He found his aunt ascending the main stair-case, shouting, "Where is my nephew?"

"Aunt, what possible reason can there be for this unseemly display?" he barked.

"Aha!" she hurried up towards him. "There you are. We must speak on a matter of grave importance."

"I ask you again, Lady Catherine, why have you decided to mortify me by carrying on in this manner in my home?"

She stopped before him, her expression mutinous. "Because I come on business which cannot be delayed. I must speak with you this instant!"

"You will not say another word until we are in private," he replied in a tone which brooked no dissent.

"Darcy—" she began but was immediately interrupted.

"Not one word!" he roared, in no mood for his aunt's antics. "We shall go to the parlour and sit down and discuss whatever this emergency may be like rational people." He strode past her to the stairs, leaving her no choice but to follow. Once in the parlour, he closed the door and gestured her to a chair. When she was seated, he took his own place across from her.

"Now," he said. "Tell me—without histrionics, if you please—what has happened."

She reached into her reticule and withdrew a letter, handling it as though it were tainted. "My rector gave me this two days ago, and I knew I must at once act upon the information contained therein."

Darcy unfolded the paper, read with bewilderment the salutation '*My dear Charlotte,*' and flicked his gaze to the signature: *Elizabeth Bennet.* He dropped the page as though it had scalded him. "This is a letter from Miss Elizabeth Bennet to her friend Mrs Collins! I most certainly shall not read it without the explicit permission of one—or preferably both— of those ladies!"

"Mr Collins had every right to read his wife's letters, and

he was absolutely correct to bring this one to me. We have his permission to read it and need nothing more."

"I shall not." He did, however, pick it up from the floor, fold it, and place it next to himself, out of his aunt's reach.

His aunt said contemptuously, "Your notions of morality have become positively middle class, Nephew. Very well, I shall tell you the contents which so disturbed me. Miss Bennet said that you and your sister call upon her quite often at her uncle's home. The home of a tradesman! I expected to find that this was a falsehood, perpetuated by that little nobody to aggrandize herself in her friend's eyes, but when I lowered myself to visit that part of town and confront her with her lies, who do I find with her but my own niece, your sister!"

Darcy paled. "You visited Miss Bennet at the Gardiners' home?"

"Certainly, I did! I could not allow Miss Bennet to start rumours which might lead to aspersions being cast upon your honour! Never did I expect to find my niece in the home of a tradesman. I am most seriously displeased with you, Darcy."

"Not half so displeased as I am with you, I suspect," Darcy replied sharply, causing his aunt to gasp with affront. "Tell me everything that was said and, if you will, your reason for interfering."

"I interfere, as you put it, because I am nearly the closest relation you have, and am entitled to know all your concerns." She chose to ignore Darcy's heavenward glance at that piece of effrontery. "And because I am Anne's mother and will not allow some market-town hussy to disrupt your engagement!"

Darcy rose from his seat, paced across the room once, twice, then abruptly sat again. "For the last time, Anne and I are not engaged, nor shall we ever be."

"You most certainly are! It was the dearest wish of your mother and hers."

"And yet we are not engaged, for the question has been neither asked nor answered, and neither my father nor hers ever entered into such an agreement for our futures," Darcy replied with strained patience. "Anne does not wish to be married, not to me and not to anyone. She is aware that carrying a child would most likely kill her, and confined though her life is, she is unwilling to end it. This discussion is over. You will tell me what you have said to Miss Elizabeth Bennet and what my sister was forced to witness."

Lady Catherine raised her chin, unabashed. "I told her that a report was abroad of your regular attentions to her—I did not disclose my source—and let her know that a schemer such as herself could not and would not succeed in attaching the honour of a man such as you. She denied any such arts, of course, but I let her know that the world is aware she and her sisters have learnt such things from her mother, a tradesman's daughter who had captured a gentleman, and that her sister's recent engagement far above her station only confirmed that Mrs Bennet has passed her tricks on to her daughters."

Darcy was by now pale with anger but with some effort held his tongue and allowed her to continue.

"I was able to bring her to confess that she is not engaged to you—as if she could be—but the little harlot would not promise me never to enter into any such engagement, should you be weak enough to proffer it! You see, nephew, she is determined to have you! Whatever infatuation you have been labouring under, let it end now that you know what she is. I have done you a service in revealing this, and I should have had that promise from her one way or another, had not her lowborn relation interfered!"

"Mr Gardiner?" Darcy replied in a strangled tone, torn

between the angry mortification induced by his aunt's actions and the wild hope engendered by Elizabeth's refusal to disown his suit entirely.

"Mrs Gardiner," Lady Catherine sniffed contemptuously. "She had the nerve to threaten to have her servants carry me from her home! Does she not know who I am?"

"Oh, I imagine she knows quite well," Darcy muttered darkly, then rounded on his aunt. "Aunt, you have shamed me beyond bearing. You have insulted and abused two excellent ladies and subjected my tenderhearted sister to a scene which can only have distressed her. Your manners are those of a drunken sailor, barrelling into situations which are no concern of yours and wrecking everything in sight! I am ashamed to be connected to you and ashamed of anything I have ever done to make people believe I resemble you in any particular!"

His aunt was pale and trembling with offence and attempted to speak, but he would not be stopped. "You will leave my house this instant, and until you have apologised both sincerely and profusely to myself, Miss Bennet, Mrs Gardiner, and my sister for the scenes you have enacted today, you will not be welcome in any of my homes, and I most certainly shall not be visiting you!" He pointed sharply to the door.

"Not so hasty, if you please," his aunt cried. "I have by no means done. I see you are determined to have her, that you have no regard for your own honour and credit. The niece of a tradesman—is such a girl to be my niece's sister? Heaven and earth! Of what are you thinking? Are the shades of Pemberley to be thus polluted?"

"Enough, madam. You have insulted me in every possible method. You will leave my home or, like Mrs Gardiner, I will have you carried out. Dunleavy!" he called, and that good servant promptly appeared in the doorway. "Fetch our two strongest footmen and have my aunt removed from the house. She is not to be readmitted without my express permission."

The butler bowed and quickly left, and for the second time that day, the great Lady Catherine de Bourgh was forced to leave a house before her business was completed to her own satisfaction, lest she lose her dignity in the pursuit.

CHAPTER TWENTY-THREE

D arcy hurried back to his study, where he penned a quick note and rang for a servant to bear it to his uncle, the Earl of Matlock, who was usually to be found at Brook's of a Tuesday afternoon. Hurriedly finishing the letter to his steward, he saw it sent off express before returning to his chambers only long enough for his valet to fling a jacket onto him and run a comb through his hair before he was off to Gracechurch Street.

In the Gardiners' parlour, he found his Elizabeth upon the settee, gazing contemplatively out the window and sipping some chocolate as his sister, next to her, read softly from Wordsworth.

> Though absent long,
> These forms of beauty have not been to me,

As is a landscape to a blind man's eye:
But oft, in lonely rooms, and mid the din
Of towns and cities, I have owed to them,
In hours of weariness, sensations sweet,
Felt in the blood, and felt along the heart,
And passing even into my purer mind
With tranquil restoration:—feelings too
Of unremembered pleasure; such, perhaps,
As may have had no trivial influence
On that best portion of a good man's life;
His little, nameless, unremembered acts
Of kindness and of love. Nor less, I trust,
To them I may have owed another gift,
Of aspect more sublime; that blessed mood,
In which the burthen of the mystery,
In which the heavy and the weary weight
Of all this unintelligible world
Is lighten'd:—that serene and blessed mood,
In which the affections gently lead us on,
Until, the breath of this corporeal frame,
And even the motion of our human blood
Almost suspended, we are laid asleep
In body, and become a living soul:
While with an eye made quiet by the power
Of harmony, and the deep power of joy,
We see into the life of things.

— WM WORDSWORTH, 1798

Georgiana glanced up then, perhaps seeing in the corner of
her eye some slight motion of his, and gave him a quick,

strained smile before touching the back of Elizabeth's hand and saying, "Lizzy, my brother is come."

Elizabeth startled, and paled, and then roused herself to greet her visitor with a curtsey and a simulacrum of her usual smile. "Mr Darcy, we did not expect you today."

He rushed across the room to take her hand and bow very low over it. "You did not expect my wretched, interfering aunt, either, but I dare hope my presence will be at least a little more welcome." He turned to his sister. "Georgiana, dear, I thank you for remaining with Miss Elizabeth after what was no doubt a distressing scene to you both. I have some information for Miss Elizabeth which she may prefer to hear in privacy. Would you mind very much sitting across the room for a few moments?"

"Of course, Brother," Georgiana agreed readily, taking herself to the farthest part of the room and bending with apparent concentration over the volume of poetry.

"Miss Elizabeth," Darcy said in a low tone. "I must apologise, again and again, for the insults and abuse you have today endured at the whim of my aunt. She came directly to me, I think, when she left you, and gave me to know enough of the matter that I have barred her from my homes and my company until such time as she sees fit to apologise to everyone she has offended today. I hope that you will acquit me of being in any way in agreement with her, and if you cannot, that you will at least do so for Georgiana, who loves you as a dear friend."

"Of course, I do not think either of you complicit, in deed or in thought, with your aunt's actions and words today. You both have shown me and my relations nothing but sincere friendship since our acquaintance was renewed."

His shoulders sagged with relief. "I have some property of yours to return, which had come into my aunt's possession."

He reached into his pocket and produced the letter. She opened it, glanced at the salutation, and blushed with mortification.

"So this is the source of her 'rumours'. How did she come to have it?"

"Mr Collins," Darcy replied shortly, distaste evident in his tone.

Elizabeth closed her eyes and sighed. "Of course. Why did I not think of that? But you have read it, sir, and know that I spoke nothing more than the truth—less, perhaps, for I made it to sound as though Georgiana was my particular visitor—and that, in confidence to a friend," she turned pleading eyes on him. "Surely you understand I had no notion of generating gossip to force your hand."

"Indeed, I have not read it," he replied. "It was not mine to read, and I am ashamed that my aunt did so. But it never so much as crossed my mind that you should attempt such stratagems, for they are quite contrary to your nature." He took her hand again and looked at it rather than her face as he continued. "And surely you know—surely by now you understand—that my affections and wishes are unchanged, and if you ever wish me to speak again on the subject I raised last April, you need only drop a hint. But perhaps a rather large one, for we both know that I can be somewhat obtuse."

She smiled softly at him, understanding in a swell of gentle feeling how much she had come to care for this dear, difficult, kindly man when she had thought herself to be merely enjoying his friendship.

Elizabeth would not, afterwards, be able to recall precisely what she meant to say in reply to that declaration, for at that moment her aunt's personal maid rushed into the room. She dropped a hasty curtsey to them all.

"Begging your pardon, Miss Elizabeth, but you are urgently needed upstairs."

"Is it time? No, it cannot be—not for three weeks at least!"

The maid nodded anxiously. "I'm afraid it is, miss, and your aunt wishes to speak with you before...before matters progress."

"I beg you will excuse me," Elizabeth said distractedly to her guests and quickly followed the servant from the room.

When she returned half an hour later, only Mr Darcy remained. He stood and bowed when she entered and said, "I have sent my sister home and remained only to enquire if I might be of any assistance."

"I thank you, sir. I...I believe I would like some company until my uncle arrives, if you would be so kind," she answered.

"Of course." He waited until she had summoned a maid to keep propriety for them and had taken a seat before resuming his own. "I apprehend that the child is coming?"

"Yes." Elizabeth brushed a curl away from her face with a shaking hand. "We did not expect it just yet, and she has been so frail throughout..." She caught a breath that was nearly a sob and continued. "But the midwife has been summoned and a chamber prepared for the birth. A servant goes even now to fetch my uncle, and I may do nothing more to comfort my aunt."

He read the frustration in her tone and expression and said gently, "You may comfort your uncle, and it will give her peace to know that he shall not be alone in his waiting."

"That is almost exactly what she said when I tried to insist upon staying with her," Elizabeth answered with a tremulous smile. "She thinks of everyone but herself. She asked me to attend her so that she might instruct me in what ought to be done for the comfort of her children if she...if she..." Elizabeth allowed her head to fall into her hands and wept.

Darcy wished very much that he might take her into his arms and console her, but mindful as he was of Mr Gardiner's expectations, he would take no such liberty even for an innocent reason. He was therefore forced to content himself with offering her his handkerchief.

"I shall not say that it cannot be so, for such a blatant falsehood can offer no solace, but I will tell you in all honesty that your aunt has struck me as a lady with a will of iron, and I believe that she will come through this if anyone could."

Elizabeth raised her head at that, saw the offered handkerchief and gratefully accepted it. Dabbing at her eyes, she said, "That is true. I only wish there were more I could do. I shall feel so helpless sitting here, waiting for word. Indeed, I already do!"

"The midwife, is she known to your aunt? Is she trustworthy?" Darcy asked curiously.

"Oh, yes, she has attended my aunt every time."

"Has any thought been given to bringing in an accoucheur, under the circumstances?"

"My uncle interviewed several last month, but he said... well, I shall not repeat exactly what he said, but he was not impressed with their intelligence or their manners."

"Ah. I know little of such matters, except that the wives of my London acquaintance all seem to have one."

Elizabeth's lips twitched. "My uncle seemed to think they were more fashionable than useful."

"That is a dashed silly thing to try to be fashionable about," Darcy muttered, surprising a laugh from Elizabeth.

He turned the subject then to books, hoping to distract her from her worries. They spoke rather disjointedly on the subject—her attention was not truly on the conversation—for nearly half an hour until her uncle arrived, desperate for news of his wife. Darcy waited patiently as Elizabeth told her uncle all she knew, and when he had run out of questions she could answer, Darcy spoke.

"Mr Gardiner, sir, I understand from your niece that you interviewed several accoucheurs before concluding that your wife would be safer in the hands of her midwife. I wonder, however, if I might introduce to you the physician our family uses when we are in town? It is my understanding that he will occasionally attend the lying-in of a patient if there is reason to believe the delivery will be difficult or unusual in some way."

Mr Gardiner hesitated only a second before he replied, "If this physician will come here, I will meet him, but I do not intend to stir from this house until my wife's labours are at their end."

"I expected nothing else." He bowed. "If you will excuse me, sir, Miss Elizabeth, I shall go now and try to find him. If we are lucky, he will not be out on a call."

Elizabeth and her uncle bade him farewell and good fortune in his search, and he left swiftly, happy to have this chance to be of use.

An hour later, Darcy returned, followed by a well-dressed, grey-haired man whose eyes gleamed with intelligence behind the lenses of his spectacles. Behind them, a younger man carried a large satchel. Darcy introduced them as Mr Holcomb and his assistant, Mr Greeley.

They sat, and the history of Mrs Gardiner's expectancy and illness were related to the physician. Mr Gardiner ended with the question, "What might you be able to offer in such a case, in the way of assistance?"

"I am of the opinion that birthing is, in general, best left to the ladies and the midwives," Mr Holcomb replied. "What a competent physician—and I count myself among their number—may offer is the possibility of surgical intervention in a critical case."

Mr Gardiner paled and swallowed. "Elizabeth, I must ask you to remove yourself from the room until we have finished discussing this." Her lips tightened but she rose, curtseyed, and left without a murmur. Mr Gardiner turned back to the doctor. "You are speaking of surgical removal of the babe?"

Mr Holcomb nodded. "I will be blunt—the procedure does not often end happily, but in extremity it does offer one last chance for mother and child. It is to be hoped that, if you choose to have me present, I shall be nothing more than an assistant to the midwife, but I can and will intervene if matters come to a crisis."

Mr Gardiner rubbed a hand over his mouth, looking uncertain for the first time in Darcy's acquaintance with him. "Very well, sir," he answered after a long moment. "If my wife is willing to have you in the room, you may attend her. But if it should come to a choice, sir, I will ask for your word as a gentleman that you will do everything possible to save my wife, even if you must sacrifice the babe."

Mr Holcomb stood and bowed sharply to Mr Gardiner. "Sir, you have my word as a physician, which I fancy carries rather more weight in the present circumstance."

Mr Gardiner stood also and walked with the doctor to the

door. Finding his niece in the hall as he expected, he enjoined her to convey the doctor to the birthing chamber and ensure that Mrs Gardiner was content with his presence before returning to wait with him.

"Should you care for a glass of brandy, Mr Darcy?" he asked upon his return. "Or I have a bottle of Irish whisky, if that is more to your taste."

"I shall be happy to join you in a glass of whatever you are having, sir," Darcy replied. Generally, he did not care to imbibe before dinner, but sensing the other man's anxiety, he would not for the world do or say anything that was less than easy and agreeable.

Mr Gardiner selected the whisky, and they sat for a time speaking of ordinary things, such as the weather and the difficulty of acquiring good brandy as the war stretched on. Darcy was glad to see that the other man sipped at the strong drink only occasionally, and he did likewise. In time, Elizabeth joined them and said that her aunt had put several questions to Mr Holcomb and, approving of his answers, had allowed that he might remain. She then turned to Darcy.

"I must thank you, sir, for thinking to bring him. He seems a very learned gentleman and I will feel easier knowing that my aunt shall have two experienced people looking after her."

"Indeed, my niece is correct. I think I have neglected to give you my thanks, but please allow me now to do so—thank you, sir, from the bottom of my heart, for the care and concern you have shewn to us, and for the practical help you have provided in the form of the good doctor."

Darcy blushed and waved off their thanks. "Truly, it was the least I could do after the trouble my family caused yours today. I only hope that my aunt's actions did not upset Mrs Gardiner so much as to hasten her lying-in."

Mr Gardiner sat upright abruptly. "What is this about your aunt?"

Elizabeth hastened to say, "I am sure the timing is merely a coincidence, and my aunt did not seem at all distressed— perhaps a little angry, but that is all." She explained briefly to her uncle what had transpired earlier, and her aunt's involvement.

Mr Gardiner turned to Darcy. "A relation of yours so disapproves of your attentions to my niece that she has entered my home, insulted both my niece and my wife, and desisted only upon threat of force and humiliation?"

"My aunt would disapprove of my attentions to a duke's daughter, for she would not be *her* daughter. She has long wished for a match between myself and my cousin Anne, but neither of us shares this desire."

"I find it hard to believe any lady would behave in this fashion if she had been informed that her wishes could not come to fruition."

"She has been so informed, though perhaps not so forcefully as now, in hindsight, seems to have been necessary. That is an error which I have already endeavoured to correct." Darcy set his glass down and stood. "I feel I have overstayed my welcome. This is a time for your family to draw together and mine may require my assistance with my aunt. Mr Gardiner, Miss Elizabeth, please allow me to apologise again for her actions today and her offences against you."

He looked down at his hands, swallowed, and added, "I have no right to ask any favours of you now, but I hope that when it is convenient you might be kind enough to send me a note and tell me how Mrs Gardiner does."

Mr Gardiner, clearly not yet disposed to be conciliatory, must have seen the look on his niece's face—half pleading, half stern—for he nodded grudgingly. "I shall be sure to inform you of the outcome," he said shortly, rising to his feet. Darcy bowed to his hosts and left, pausing in the door to cast a lingering look over his shoulder at Elizabeth before vanishing from their sight.

Just before the front door closed, he could hear Mr Gardiner's voice. "I do like your young man, Lizzy, but if this is how his relations behave, I may have to reconsider his welcome here."

CHAPTER TWENTY-FOUR

D arcy had been home little more than half an hour and had just begun a strongly worded letter to Lady Catherine after informing Georgiana of the events following her departure from Gracechurch Street, when his butler entered and announced that the Earl of Matlock was below and wished to see him.

"Thank you, Dunleavy, you may bring him here." Darcy put away his writing supplies and rose to greet his uncle as he was shown in. The earl was a hale and vigorous man who looked a decade younger than his eight and fifty years, his face hardly lined and his blond hair only touched with grey at the temples and showing no signs of thinning. He greeted his nephew with a firm handshake and gladly accepted the offer of a glass of brandy.

When they were seated, he eyed his nephew speculatively.

"Well, my boy, you have set the cat among the pigeons, and my wife is not best pleased that my sister is under our roof and spewing more spite than usual. Are you certain you know what you are about, courting this unknown country girl?"

"I am," Darcy replied shortly. "I am pursuing my own happiness and that of my sister."

"Well, the good Lord knows you both deserve that." Matlock sipped at his brandy. "I will not attempt to dissuade you. You are the head of your family, regardless of the nonsense Catherine spouted while she tried to badger me into 'exerting my authority' over you to force you to desist in pursuing this alliance—as though I could!" Both men rolled their eyes. "You are aware that your aunt and I hoped you would make a more eligible match with regard to status, but you have met with every debutante the last five Seasons have offered, and none of them drew your attention. That you found a lady who captured your interest in the country... perhaps it should not come as a surprise. And I understand the sister is betrothed to Lyfford?"

"That is so."

"Well, then, that is a connexion I may be able to approve most heartily. Rumour has it that young Lyfford will declare for my party when Parliament opens. We should be happy to have him, and if he is half the orator his father was, our side can put him to very good use. You would not happen to have any intelligence on the matter for your old uncle, would you?"

Darcy shook his head and chuckled. "It all comes back to politics for you, does it not?"

The earl grinned. "Indeed, it does. Parliament! The greatest chess match in all the empire!" He sobered and cast a serious look at his nephew. "My sister tells me that you have barred her from your homes and that your young lady's relation was forced to threaten her with bodily harm to get her out of their house—though that is not quite the way she put it, you understand."

"It is quite true that she is no longer welcome in my homes and that she will not be afforded my company or that of my sister for any reason other than a thorough apology, which I do not expect shall be forthcoming in my lifetime. But that is the least of it, Uncle." Darcy looked more grave than usual. "Mrs Gardiner is with child and has been very ill. Not two hours after she was forced to deal with my aunt, her lying-in began, some weeks early. I worry that the commotion my aunt caused and the strain of arguing with her may have... hastened matters. Holcomb now attends her, but I truly fear what my aunt has wrought this day."

Lord Matlock shook his head. "I beg you will let me know how that business turns out. I shall pack my sister off to Rosings first thing in the morning, and then perhaps you might visit us later in the day? Lady Matlock will wish to hear of this Miss Bennet from you, and we may discuss how to keep Catherine in check until you are safely wed."

"You are rather ahead of me, Uncle. Miss Bennet and I are not engaged, and I am by no means certain she will accept me when I ask."

The earl's eyebrows rose sharply. "You think a country girl of little fortune or standing might refuse Darcy of Pemberley? I find that difficult to imagine."

"I shall tell you all over tea tomorrow," Darcy said. "For now, let it suffice when I say that Miss Elizabeth Bennet is no ordinary lady."

The older man rose, and Darcy followed suit. "I shall hold you to that promise, my boy," Lord Matlock said. "Look for my note tomorrow. I shall inform you when Matlock House is safe." He made his way to the door, paused, and turned.

"I almost forgot thank you for having the forethought to

send that message to my club. It allowed me to reach Matlock House before Sarah entirely lost patience with Catherine. Although I believe it was a close thing." He shook his head. "Thirty-two years of marriage, and I swear that half my apologies have been for my sister's behaviour rather than my own."

"I had not thought you visited with her so often."

"We do not. Catherine is a virtuoso of offensive correspondence, as you will likely soon learn for yourself."

Darcy grimaced. "Excellent, something new to look forward to."

"You know, my boy, there were those who called my marriage a mistake—Lord Matlock's heir marrying the daughter of a baronet with only four thousand pounds. It was the best mistake I ever made. She brought me little in the way of status or funds, but she was the making of me as a man."

Darcy smiled faintly. "Miss Elizabeth Bennet has already worked a change in me for the better. If I should be so fortunate as to win her, I can only imagine that my improvement would continue."

Lord Matlock returned to Matlock House to find his sister and his long-suffering wife awaiting him.

"Well?" Lady Catherine barked. "Have you convinced my nephew to think as he ought?"

"No need, no need," he replied cheerfully, taking a seat and accepting a cup of tea from his wife. "Darcy is an intelligent fellow, and he knows what he and Pemberley require." His sister's face was a study in smug satisfaction, and he winked at his wife before he continued. "One might, perhaps, wish for more in the way of fortune, but this Miss Elizabeth

Bennet is a hearty country girl who will not badger him to be always in town, and would, one hopes, bear him a number of children. It is past time that there were more than two Darcys of Pemberley! And she brings a connexion to Lyfford through her sister, which is not to be cavilled at. I shall have to meet her to be certain, but it sounds as if Darcy has made a good choice for himself."

Lady Catherine had slowly turned purple as he spoke, and when he was done, she could contain herself no longer. "Brother! I am astounded at you! That you could even consider approving of his casting Anne—and Rosings!—aside for a girl of no fortune or standing!"

"Good God, Cathy, how many times must we all repeat it —Darcy and Anne are not and never have been engaged. Had my nephew ever contemplated entering into such an engagement, I should have advised him against it!" His sister gasped with outrage and attempted to speak, but he raised his voice and overrode her. "Anne is not well enough to bear an heir for Pemberley, and Darcy is the sort of man who will be happiest if he may spend ten months of the year ensconced in the country surrounded by his children. For that to happen, he requires a healthy wife who enjoys the country. He has, from what he has told me, selected just such a lady and I, for one, am prepared to embrace her as a niece if she makes him happy. Lord knows there has been little enough happiness in that family since our sister died."

"Oh, yes, our sister," Lady Catherine said bitterly. "Sweet, gentle Anne who everyone loved; pretty, insipid Anne who had all the fortitude of a butterfly! She had everything— George Darcy, Pemberley, and a son and heir—and was too weak to hold it. How fitting that my weak, insipid daughter was named for her!"

"Catherine!" Lady Matlock snapped. "How dare you speak

of your sister and your own daughter in such a manner! Anne was my dearest friend and a true sister to me, and neither she nor your daughter deserve your vitriol!"

"She stole George Darcy from me!" Lady Catherine screeched. "My father and his were near an agreement when he caught sight of Anne—pretty little Anne, only fifteen years old—and declared that he would wait for her. He cast me aside as though I were nothing—me, the eldest child of the Earl of Matlock!"

"He loved Anne from the moment he first laid eyes on her," Lord Matlock said.

"What has love to do with anything?" Lady Catherine spat. "Marriage in our circles is a joining of families and fortunes. Love is for poets and fools."

"Then you may call me a fool, with my blessing. I would not be the man I am today without Sarah." He cast a fond look at his wife. "I only hope Darcy may be as contented as I in his own union."

"He should be contented with uniting two great estates! I married that old lecher to get Rosings for this family, and Darcy has no right to discard it!"

Lord Matlock had reached the end of his considerable patience. "Rosings belongs to Anne, not to you! You have no say in its disposition! And now that I know the contempt you feel for your own daughter, I believe I shall exercise my privilege as head of the Fitzwilliam family and Anne's trustee to remove her from your care." He stood, a dangerous glint in his eye. "Have your maid pack your things, Sister, we depart for Rosings in an hour. Anne shall return here with me, and you may stew alone in your spite amid the cold ostentation of the house your marriage brought you."

"I will not be badgered like this! And I shall not give my daughter over to you."

The earl was a man whose fiercest anger came wrapt in quiet, and the very air seemed to still when his voice dropped near a whisper. "You shall if you wish to receive your quarterly funds. Or had you forgotten that Lewis made me your trustee, as well? What will your neighbours think of the great Lady Catherine when she no longer has funds for new gowns and dinner parties?"

Lady Catherine paled, and Lord Matlock rang the bell for a servant. When a footman arrived, he gave orders that his sister's bags were to be packed as well as a valise for him, and the traveling coach readied to depart in one hour. Defeated, his sister hurried to oversee the packing of her gowns.

When they were alone, he turned to his wife. "My dear, I must leave the preparation of a suite for Anne in your hands, and another matter as well." He explained what Darcy had said about Lady Catherine's visit to the Gardiner home only a few hours previously, and the possibility that it had hastened Mrs Gardiner's lying-in. "I will ask that you communicate with Darcy on the matter, and when it is appropriate, I know you will find the best method of conveying our family's apologies to theirs."

"You may rely upon me," Lady Matlock said with a reassuring smile. "Now, go see to your arrangements, and come back to me with our niece as soon as you may."

"I shall. Oh, and please inform Darcy of what has occurred immediately. When I left him, he was expecting to visit us tomorrow." With a last fond smile, he hurried off.

Two days later, just before midday, Lyfford entered the library where Jane was reading on a settee in the morning light while

Kitty practised her figure drawing by sketching her sister. Both looked up upon hearing his steps.

"My dear, an express is come from London."

Jane paled and sat up abruptly, while Kitty hurriedly set her pencil aside and joined her sister on the settee. The sisters clasped hands and Jane said, "Would you read it to us?"

"Of course." Lyfford took Kitty's abandoned seat and broke the seal. "It is dated yesterday. 'Dear Jane and Kitty, Yesterday, my aunt was brought to bed, and early this morning was safely delivered of two darling daughters.'"

He glanced up, smiling, as the ladies exclaimed, "Twins!"

"So it would seem." He returned his gaze to the letter and continued, "'The babes are small and my aunt quite weak, but both the midwife and the physician have said they hope all three will do well with rest and good food. They are both to visit daily for the next week, at least, so be assured that my aunt and new cousins are receiving the best possible care. I will leave the details for your return, in the interests of seeing this note into your hands with all possible speed. Your loving sister, Elizabeth'."

"Oh, I am so relieved!" Jane exclaimed.

"As am I," Kitty agreed. "Oh, I should so like to see the babies! I wish I might go to town with you when we leave."

Lyfford and Jane looked at each other. "I see no reason why you should not," Jane said slowly after that unspoken communication. "You might help our aunt and uncle with the children, which would allow Lizzy to accompany me as I shop for my trousseau."

"I should be delighted," Kitty replied promptly.

"You should not mind missing the shopping?"

"Not very much," Kitty admitted. "I cannot be two places at once, and I have already had this lovely trip. If I may assist our aunt, it will give Lizzy the chance to have some fun."

"I am certain she will appreciate it, Kitty."

"My business here is more or less done. We might leave on Saturday if you like, which would put us in Coventry the whole of Sunday and in London on Tuesday, with good roads," Lyfford offered.

"That seems an excellent plan. I will write to my father and mother to tell them that we shall be keeping Kitty with us a little longer."

Darcy had been pleased to learn from his aunt that his cousin Anne was to be removed from Rosings and into the more affectionate care of her Fitzwilliam relations. When the anxiously awaited note from Mr Gardiner arrived announcing the relative safety of Mrs Gardiner and her babes, he shared that information with Lady Matlock, according to her desire.

Several days after the birth, the Gardiners were surprised to receive a large basket containing a bowl of hothouse strawberries, a tin of a particular variety of Swiss drinking chocolate sold only by the most exclusive shops, a box of small cakes from Gunter's, and two exquisite blankets woven of soft wool. Enclosed was a letter written in a fine copperplate hand.

Matlock House, Grosvenor Square

Mrs Gardiner,

We pray you shall condescend to accept our most sincere apologies for the uncouth and unconscionable behaviour of our sister, Lady Catherine de Bourgh, on her recent visit to your home. Were it within our power to ensure that she would give her own apologies to you, it would be so, but as that has proved impossible we have secured her removal from town and arranged matters such that her stay in the country will be of some duration. Be assured that she will not trouble you again and that all her family are shocked and dismayed by her actions and the sentiments which inspired them.

It is our hope that the delicacies enclosed will assist you in your recovery and that it shall be swift and complete.

Yours,

Edmund Matlock

Sarah Matlock

The letter and the gifts were both passed round and exclaimed over by the adults, and while it was wondered how much influence, if any, Mr Darcy had in its creation, it was agreed that every item was thoughtfully selected and the letter was gracious and humble. Mr Gardiner's view of Mr Darcy's family, jaundiced by the actions of one relation, was softened by this gesture from others.

CHAPTER TWENTY-FIVE

Mr Darcy, with uncharacteristic impatience, found himself unable to stay away from Gracechurch Street and called upon Elizabeth on the fifth day following the birth of the twins, expecting only to leave his card but finding himself instead ushered into the parlour to wait for her.

Jane's letter which had concluded with her advice on matters of the heart had been received several days previously, and much thought upon since. Elizabeth, a little sleepless from the business of caring for five cousins, had arrived at no definite conclusions, but she felt herself to be strongly inclined towards the gentleman who leapt to his feet as she entered the room and searched her face, a solemn, anxious look upon his own.

He asked after Mrs Gardiner immediately following the

exchange of greetings and expressed his relief that she continued well.

Elizabeth smiled softly. "Your Mr Holcomb has been a great reassurance to us all, though in the event itself he was not really needed. But we were very glad to have him there and he has visited daily since, as has Mrs Ellis, the midwife. With two experts looking after her and the twins, we have all been put quite at our ease!"

"I am very glad for it," Darcy replied. "I do not think I should ever have forgiven myself had something gone awry, for the more I think on it, the more likely it seems to me that my aunt's actions that day must have contributed to Mrs Gardiner's early lying-in."

"And how, pray tell, would that have been your fault?" Elizabeth wondered with some astonishment. "For all our brief acquaintance, I fancy I know Lady Catherine well enough to say that only extraordinary measures will divert her once she is set upon a course."

"I ought to have been firmer with her in rebuffing her attempts to engage me to my cousin."

"I should think a simple refusal would have been enough for any reasonable person," she said, laughing.

"But my aunt is not reasonable, particularly on that subject," he retorted with a wry look.

"And that is a fault in her for which you bear no responsibility, and no one here blames you for her actions. Indeed, we cannot even say that there was more to the business than an unpleasant visit, for both the midwife and the physician have said that twins usually come a little early." She smiled kindly at him and was rewarded with a tentative smile in return. "Now, I shall thank you to cease tormenting yourself with conjectures which cannot be proved, or else I shall be very cross," she declared briskly, and surprised a chuckle from him.

"It is a sunny day, though cool," he said. "Might you care for a turn about the park down the street?"

"Oh, yes!" she exclaimed. "I have hardly stirred from the house since Jane left, and a walk would suit me exceedingly." She excused herself to don her walking attire, ensure that her aunt was well-tended, and find a maid to accompany them, re-joining Mr Darcy in only a few minutes with a sparkle in her eye and a spring in her step.

She took a deep breath of autumn air as the door closed behind them and then smiled up at him, saying, "I shall depend upon you, Mr Darcy, to keep our excursion at a proper length, for I shall not wish to return indoors!"

He smiled and made a show of checking his timepiece before assuring her that although he would not like to curtail her enjoyment, he was far too afraid of Mr Gardiner to keep her out over-long. She laughed and asked after Georgiana, and they fell into easy conversation.

He returned her to the house at the end of half an hour, but visited the next day with his sister, and they all three walked out together. They spoke of many things—of town and country, of Georgiana's studies and Elizabeth's letters from Staffordshire, of the coming Christmas season and their differing family traditions around it. So absorbed were they in speaking of anything and nothing, in enjoying each other's company, that they were all quite chilled when they finally returned to the house and the Darcys bid their farewells.

Elizabeth would reflect that evening in her chamber on the pleasure she found in their company, and in his most particularly, and came to understand that her greatest desire now rested in what she had so vehemently spurned only a season ago.

Lord Matlock returned one week to the day from his departure. Anne de Bourgh was quickly settled into chambers much more airy and cheerful than her own at Rosings and, after fond greetings from her aunt, was left to rest from her travels. Her aunt and uncle took the opportunity to confer in the seclusion of their private sitting room.

"We must have Holcomb to see her as soon as may be," the earl said in a tone of mingled exasperation and worry. "While I was in Kent, I had the displeasure of meeting the fellow who has been treating her, and I cannot call him aught but a thoroughgoing quack!"

"I thought she might require a physician after the journey, my dear—Mr Holcomb awaits only word from me. I shall send for him now, if you like."

He clasped her hand and sighed with contentment. "I am a lucky man. I believe the summons can wait just a bit longer. I have a great need to bask in your company after so much of Catherine's."

She replied with a fond smile and a slight change of subject. "You received my letter?"

"Yes, and was glad to hear that Mrs Gardiner survived. You sent our apologies?"

"Of course, and received a very polite response. I kept it for you to read, if you like."

"Well, we have made the best of a bad business, I think. Let us hope it has not entirely scotched Darcy's chances with the young lady."

"I believe she is made of sterner stuff than that, my dear. I had Darcy to tea while you were gone, and cajoled from him the story of their acquaintance, which I have his permission to relate to you. Prepare yourself for something very shocking. Before they ever met, he insulted her…"

The following day, in accordance with Elizabeth's hopes, Mr Darcy appeared alone. The wind had taken a cold turn, and they stopped at a vendor's cart for cones of hot roasted chestnuts to warm them as they ambled through the park. He had been telling her of his visit earlier in the day to his cousin, Anne de Bourgh, who was settling in at Matlock House and under the care of his physician, Mr Holcomb.

"I hope she will be happier and healthier with Lord and Lady Matlock than she was at Rosings," Elizabeth said. "Do you know, I have been thinking of your problem in persuading your aunt, Lady Catherine, to acknowledge that her plans for you and Miss de Bourgh shall come to naught, and I believe I have hit upon a solution she cannot ignore or deflect."

He saw the teasing light in her eye, and answered gamely, "I shall be happy to hear it."

"Why, it is very simple, Mr Darcy—you must marry someone else!"

He stopped and faced her and said, "Ah, but what lady would have me, taciturn and unsociable as I am?"

"Oh, I do not know," she said breezily. "Perhaps a lady who would like to walk your extensive paths at Pemberley and does not mind the effort required to tease you into smiling. A lady who understands that if she is going to give you a hint, it must be very obvious indeed."

The expression of heartfelt delight diffused over his face became him excellently well, and though he had not always understood her wishes, he understood them now and had no compunction in dropping to one knee in the middle of a public park and clasping one of her hands between his own as he declared, "Elizabeth Bennet, will you be so kind as to accept my hand in marriage, on the understanding that henceforth all my pride and vanity shall be centred on the very great honour of being your chosen partner in life?"

Tears of happiness welled in her eyes as she replied, "On the understanding that henceforth all my hasty judgments and ill-humoured remonstrances shall be directed at those who do not appreciate your worth, Mr Darcy, I do accept."

They beamed at each other for a moment in silence, until their blissful reverie was broken by the applause of an elderly couple sat upon a nearby bench, who had gone completely unnoticed until then. Darcy scrambled to his feet and hid his reddening face by bending to brush the soil from his knee.

"Allow us to wish you, sir and miss, all the happiness my Agnes and I have known in fifty-one years of marriage!" the gentleman called cheerfully.

"Fifty-two," his wife corrected in a carrying whisper.

He turned to her. "Is it fifty-two already? How the time does fly."

Elizabeth laughed. "I cannot think of a finer blessing on our betrothal, sir, and I thank you for it." She curtseyed to them and took Darcy's arm. He nodded to the couple with a rather embarrassed smile, and they walked on. When he enquired whether he ought to ride to Longbourn in the morning, Elizabeth was of the opinion that as she was now of age, they might as well announce their betrothal as a fait accompli and ask her uncle and father for their blessings rather than their permission.

He feared they would be offended; she was certain they would not. "But, if you like, we shall speak with my uncle upon our return to the house, and if he does not object as you fear, we might immediately write to my father, and hope that your suspense will be of short duration," she continued on a teasing note. "Having finally secured you, I am in no mood to surrender your company just yet."

Suiting action to words, they returned to her uncle's home and disturbed him in his study. Upon receiving their news, he said only, "I cannot say I rejoice that our Lizzy is acquiring that aunt of yours as a relation, but we shall repay you with my sisters and Lydia, so perhaps it is best to speak no further on that subject. Welcome to the family, Mr Darcy."

Darcy thanked him and they shook hands on the business before the couple left him to his work. Loath though they were to be parted, he had a sister at home and other relations in town who ought to be informed, and she an aunt upstairs who would be glad of the news. So, they took only another half hour to themselves, much of that spent penning notes to Mr Bennet, before Mr Darcy bade her farewell.

Mrs Gardiner was delighted by the day's events and wished only that she were strong enough to come downstairs on the morrow to personally greet her future nephew. Instead, she entrusted all her pleasure and good wishes to her niece and enjoined her to relay them to her betrothed at the first opportunity.

Georgiana received the intelligence of her brother's engagement with a squeal of delight, and nothing else would do but that she accompany Darcy to Gracechurch Street the next day and to Matlock House that afternoon. Their arrival there was a surprise, but fortunately both their aunt and uncle were home, and as soon as Anne could be summoned to the parlour, Darcy's news was given. His relations could not but be pleased by the sheer joy on the faces of both Darcys, and though they wished they might have met the lady before such a step were taken, their congratulations were sincere.

If Anne's good wishes comprised of equal parts pleasure for her cousin and relief on her own behalf, that was easily understood by all and censured by none. Upon learning that Lord Lyfford and Miss Bennet were expected back in town as early as the following day, Lady Matlock immediately settled on a date five days hence when the Miss Bennets, the Darcys, and Lord Lyfford were to be invited to a private tea.

CHAPTER TWENTY-SIX

The party from Staffordshire were delayed a day by a cracked wheel, arriving at the Gardiner home late Wednesday afternoon, rumpled and relieved to be at last free of the carriage. There they found not only the Gardiners and Elizabeth, but Mr Darcy and his sister, who had been invited to dine. News of the new betrothal was shared with the travellers. Jane, seeing the confidence and genuine happiness in her sister's air, rushed to embrace her.

"Oh Lizzy! I am so happy for you, and you are positively glowing!" She kissed Elizabeth on both cheeks. "And I am happy for myself as well—we shall be settled within twenty miles of each other! Can there be any greater felicity?"

Lyfford grinned and approached Darcy, hand outstretched. "Congratulations, Darcy. I shall be pleased to call you brother."

Darcy clasped Lyfford's hand firmly, his own smile broader than his old friend had ever before witnessed. "And I you, my friend."

When Jane let go of Elizabeth, Kitty came forward to offer her own congratulations. "This does not seem to come as a surprise to Jane, but she has been very sly, for I knew only that he had brought his sister here once to meet you both!"

Elizabeth laughed and said that it was a long story she would tell her younger sister another time. "It is good that you are here, Kitty," she said with a laugh, "for Jane and I shall require you to mediate when we begin to quarrel over which of us is to be happiest!"

"Oh, I shall side with Jane, for I hope to visit Lyfford often," Kitty said with a giggle.

Elizabeth could only laugh and concede defeat—and privately rejoice in the knowledge that her most sensitive sister had learnt the confidence to tease. She then got the attention of the group and announced, "We are having a little celebration, for the doctor has said my aunt has recovered enough to walk about the house as her strength allows, so she has decided to come down to dinner tonight. Will you join us?" She smiled at Lord Lyfford and Mrs Swindon, who accepted.

Darcy then cleared his throat and said, "There is a matter Elizabeth and I should like to discuss with you. Or perhaps I should say, a favour we would like to ask."

"We will be happy to hear any request of yours," said Lyfford.

"We do not expect your answer immediately, of course, but hope you will at least consider the idea of sharing your wedding day with us," Darcy said, briefly and to the point.

Jane's delighted expression gave her part of their answer, and Lyfford, seeing this and being of like mind, smiled at his betrothed before turning to his future sister and old friend. "You may find Mrs Bennet more difficult to persuade, but I think it apparent that neither Jane nor I can regard the notion with anything but pleasure."

"Oh, a double wedding, how romantic," Kitty sighed dreamily.

"I believe that if my mother objects, we shall find an ally in my father," Elizabeth suggested, "for one wedding must always cost less than two!"

Lyfford and his aunt went briefly to Markham House to refresh themselves and change for dinner, while Jane and Kitty did likewise upstairs. When all were assembled once more, Mrs Gardiner came slowly down the stairs on the arm of her husband, and her first action was to personally welcome Mr and Miss Darcy to the family. The meal was a merry one, as tales from Staffordshire and London were exchanged. In the parlour afterwards, the twins were brought down to meet their newly arrived cousins, and to be cooed over by all the ladies. When the babies returned to the nursery, Kitty's sketches were passed round, and the scenes they depicted elaborated upon by those who had witnessed them.

Praise of Kitty's artistry rendered her blushing quite early on, though she tended to disbelieve half of it as stemming from the fondness of her relations. When Miss Darcy, who had been under the instruction of a master from the age of seven, praised her use of light and shadow and enquired after the technique used to produce the effect of motion in the depiction of a trotting horse, however, Kitty could hardly reply. She did manage to make it known that the master she studied with in Hertfordshire had been working with her on capturing active scenes.

"My drawing master comes on Wednesday mornings," Miss Darcy said. "If your aunt can spare you, Miss Catherine, I should be more than happy to share my lessons while you are in town."

"A London master!" Kitty exclaimed in tones of awe. "I should very much like that. You are generous, Miss Darcy, and I thank you. I shall ask if it may be possible."

After the Gardiners retired, the three sisters gathered in the room Jane and Elizabeth shared, and Elizabeth was prevailed upon to share the story of her courtship and betrothal. Her sisters were shocked, and Kitty angered, by the tale of Lady Catherine's visit, but their respect for their future brother was only enhanced when they heard of his bringing Mr Holcomb to tend their aunt. Kitty giggled and Jane smiled as Elizabeth related the bold hint she had given her suitor, and they both laughed at the reaction of the elderly couple who had witnessed the proposal.

When the carriage pulled up at Matlock House the following day, the sisters were pleased to note that it was not so very different from the London homes they would soon inhabit. It was large and fine, as one would expect of an earldom, well-maintained, which the Fitzwilliam wealth allowed better than that of many other aristocratic families, and newer than Markham House but older than Darcy House. Though it was impossible to banish nerves entirely at the first meeting of an earl and countess to whom one would soon be related, the Bennet sisters had no reason to believe that Lord and Lady

Matlock would be less kind to them than to their aunt in trade. Placing their faith in the fondness the Darcys expressed for their relations and in the graciousness of their letter to the Gardiners, Jane and Elizabeth held their heads up and smiled as they were ushered into Lady Matlock's parlour.

After the introductions had been performed and everyone was seated and provided with a cup of tea and had made their selections from the tray of sandwiches and cakes, Lord Matlock turned to Lyfford. "There is talk, Lord Lyfford, that you have been seen in conference with more than one member of my party of late and may declare for our side when we open in January."

Lyfford smiled slightly and took a sip from his cup before replying. "Then gossip has, for once, got something right."

"Oh ho!" the earl chuckled. "Excellent! And what issues do you hope to pursue?"

"I shall gladly bend my efforts to anything that will benefit our empire and its people, of course, but there is one problem which is nearest my heart at this time." He set his cup aside and fixed the other man with a serious look. "You have, I believe, a son in the army?" When the earl nodded, he continued. "And I, a brother. Should one of them, God forbid, return grievously injured, our families could support them in comfort for the rest of their lives. But what of the tinker's son, or the butcher's, or the grocer's, who returns blind or maimed? What happens to them? I tell you, my lord, you may see them now, begging in the streets. These men who gave so much for king and country at this very moment starve and die in the gutters because no provision is made for them, and likewise their wives and children, and the wives and children of those who do not return at all. I call it a sin and a shame, and a stain on this great kingdom."

A satisfied smile spread slowly across the earl's face as

Lyfford spoke. "You will do very well," he commented at the end.

Across the room, the countess set about getting to know the Bennet ladies, in particular Miss Elizabeth Bennet. Both girls were pretty and well-mannered, she thought, and if their gowns lagged behind the current fashion that could be easily remedied after their marriages to such wealthy men. She was a bit startled at first by Elizabeth's easy, sportive manner of conversing with the Darcys, but soon came to appreciate the lightness and laughter this brought to the reserved pair.

As was her custom, Anne said the least of the company, but Lady Matlock noted that her niece could often be found smiling at something which had been said by one of the others. During one slight lull in the conversation, Elizabeth turned and commented, "May I say, Miss de Bourgh, how well you are looking today? I believe London must agree with you."

In reply, Anne ducked her head and murmured, "I think it is the company of my Fitzwilliam relations which agrees with me, but I thank you."

"I always find it pleasant to visit my aunt and uncle, too," Elizabeth replied cheerfully. "Have you any excursions planned while you are here?"

"Oh..." she glanced uncertainly at Lady Matlock, who smiled encouragingly, pleased by the exchange between the two young women. "Well...we have spoken a little of doing some shopping. I should like some new gowns in colours I prefer."

Lady Matlock observed the Bennets exchange a look

before Elizabeth turned back to Anne with a smile. "Perhaps you might like to come out with Jane and myself tomorrow? We are shopping for our trousseaux, and Georgiana shall accompany us also. You would have a chance to look through the fashion plates at your leisure while the modiste is busy with us."

"Oh, do come, Cousin," Georgiana urged. "It shall be great fun."

"I—" Anne looked at the other three young ladies, who all smiled back at her with every appearance of genuinely wishing for her company, a novel experience for her. "Yes, I thank you, I should like that."

Arrangements were quickly made for the Darcy carriage to stop at Matlock House for Anne before meeting the Bennets the following morning. Lady Matlock now understood what a wise choice her nephew had made, for his betrothed had a talent for drawing out and pleasing the reserved members of the family. As their guests were preparing to leave, she found a moment to draw Darcy a little aside.

"I can only approve of your betrothed, Nephew. She will bring laughter to your life. If I may assist in any way as she is introduced to the *ton*, you have only to ask."

He smiled and kissed her cheek. "Thank you, Aunt. Your support means a great deal to me."

CHAPTER TWENTY-SEVEN

L ate the next morning Mrs Swindon, Jane, Elizabeth, Georgiana, and Anne met in the shop of Mrs Gardiner's modiste, Mrs Carmichael. The establishment catered to those with the taste and money for truly fine apparel but without the connexions to acquire appointments with the more coveted modistes in Bond Street. The fabrics Jane and Elizabeth had selected had been delivered, and the ladies set about the business of matching them to patterns. When a selection was made, the modiste's assistants would note any alterations requested and then fetch a selection of complementary trims for the lady's perusal. When all the details were fixed, the fabric, trims and notes for the gown were borne away to the back. The process continued until all of the fabrics had been so disposed of, and the brides were then whisked off to fitting rooms to have their measurements taken.

When they returned from their shopping, Elizabeth poked her head into the nursery to check on the twins, and found Kitty there, bent over her sketching book. She went up to the crib and saw that the babes were fast asleep, their little limbs intertwined, and her sister was using the opportunity to take their likenesses.

"Oh, Kitty," she whispered, "that is very fine. You shall have to show our aunt and uncle when it is complete."

"Mr Ewing, Miss Darcy's drawing master, gave me some hints about rendering faces," Kitty whispered back, beaming. "I have used his suggestions and I believe my style has been much improved by them."

When they had left the sleeping twins, Elizabeth turned to her sister and said, "As proud and delighted as I am with your talent and dedication, I am even more glad, Kitty, that you have found something you love more than ribbons and officers."

"I cannot say that I am not still very fond of ribbons, Lizzy," Kitty replied with an impish grin, "but I think you may safely believe me cured of running after officers! My ideas of my own future now stretch beyond the delights of courtship to what I want for myself after the wedding, and I most emphatically do not wish to follow the drum. A comfortable home, an amiable husband, regular society, and sufficient pin money to keep myself in paper and charcoal—that is what I wish for now."

"And I hope most devoutly that you shall find it!" Elizabeth said, embracing her sister and blinking away the beginnings of happy tears.

When the shops and pattern books had been conquered,

there were tours to be taken. The Bennet sisters toured Markham House, where Elizabeth's stifled laughter at the previous Lady Lyfford's many gilded accoutrements caused Jane similar difficulties and somewhat offended the housekeeper, who considered the late lady's chambers to be everything they should be. Then they toured Darcy House, where Lady Anne Darcy's taste could not be faulted, but the condition of her fabrics and papers after fifteen years of disuse were no longer acceptable. After that, it required the combined resources of several shops and a full day's search for both ladies to find all the fabrics and paper required to refresh their chambers in London and Jane's in Staffordshire.

During this time, a letter had been received by Elizabeth from her father. In it, he gave his blessing to the betrothal which, she had given him to know in the most heartfelt terms in her own letter, she had entered into for only the very best of reasons. Another missive from Mr Bennet reached Mr Darcy on the same day, and although he chided his future son for taking his beloved Lizzy so far away, he allowed that the young gentleman might have her so long as her father would thereby gain unfettered access to the fabled Pemberley library.

The following day, as Bingley, his sisters, his aunt, and Mr Hurst ate breakfast, the peace of the morning was broken by an ungodly screech. Caroline stood, face red with anger and surprise, waving the newspaper as though shaking it hard enough might alter the news it contained.

"No!" she cried, "It cannot be true! It must be the foulest sort of joke!" She would have continued in this vein had not Mrs Bingley snapped her name in a tone that would not be gainsaid.

"Sit down, girl!" the old woman barked, and Caroline dropt into her seat as though she had been cut off at the knees. "Take a breath. Now another. And another. Now, tell us, in a reasonable tone, what has you so overwrought."

"It says—it cannot be true!—that Mr Darcy is engaged to Eliza Bennet," she gasped. "That impertinent hussy! That countrified wench! That—" She sputtered as her aunt calmly upended her morning glass of ale over her great-niece's head.

"Refined ladies do not use those words, Caroline," she commented coolly. "Go upstairs and repair your appearance. And then you may stay within your chambers until I come to speak to you."

Taking a cue from his aunt, Bingley added in a similar tone, "And if you wish to break anything to relieve your feelings, be aware that the costs of replacement shall come out of your next quarter's funds."

Blinking, dripping, and furious, Caroline looked to Louisa, who was studying the muffin upon her plate as though it held the answers to all the mysteries of the universe and did not so much as glance in her sister's direction. Mr Hurst grinned at the scene as if it were an entertainment he had long been anticipating and which had exceeded his expectations. With an inarticulate cry of rage, she stormed from the room.

Mrs Bingley turned to the footman, who was struggling to maintain his impassive mien. "I shall require a fresh glass of ale."

Mrs Honingsby was the daughter of a country gentleman and the wife of a man whose father had been a wealthy brewer. Mr Honingsby the elder had his son educated as a gentleman and, upon his marriage, had gifted him and his bride with an estate in Nottinghamshire which brought in three thousand pounds a year. Mr Honingsby the younger, upon the death of his esteemed sire, had used a not-insignificant portion of his inheritance to nearly double the size and production of his estate. He had then stood for the local seat in the Commons when it came open and, in no small part thanks to the patronage of Lord Matlock, won the election.

In light of these events, Mrs Honingsby's happy shock upon the occasion of being paid a private call by Lady Matlock may be readily understood. So, too, was the delight she took in acceding to the countess's request that she extend an invitation to her ball, which was to take place in less than a week, to the great lady's nephew Mr Darcy, his betrothed, Miss Elizabeth Bennet, and her sister, Miss Bennet, who was betrothed to Lord Lyfford. That she knew of Mr Darcy went without saying; that her ball would mark the first public appearance of that great gentleman with his betrothed was very nearly enough to send the usually sensible lady into a fit of ecstatic nerves which would have put Mrs Bennet to shame. She also apprehended that her compliance with this request would ensure the acceptance of her earlier invitations to Lord and Lady Matlock and Lord Lyfford, which would please her husband exceedingly.

It may also be readily understood with what extreme delight Mrs Gardiner's modiste accepted an extravagant gratuity to hurry the creation of one ball gown from each Miss Bennet's trousseau order, that they might be ready for this event. Within a few days, on the morning of the ball, these gowns arrived in Gracechurch Street, accompanied by the modiste herself and her two best assistants, to accomplish the final fittings and alterations.

Each gentleman arrived in Cheapside that evening

bearing a jeweller's box containing a newly cleaned item from their family collections, for Mrs Gardiner had taken it upon herself to send each of them information as to the colours his betrothed would wear as soon as the ladies themselves had decided which gowns would be finished for the ball. Lord Lyfford presented Jane with his grandmother's sapphire necklace and bracelet set, the deep blue of the stones setting off her eyes and giving the impression that the rose velvet gown had been given its blue silk sash and embroidery for the express purpose of being worn with those jewels. Mr Darcy presented Elizabeth with his mother's diamond and pearl teardrop on a golden chain, which looked exceedingly elegant with her apricot silk gown and its ivory trim.

Mrs Gardiner blinked back tears to see her favourite nieces so finely attired and bejeweled upon the arms of their handsome and worthy suitors. Kitty sighed dreamily over the jewellery as she played lady's maid and helped her sisters don the sparkling pieces. She begged them to remember every detail for her sake and vowed that she would stay up to meet them when they returned.

When they arrived at the home of the Honingsbys, both ladies relaxed perceptibly, for though the address was much more fashionable than Cheapside, the house itself was no finer, and little larger, than their uncle's. Their host and hostess met them with every evidence of real pleasure, and Lord and Lady Matlock signalled their approval of their nephew's betrothal by spending some minutes in conversation with the pair before the countess bore Elizabeth off to personally introduce her to those she deemed important as Darcy trailed, rather disgruntled, behind.

Lyfford managed to spend half an hour introducing Jane to his friends before he was called away by Lord Matlock to speak to several high-ranking Whigs. Jane was left to make conversation with Lady Juliana Wembley, the daughter of one of those men. Fortunately, the lady was pleasant, if perhaps too eager to speak of her own wedding some six months previous, which she assumed must be of great interest to any lady whose own nuptials were approaching. Knowing that not every lady present was likely to be so friendly, Jane was perfectly happy to listen to Lady Juliana's advice and stories until Lyfford returned to her, if need be. As it was, they spoke for less than ten minutes before they were interrupted.

"Miss Bennet!"

Jane knew that voice, and though she inwardly cringed, she kept her expression carefully placid as she turned to see Caroline Bingley gliding up to her, smiling in feigned delight, her hand outstretched.

"Miss Bennet, my dear Jane, how delightful to see you again after all this time!" she exclaimed with apparent joy.

Jane had not the ability her sister Elizabeth possessed to smile and deliver insults wrapped in pleasantry. Nor would her innate modesty and courtesy allow her to voice any of the unpleasant thoughts which came to her as she looked into the face of a woman she had once thought of as a bosom friend. Yet there was one response still open to her, if only she had the fortitude to make it. Miss Bingley stood before her, certain of her reception from the little fool she had so easily gulled the previous autumn, and Jane found that she did indeed possess the necessary will.

Jane Bennet met the eyes of her erstwhile friend, raised her eyebrows slightly, and deliberately turned her back. "Pardon me, Lady Juliana, you were saying?"

Miss Bingley stood frozen, hand held out towards nothing for some seconds before she became conscious of the whispers and titters all about her.

It is a truth universally acknowledged that it is almost

impossible to both enact a hasty retreat and behave as though nothing untoward has occurred, and Miss Bingley failed rather dreadfully on both fronts as she scurried back to her great-aunt, who coolly latched onto her arm and, under the guise of a turn about the room, pulled her niece away from the others and into a secluded spot behind some very tall plants.

"I suggested you make amends with the future Lady Lyfford, not a spectacle! You ought to have apologised."

"I was not given the chance," Caroline began, but her aunt waved impatiently.

"Faugh! You greeted her as though you were the best of friends, and she—clever girl!—saw your pretence for what it was. Had you approached her humbly, with words of remorse, she might have forgiven you, but you chose to pretend that all was well between you in hopes that she would blindly follow your lead." The old woman pierced the younger with her gaze. "Tell me, niece, can your ambitions withstand the enmity of Lord and Lady Lyfford?"

Caroline wilted under the weight of her aunt's glare and her own error and said nothing.

"Well, the only course left to you now is to pen a very pretty letter of apology, and hope that she actually reads it!"

"I should like to leave now," Caroline said in the most subdued tone her aunt had ever heard, though whether it stemmed from a real depression of spirits or simply a desire not to be overheard she would not care to wager.

"You shall do no such thing. You have put your foot in it, and now you shall deal with the consequences," Mrs Bingley said firmly, though in a similarly discreet tone.

Mrs Bingley watched the subtle signs of her great-niece's emotions play across her face—anger, insult, confusion—and wondered, not for the first time, how to persuade the stubborn girl to release her wrong-headed ideas and face the reality of her situation. Privately, she thought Caroline could have been well-married after her first Season if she had not got it into her head that she deserved a place in the first circles. She had acquaintances there, which was a very fine thing for the daughter of a shipping magnate, but she could not reasonably expect to marry into the elite without some extraordinary quality of her own. Caroline's conceit might see her a spinster despite her excellent dowry, Mrs Bingley concluded with a sigh.

"Try to avoid her, and let us see what your brother's charm and my good sense might do to mitigate this latest stumble of yours. Go on, now."

Caroline slunk away into the crowd in search of a sympathetic friend or a hiding place—she cared not which. Mrs Bingley sighed under her breath and resisted the urge to rub her temples. She looked about for some time before she spotted her nephew, and it was some moments longer before she was able to manoeuvre herself into a position to discreetly catch his eye and summon him with a look. When he reached her side, she succinctly described his sister's newest mis-step, eliciting from him a groan and a shake of the head.

"For all the money my father paid out to that seminary she attended, one would think she would have better manners," he grumbled.

"She learnt the manners of those above her, I am afraid, and what is acceptable in the daughter of a peer is not to be borne from the daughter of Mr Josephus Bingley, shipping magnate," she replied practically. "That is the thing she failed to learn. She is not a stupid girl, but she is remarkably lacking in sense. I have told Caroline to avoid Miss Bennet, and now the next move must be ours. Let us give it a bit of time and then see if we can contrive to encounter her."

CHAPTER TWENTY-EIGHT

The dancers assembled for the first set of the ball, and Lyfford and Jane faced each other from their positions next to Darcy and Elizabeth. When the first notes sounded, she took his hand and stepped into the figures of the dance, her bright smile reflected on the face of her betrothed.

Nearby, Elizabeth had teased a smile from Darcy, and that event, never before seen in a London ballroom, attracted the attention of a number of observers, including the gentleman's relations.

"Goodness, would you look at Darcy?" commented Viscount Selfridge, the eldest son of Lord and Lady Matlock, to his friend Sir Hubert Wallingford. "Smiling as he dances! I had my doubts about the wisdom of his betrothal to a lady from outside our circles, but perhaps he knew what he was about after all."

Caroline Bingley saw and seethed, for Mr Darcy had never appeared more than mildly amused during their sets together. He had certainly never looked at her as he did at Eliza Bennet, as though she had hung the stars. How dare that pert country miss so easily snatch the prize that she, the wealthy and accomplished Miss Bingley, had worked so long and diligently to capture? And how dare her brother speak to her as he had earlier—did he have no care for his sister, who wanted only for their family to prosper? Where had it all gone so terribly wrong? Cut by Jane Bennet, of all people! Bedecked in a new gown, her hair in the latest style, yet her dance card remained empty save for the additional mortification of her brother's name in the spot for the supper dance.

Lady Matlock, meanwhile, drew her husband's attention to the scene. "Do observe our nephew. Did you ever think you should see the day?" She smiled with fond delight, and he smiled down at her.

"I dare say I did not, my dear."

As Mr Darcy escorted Jane off the floor after the second set, they came face to face with Mr Bingley and a well-dressed elderly woman who hung lightly from his arm and made little use of the fine ebony walking stick in her other hand. Mr Bingley released the lady and bowed to them.

"Darcy," he said briefly, before turning his earnest gaze to Jane. "Miss Bennet, good evening. I have been hoping for some time that we might encounter each other. I believe we both understand that I owe you an apology and an explanation, but first, I hope you will allow me to introduce my aunt to your acquaintance."

Hesitating only briefly, Jane nodded her acceptance.

Bingley positively beamed. "Miss Bennet, may I present Mrs Theodora Bingley." The ladies curtseyed to each other. "Aunt, this is Miss Jane Bennet of Longbourn, and of course you know Mr Darcy." The gentleman bowed to her.

"I am pleased to meet you, Mrs Bingley," Jane said politely.

"And I am very pleased to meet you, Miss Bennet. I have heard such different accounts of you as might have puzzled me exceedingly, did I not know my nephew Charles to be a better judge of character than his sister," Mrs Bingley said with a hint of mischief to her smile.

Jane's eyebrows lifted slightly before she smoothed out her expression. "I hope you will form your own judgment rather than relying on the impressions of those who knew me only briefly some time ago," she replied pleasantly, and the older woman grinned with delight.

"A hit, Miss Bennet, a palpable hit, and so sweetly spoken. I believe I shall like you."

"Miss Bennet, if your card is not yet full, might I request the honour of a set?" Bingley asked. Jane, secure in the knowledge that Lyfford had claimed the supper set and Viscount Selfridge would honour her with the last, handed Bingley her dance card with hardly a qualm. He added his name to a quadrille after dinner, and thanked her as he handed it back. He then bowed, bade his brief farewells and, collecting his aunt, moved off.

In her preoccupation with avoiding Jane, Caroline was perhaps less attentive to her immediate surroundings than she ought to have been, which led to her nearly colliding with the other Bennet present. Miss Bingley's abrupt stop mere inches from Elizabeth's person drew not only her attention, but that of her betrothed, with whom she had been quietly speaking. Mr Darcy broke the frozen moment with a curt bow, and Caroline had no polite choice but to curtsey to the couple.

"Mr Darcy. Miss Eliza Bennet."

Elizabeth curtseyed and smiled. "Miss Caro Bingley," she replied pleasantly.

Her temper already in a fragile state, it was all Caroline could do not to unleash her wrath upon the woman who had gained everything she herself had sought. "Please excuse me, I have been tasked to fetch a drink for my aunt Bingley," she murmured as she continued on her way. Mr Darcy and Elizabeth both glanced at the table of refreshments, which lay in the opposite direction to Miss Bingley's flight, smirked briefly, and resumed their interrupted conversation.

Caroline realised her mistake only a few steps away and momentarily closed her eyes as a fresh pang of humiliation seared her breast. On the chance that either of the two might yet be observing her she circled nearly the entire ballroom, pausing here and there to greet acquaintances, before she reached the refreshments. She decided that a glass of wine was exactly what she needed and made quick work of it before returning for another.

A pleasant sense of detachment, lent to her by the wine, soothed her battered nerves and somewhat restored her sense of self-worth. She watched the dance go by and contemplated how she might yet trade her fortune for a marriage equal to or better than those her rivals had secured. Some minutes later her plotting was interrupted by the approach of Miss Augusta

Spencer, the daughter of a wealthy member of the Commons, who had spent nearly as long attempting to capture Lord Lyfford's interest as Caroline had Mr Darcy's. She and Caroline were somewhat acquainted due to Miss Spencer's older sister's attendance at the same seminary as Caroline.

"Miss Bingley, how pleasant to encounter you. It has been two months at least."

"I believe you are correct, Miss Spencer. How do you do? Are your family well?"

"Oh, yes, all very well, and yours?"

"Quite well, I thank you."

Miss Spencer lowered her voice. "I have heard you are acquainted with the Miss Bennets?"

Caroline's lips pressed into a hard line. "Unfortunately."

"Well do not keep me in suspense, my dear Miss Bingley! Tell me of them." Miss Spencer's eyes glittered in anticipation of a thorough dissection of the character of the ladies who had come seemingly out of the ether to snap up two of the most eligible bachelors in England.

Caroline was chastened enough by earlier events to avoid embellishment or outright lies, lest they become rumour and be traced back to her, but her sense of ill-use spurred her to speak what she thought of as the truth. "Country girls," she said dismissively. "From a savage little nothing of a town. Their father prefers his books to his family, and their mother is frantic to get them married off to anyone at all. Their connexions are an uncle in trade and another who is a country attorney. How the Bennet girls caught the attention of anyone better than a tradesman I shall never understand— they have few accomplishments and less education, and no dowry to speak of save wide hips and large..." She gestured discreetly toward her upper body.

Miss Spencer was leaning towards her, gratifyingly attentive, and Caroline was drawing breath to continue when a heavy hand landed on her shoulder.

"Pardon the interruption, Miss Spencer, but I am afraid my sister is needed elsewhere," Bingley said with a pleasant mien and pulled his sister away to an alcove before either of the ladies could say a word.

He turned to face her there, and his expression was one she had not seen upon her brother before: severe and stern, almost cold, a muscle pulsing in his clenched jaw. He spoke in a clipped, precise tone.

"Caroline, you will hear me. You never had the slightest chance with Mr Darcy. Your dislike of Miss Bennet and Miss Elizabeth was ridiculous a year ago and has now become insupportable. If you do not immediately cease to speak poorly of them, I shall no longer bring you out to events such as this. I am the head of this family, and by God, you shall obey me or suffer the consequences."

"I said nothing untrue," she replied mutinously, crossing her arms over her chest and glaring at him.

"What little I heard was more opinion than fact, dear sister, and I will not have you sink my credit for the sake of relieving your own spleen over your failed attempt to capture my friend, nor will I allow you to damage that friendship! You shall speak of Miss Bennet and Miss Elizabeth in pleasant terms or decline to discuss them at all."

"You cannot prevent me from speaking my mind!"

His eyes narrowed. "Perhaps not, but I control your funds. For your defiance and poor judgment tonight, you have lost your next quarter's pin money. The following quarter's hangs on your obedience, as does your continued residence in London for the upcoming Season."

"I am of age! You cannot treat me in such an infamous manner!"

He smiled at that, the same broad and faintly smug smile their father had worn after getting the best of a business rival. "Oh, Caroline…I think you will find that I can."

He stayed near his sister until the supper dance ended. Then he and his aunt steered Caroline to a table some distance from that occupied by the Bennets but were unable to cajole her into a more sanguine state of mind. She hardly moved her gaze from Mr Darcy and his companions, and every smile or laugh at that table fanned the flames of her indignation.

The two couples sat down to dinner with Lord and Lady Matlock, the viscount, and Miss Vivian Ponsonby, with whom the viscount had danced the supper set. Miss Ponsonby was a pretty, fashionable girl about to embark upon her third Season. This was not due to any deficiency in her person, her lineage, or her dowry, but simply because she lacked the inclination to accept any of the several gentlemen who had requested her hand. Lady Matlock, whose eagerness to become a grandmother was tempered only by the wish that the next generation of her descendants not be borne by feather-wits or harpies, had encouraged her son to dance with the young lady. They were known to each other, and though Viscount Selfridge had not found her to be particularly compelling company he had no objection to the lady and so complied with his mother's wishes.

While the viscount spoke of horses with Lyfford, Miss Ponsonby fell into conversation with Elizabeth, who was seated on her other side. The two quickly discovered a mutual love of Shakespeare, and soon embarked upon a fast-paced and witty exchange of quotations from the plays of the Bard, which ended when Miss Ponsonby looked Elizabeth in the eye and proclaimed solemnly, "More of your conversation would infect my brain," and Elizabeth could not cease her laughter long enough to form a reply.

"I am truly bested," Elizabeth conceded in time, wiping at her eyes. "I can see I shall have to sharpen my wits before I meet with you again, Miss Ponsonby."

"You very nearly had me with 'I was seeking for a fool when I found you,'" Miss Ponsonby said modestly.

The viscount, meanwhile, was looking at his partner with new eyes. He saw now that when they had met before, she had been displaying the behaviour Society decreed was right and proper in an unmarried lady, veiling her wit and speaking largely of commonplaces. Witnessing the sparkling repartee between the two women, he considered that perhaps his mother had been correct to suggest he get to know the lady better.

"How is it that you know our hosts?" Jane asked Mr Bingley as their set together began, shortly after dinner.

"Mr Honingsby is, like myself, the son of a tradesman. Since his elevation to the gentry and now Parliament, he has made a point of including those of us who are still making our way into the gentry in his invitations. My connexion to the Darcys no doubt ensures that mine are all the more frequent," he concluded with a wry smile.

"That is very kind of him," Jane remarked. "So many in his position would choose to forget whence they came."

Bingley wondered if that was a reference to his sisters and

hoped that it did not encompass himself. He had none of his sister's bitterness. For all his regrets over the events of the previous autumn, he had never wished Miss Bennet anything less than real happiness.

"He is an excellent fellow. His wife is from a family similar to yours—she may prove a friend to you as you make your place in Society."

"I thank you for the information and shall remember it when I call upon her."

He smiled and asked after her parents and sisters, and she told him all the news from Meryton that might be of interest to him and was suitable for a ballroom floor, which occupied them pleasantly until the end of the dances. As he escorted her off the floor, he summoned up his courage and spoke.

"Miss Bennet, I owe almost everyone in Meryton an apology for leaving without notice or farewell last autumn, but you most particularly. I had intended to return after my business in London was complete, but with a bit of distance I found I had doubts about the direction in which our acquaintance seemed to be moving. I ought to have come back and discussed them with you and tried to salvage our friendship, but I was a coward. I was afraid the pleasure of your company would once again make me disregard the truth that I am not intellectual enough for you, and you are perhaps not sociable enough for me. I did not act the part of a gentleman, and I am certain my failure to return or send word caused you great confusion and perchance some pain. I am most dreadfully and utterly sorry, Miss Bennet, and I hope you might one day forgive me."

Jane smiled faintly. "You were not incorrect in your reasoning when you decided that we would not suit. I arrived at a similar conclusion in time." She looked him in the eye then, for the first time that evening, and was relieved to feel not the faintest spark of that attraction which had so consumed her thoughts a twelvemonth before. "We were good friends, Mr Bingley. Perhaps we shall be again one day."

He cast her a look full of affection and regret. "You are too generous. Be assured that given the chance I shall prove a better friend to you than previously." He bowed deeply and, straightening, offered her his arm and escorted her directly to her betrothed. "Good evening, Lord Lyfford," he said as Jane took Lyfford's arm and smiled up at him to demonstrate that dancing with her erstwhile suitor had not distressed her.

"Good evening, Mr Bingley," Lyfford said after returning Jane's smile. "How do you do?"

"Very well, my lord, I thank you. May I congratulate you both on your betrothal?"

Jane and Lyfford thanked him for the sentiment and chatted about nothing of importance for a few minutes, until it was time for them to find their partners for the next set.

The rest of the evening was uneventful for Jane, save for a less than pleasant set with a leering knight. She met a number of parliamentarians and their wives and adult children. These meetings, in a crowded ballroom, were perforce brief and superficial, so she formed no solid impressions save that her betrothed was well-liked among the members of his future party and that his political allies, at least, were happy enough to welcome her into their circle.

Elizabeth and Caroline encountered each other again late in the evening. Buoyed by having just danced a set with a baronet, and entirely ignorant of the fact that her brother had very nearly begged the gentleman to ask her, Caroline smirked as she dipped an insultingly shallow curtsey to her rival.

"Well, Eliza, you must be feeling very proud of yourself; you have captured the prize. How ever did you manage to secure an offer from such a famously elusive man?" she asked with a sneer.

Elizabeth was surprised to find she felt a certain amount of pity for the bitter lady before her, suffocating in her own disappointment, but she knew that it was past time to make it clear that it was not Caroline Bingley who held the power here. "Well, you see, Miss Bingley, it was more a matter of what I did not do than what I did. I did not cling to his arm like a limpet at every turn, nor ostentatiously praise his penmanship, his sister, and his estate. I did not voice my agreement with every commonplace that dropt from his lips, nor pursue him so blatantly that I became an annoyance to him and a joke to his friends." She smiled pleasantly. "I must, however, thank you, dear Caro, for the extensive descriptions of Pemberley which you related last year. Because of your information, I am able to quite look forward to my new home, though I have yet to see it myself. Perhaps one day we shall meet there…if you are fortunate enough to secure an invitation from the mistress of the house."

With that last, devastating remark, Elizabeth dipped a proper curtsey at a red-faced and sputtering Miss Bingley and returned, smiling, to the side of her betrothed.

CHAPTER TWENTY-NINE

T he day after the ball, Jane and Elizabeth called upon Mrs Honingsby. That this courtesy was rather early could not be avoided, for they were to depart for Hertfordshire the following morning. Mrs Honingsby happily accepted this explanation, for aside from the fact that the future Lady Lyfford and the future Mrs Darcy were not to be offended, she was of a complying and amiable temperament by nature, traits which her rather more rigid and suspicious husband encouraged in her, to the benefit of both. The half hour of their visit passed very pleasantly as the Bennets encouraged Mrs Honingsby to wax lyrical on the joys of motherhood. Her eldest was twelve years old, and a place had been secured for him at Harrow in the coming autumn. Her two daughters, at ten and six years old, were both much engaged with their governess, and the youngest, a boy of only two, still resided in nursery. That she was a fond and doting mother was beyond question; that her affections were enhanced by having given the troublesome aspects of child-rearing over to nurses and tutors was probable. Still, she was a likable woman and a pleasant hostess, so neither of the Bennets could regret the acquaintance.

They returned to Gracechurch Street to discover that Jane had a caller of her own waiting in the parlour. She showed the card to her sister, and they agreed to receive the call together. The visitor was standing by the window when they entered and turned to them with a smile.

The Bennets curtseyed. "Mrs Bingley, this is an unexpected pleasure," Jane said.

"As was not being turned away at the door, Miss Bennet," said the old woman, surprising a laugh out of Elizabeth while even her more controlled sister could not restrain a brief smile.

Jane offered tea, which was gladly accepted, and they all sat to await the delivery of the tray. "This is a very pleasant room," Mrs Bingley commented.

"I shall tell my aunt you said so," Jane replied.

"Do you know, did your uncle purchase this home from a Mr Bollard?"

The sisters glanced at each other. "The house was purchased by his father, but the name Bollard does sound familiar," Elizabeth answered slowly.

Mrs Bingley nodded. "I thought I recognised it when I arrived. Mr Bollard was an occasional business partner of my husband's. I took many a pleasant tea in this very room when I was younger."

The Bennets politely exclaimed over the coincidence, and when the tea tray arrived Elizabeth prepared the pot. While Elizabeth was thus occupied, Mrs Bingley levelled a frank look at Jane and said, "I expect you are wondering why I have come." Jane nodded, and the older woman continued, "Aside from the pleasure of your company, which is not inconsiderable, I have with me a letter for you from my great-niece Caroline. Though I understand you may be unwilling to read it, I hope you will do so, if only to avoid refusing me to my face." Her eyes twinkled, and Jane knew that if she categorically declined to acquiesce, Mrs Bingley would not be at all offended. Strangely, that made Jane more willing to agree.

"I will read it, but I cannot promise a response she will like—or any response at all."

"That is more than fair, and I thank you." From her reticule she produced the folded sheet and passed it to Jane, who opened it up to read.

Dear Miss Bennet,

I hardly know what to write. I have been brought to understand that in my dealings with you I have been arrogant, presumptuous, and false. I am most abjectly sorry and beg that you will tell me what I might do or say to restore the friendship we once enjoyed, the ending of which has been entirely my doing.

Yours in humble remorse,

Caroline Bingley

This, Jane read without expression before silently passing the page to her sister, who read it and rolled her eyes in a most unladylike fashion. Jane retrieved the note and began to read it again, more slowly. Mrs Bingley sat, silent and apparently at ease, through these wordless interactions until Elizabeth spoke.

"How do you take your tea, Mrs Bingley?"

"A spoonful of sugar and just a dollop of cream, I thank

you," she replied, and gratefully received the steaming cup a few seconds later. Elizabeth began to prepare her sister's cup, and Jane lifted her head and addressed Mrs Bingley.

"I shall pen a response immediately, if I may."

Mrs Bingley inclined her head. "That is more than I had hoped for, but please do not concern yourself with my time. I imagine I have far less to accomplish today than you."

Jane crossed the room to the little writing desk, and Elizabeth brought her cup there before re-joining their guest and engaging her in light conversation on the subject of the previous evening's ball. Only minutes later, Jane was sanding the page and bringing it over to her sister for her opinion. Elizabeth read the brief message and nodded with a hint of reluctance. "If that is the course you wish to take, dear Jane, I shall of course support you."

Jane handed the note to Mrs Bingley, saying, "I do not know that she will be happy with my reply, but I think you will understand it, ma'am." Mrs Bingley cast her eyes to the page.

Miss Bingley,

Please allow me to correct a misapprehension of yours— we did not enjoy a friendship, for all that I thought we did at the time. Your friendship was never genuine, and so I doubt the sincerity of your apology. However, for the sake of your excellent brother and aunt, I am willing to acknowledge you in society as an acquaintance, so long as your behaviour towards my sister Elizabeth and myself is acceptable to me.

Jane Bennet

Mrs Bingley nodded once, then carefully folded the note and placed it within her reticule. "You are correct on both points, Miss Bennet—she will not like it, and I do understand.

Truly, you are more generous than she deserves, and I will remind her of that. I believe I may speak for my entire family when I say that I am most heartily grateful to you for your willingness to acknowledge her in any way. I hope we may one day be able to do you a good turn."

Jane's expression shifted, but she said nothing. Elizabeth looked at her curiously.

"Out with it, Miss Bennet. You shall have to try very hard to shock or offend me, I assure you," Mrs Bingley said with a confident half-smile.

Jane let out a breath. "Mr Bingley is Mr Darcy's great friend. He shall be invited to the wedding, as he should be. For my part, however..." She glanced anxiously at Elizabeth. "I should prefer that neither of his sisters attend."

Mrs Bingley beamed. "Is that all? Think no more upon it, Miss Bennet—it shall be as you wish."

Both sisters looked back at her in astonished pleasure. "If Mr Bingley should like to bring you, ma'am, you shall be most welcome!" Elizabeth exclaimed and her sister, laughing, agreed.

When they departed for Hertfordshire the following morning, Mr Gardiner's equipage carried only the two eldest Bennet sisters. Mrs Gardiner had asked Kitty if she would stay on until they ventured to Hertfordshire several days before the wedding, and Kitty was perfectly happy to do so, for it gave her more time away from Lydia and with the babies, whom she never tired of sketching.

The farewells indulged in by the betrothed couples were no less sincere than they were lengthy. It wanted five weeks to their wedding day, but the gentlemen would not arrive in Hertfordshire until a fortnight before the nuptials. Darcy needed to have a marriage contract drawn up and to alter his will, and both gentlemen wished to personally supervise the refurbishment of their future wives' chambers in London. It went unspoken that both also wished to procure special gifts to mark the occasion of their wedding and the days which would follow, a task better undertaken in town than in Meryton. They promised faithfully to arrive two weeks before the day; Lyfford had taken a house in the neighbourhood, a place called Purvis Lodge, on a short lease, and invited the Darcys to stay there along with his family.

When the sisters arrived at Longbourn, they were greeted with the embraces and happy tears of their family. Though Lydia did not seem truly delighted to see them, she did appear along with the others and offered a few brief words of welcome, not wishing to find herself confined to the nursery for rudeness. When they had refreshed themselves and joined their parents and Mary for tea, Mrs Bennet could contain herself no longer.

"My dear Lizzy, you must know what a surprise your betrothal was to us! We did not think you cared a farthing for Mr Darcy!"

Elizabeth smiled ruefully. "When I left Longbourn in March, I did not. And when I came back for a while in May, I did not know what I thought of him. Mr Wickham's lies had been revealed, but Mr Darcy's behaviour here had been very bad, and I was unsure of his character. But when he began to call upon me in London, I came to understand his disposition and to know that he is among the best of men. His manners have much improved since last you met him, Mama—he was unaware of how he appeared to strangers and mortified to learn they thought him conceited and ill tempered, when in fact he is only very uncomfortable around those he does not know well. He has troubled himself to improve his conduct so that it better reflects the good and amiable man he truly is in his heart, and it was that man I fell in love with." Her expression as she said the last, soft and full of tender affection, stunned her parents and Mary to silence as much as her words had. Lydia rolled her eyes but retained her place in the company by holding her tongue.

Jane glanced at her sister. She rather thought that Mr Darcy had believed himself above his company before he fell in love with an obscure country squire's daughter, and that it was love rather than reason which informed Elizabeth's present view of those events. Her gaze drifted to her father, only to find him looking back at her with a faint smirk, and she fancied his thoughts had run along similar lines.

After some moments, Mary spoke thoughtfully into the quiet. "I, too, behaved very differently a year ago, when first we met Mr Darcy, and learnt better in the intervening time. For my part, I am pleased to forget the past and welcome him as a brother. I trust your judgment and your heart, Lizzy."

"You are right, Mary, we must forgive and forget!" Mrs Bennet exclaimed. "I am sure I was very cold to him a time or two, and I shall apologise for that as soon as ever I may. We are to be family, and I hope that we may be in charity with each other."

Elizabeth was forced to produce her handkerchief and dab at her eyes. "He has told me that he hopes my family will accept him despite his past behaviour—he is really quite anxious upon the subject. Thank you, Mary, Mama, for your generosity. You have forgiven his errors much more easily than I did."

"Well, well," Mr Bennet said, patting her on the shoulder. "Had you brought home a man without flaws, we should not have known what to say to him. As it is, he has proved himself no better or worse than us, and thus he may take his place in our imperfect family with ease."

They all laughed at this dry sally, and Mrs Bennet said, "Do tell us how he proposed, Lizzy!"

"Well, we had gone walking in the park, and there in the middle of Cheapside, he went down upon one knee and asked me to be his wife! We were witnessed by the sweetest pair, who had been married fifty-two years and wished upon us all the happiness they had known, which I thought an excellent omen..."

Elizabeth tapped on the door of her father's study before dinner and was eagerly invited in. He abandoned his book to stand and extend his arms, into which she gratefully came.

"Papa," she murmured happily against his cravat as his familiar scent of bergamot and rosemary enveloped her.

"My Lizzy," he replied. "As delightful as it has been to come to know Mary and Kitty better, Longbourn has been poorer for your absence. I can hardly bear to think of your marrying and going away."

She tilted her head back and looked up into his eyes, so like her own. "I hope you will visit us—you will adore the library at Darcy House, and I am told that the one at Pemberley is very grand. You will be welcome at any time, you and Mama and my sisters. I have no intention of abandoning my current family for my new one, and Mr Darcy does not expect it of me."

"I confess I had some fears on that score," he admitted, leading her to the settee and placing himself beside her there.

"I believe his circles are very grand, and I wondered if you would be expected to cut the connexion to your less sophisticated relations."

"If anyone expects that, they will be disappointed. Papa, how could you think I would love and accept a man who would require it of me?" she chided.

"Perhaps I have been a little ridiculous," he conceded, "but no father is ever quite ready to lose his darling girl to some man who cannot possibly deserve her, you know." The old twinkle was back in his eyes, and she smiled to see it. She laid her head upon his shoulder and felt his arm come around her.

"I shall not quarrel with you over whether he deserves me or not, for your opinion flatters me quite wonderfully. Just remember—you will always be the first man I ever loved."

Jane found waiting for her at Longbourn a letter from Miss Beaton, and she saw another in the same hand atop the small pile awaiting Kitty's return. It was a pleasant, chatty communication, telling Jane of all the little happenings in and around Ardgale-on-Trent involving those she had met during her time there. The greatest news was that Miss Phelps's betrothed had been wounded in battle and was expected to be invalided out of the army. Miss Beaton speculated that the young man might now read the law and join his father's office in the village.

Jane read the letter to her family that evening after dinner, with many a digression to explain who this person was, or to describe a place that had been mentioned. Elizabeth remarked after that Ardgale-on-Trent did not seem too terribly different from Meryton, and Jane agreed that it was not.

"I expect to be very comfortable with the society there once I have come to know everyone better. Mary, when you come to us this summer, I believe you will like Mr Phelps and his wife and eldest daughter very well. They are much involved with the needs of the community, and I dare say you would consider them excellent examples of truly Christian behaviour."

Mary, pleased to be singled out and even more so to find her company wanted, murmured, "I shall look forward to knowing them."

Mrs Bennet had so many questions about Jane's future situation that the evening passed in relating all she could recall of Lyfford Hall and of Markham House, with only occasional interruptions when their mother thought of something to ask Elizabeth about Darcy House.

The morning after their return to Longbourn, the wedding planning began in earnest. First, Mrs Bennet acquainted them with all her plans and ideas, which took the whole of the morning. Much of the afternoon was spent gently bringing her to an understanding that two brides did not require twice the flowers and ribbons of one, and that the hothouses of Hertfordshire might be allowed to retain a few blooms—if only the inferior ones—for other customers when the great day arrived. Neither need she hire fancy carriages and matched pairs to bear the newly-wed couples from the church to the wedding breakfast, for the brides were perfectly satisfied with the equipages belonging to their bridegrooms.

Though Lydia had managed to maintain a weak veneer of civility the previous evening, the news that she would not be acquiring a new gown for the occasion was too much for her to bear. "Why should I even attend, then?" she cried, and ran loudly up the stairs, slamming the nursery door behind her.

Jane, Elizabeth, and Mary looked at each other in wonder, while their mother shook her head with a pained expression and slowly rose from her chair. "Excuse me, girls."

"Mama," said Elizabeth, "if you are going up to Lydia, would you be willing to let me speak to her instead?"

"I cannot think why you would wish to."

"Perhaps the novelty will spur her to listen. She has heard what you and Papa have to say several times over, no doubt. Let me try, please."

Mrs Bennet acceded, and Elizabeth made her way up to the nursery. Knocking on the door, she was greeted with a muffled, surly, "What?" from inside. Taking that as an invitation, she let herself in and found her youngest sister sat in a chair by a window, arms crossed over her chest and a sour expression on her face.

"Oh, what do you want, Lizzy? Have you come to gloat over all the gowns and jewels you shall have?"

"No, Lydia, I have come to ask how you fare," Elizabeth replied evenly, seating herself a few feet away in case Lydia reverted to her childhood tendency to punch when displeased.

"As if you cared," the girl snorted.

"I do care, Lydia. You are my sister, and my disapproval of your behaviour notwithstanding, I do love you and want you to be happy."

"Nobody wants me to be happy!" she cried, gesturing angrily. "Mama and Kitty have decided to be dull and proper, and suddenly everything I like is wrong and bad! I hate it, and

I hate this family! I cannot wait to go to school, for surely someone there will understand me!"

Elizabeth gazed upon her sister with open compassion. "I had not thought how confusing these changes must be to you, Lydia. You were never taught how important it is to behave correctly, and suddenly you are expected to do so. I am happy to answer any questions you might have."

"I don't need your help, Lizzy," Lydia replied scornfully. "I know your notion of correct behaviour isn't as important as you think, because I have always had loads of friends and admirers, so I can't be doing anything terribly wrong."

"People can find you amusing without really respecting or admiring you, you know."

"Oh, go away! What do you know? You're marrying the most disagreeable man in the world just because he is rich, but you want to pretend that you are better than me."

Offended, Elizabeth rose. It had become apparent that Lydia was in no mood to listen. Still, she kept her countenance and attempted to plant a seed that would, she hoped, be nurtured by future experience. "No, Lydia, I am marrying Mr Darcy because I love him, and he is no longer disagreeable. He has worked to better himself, and I wish you would do the same. Perhaps your schooling will inspire you to do so, where your family have failed. I will trouble you no further, but before I go, I urge you to consider the fact that your behaviour has gotten you confined to the nursery and schoolroom, while mine and Jane's have led us to happy and comfortable situations."

So saying, she re-joined her mother and sisters in the parlour below, while Lydia was left alone with her unhappy thoughts.

On their second day at home, it was necessary that the two oldest Bennet girls call upon and receive the congratulations of all their neighbours. Jane's betrothal had been known for some time, but her earlier visit home had been too brief to allow for these calls, and Elizabeth's surprising engagement was the talk of the village. Mrs Bennet was in her element, fairly bursting with pride at her daughters' matches, yet she managed to hardly embarrass them at all, content to enthusiastically agree with all the congratulations and compliments of her neighbours and to comment on how convenient it would be to visit her daughters, for there were less than twenty miles between their estates, and their London homes lay only two streets apart!

Elizabeth was a particular object of wonder to the good people of Meryton and found herself explaining time and again how Mr Darcy's extreme shyness had been misunderstood as pride and that she was certain he would be more comfortable with them on this second visit to the area. Most of them were happy to believe that Mr Darcy had never really looked down upon them, for it soothed their own pride and relieved their concerns for Elizabeth's future in one stroke.

A few days later, a letter was received by Mr Bennet, and its contents so amused him that he waited only a few hours, until they were all in the middle of their dinner, to share with his family the news that the Archbishop of York would preside over the nuptials, ably assisted—he added with a waggle of his eyebrows—by their own rector, Mr Rudolph.

When Mrs Bennet regained her faculty of speech some moments later, a look of smug glee crept over her face and she said with relish, "Well, that will show Mr Collins his place, I dare say."

Jane and Mary gasped "Mother!" as Elizabeth and her father roared with laughter. Lydia was too disgruntled by this latest honour bestowed upon her prudish and, to her mind, undeserving elder sisters to enjoy the joke.

"And yet, we must invite him," Mr Bennet said with mock sorrow. "For he is your only cousin on my side of the family. But perhaps his most gracious and condescending patroness will require his presence so close to Christmas."

"Do you remember when he introduced himself to Mr Darcy at the Netherfield ball?" Elizabeth sputtered. "I am now having visions of him doing likewise to the archbishop at the wedding breakfast!"

Mr Bennet laughed so hard tears poured from his eyes, and his wife joined him. Even Jane and Mary could not restrain discreet giggles at the thought.

CHAPTER THIRTY

M r Bennet approached Elizabeth one afternoon, a few days before the gentlemen were due to descend upon them, as she sat in the empty dining room taking advantage of the silence to pen a letter to her betrothed. She greeted him with a sunny smile and promptly wiped her pen and set it aside, so he thought himself welcome enough to take a seat.

"Well, well, my Lizzy—the great day draws near. Will your young man even receive that letter before he comes to claim you?"

She shrugged with perfect unconcern. "Oh, perhaps he will, perhaps he will not. I have nothing of great import to share, save that I am thinking of him, which he shall enjoy hearing whensoever he receives it."

Her father smiled sadly. "You are determined to leave us, then? Who will visit me in my book room now?"

"That was always the plan, was it not, Papa—we were to grow up, attach honourable men, and go away? You shall have Mary and Kitty to comfort you, for they are both coming along exceedingly well. And even Lydia has begun to sometimes pout like a schoolroom miss rather than scream like a child," she added drily, then laid a hand over his. "I will miss you—I missed you whilst in Kent and London—but Papa, I am happy. I am to have an excellent husband and a wonderful new sister. I will be responsible for so much—it will be within my power to materially affect the lives of not only my new family, but of all those who look to Pemberley for their livelihood. I shall have better uses for my energy than long walks, though I do hope I shall not be required to give those up entirely!"

He chuckled at that and replied, "I hope your husband will not mind too much if I form a habit of showing up on your doorstep at odd times and without notice."

"You shall always be welcome wherever I am," Elizabeth promised. "And I believe you and Mr Darcy will come to greatly enjoy one another. He is extremely well read and enjoys a good debate, you know."

"Well, if all is as you say then I shall have no cause for complaint. For your sake, I shall try to love him, and if that fails, he shall at least never find me less than civil so long as he is good to you."

The rage of Lady Catherine upon the announcement of her nephew's betrothal was so great as to persuade Mr Collins and his wife that a long visit to her relations was in order, and they had arrived several days before Jane and Elizabeth. So full of Christian charity was Mr Collins that they had only been at Lucas Lodge for three weeks before he allowed that his wife might call upon his regrettable relations at Longbourn.

Charlotte and Elizabeth embraced for a long moment when she came, before the matron pulled back and said, "Oh, Lizzy, I am so sorry I have not called before now and that we did not come downstairs when your family called upon mine. I hope you will somehow forgive such unforgivable rudeness."

"I know that you would have seen me that day, and come here earlier, had it been within your power. Any offence I feel is not directed at you, my dear Charlotte. Will you be allowed to attend the wedding?"

"I fear not."

"I see." Elizabeth pulled her friend over to a pair of chairs in the corner, where they might converse with some privacy if they kept their voices low while the rest of the Bennets were busy with their other callers, the Gouldings. She looked at Charlotte significantly. "I confess, I am surprised to hear that Mr Collins's disapproval is so great as to persuade him to miss the opportunity to hear the Archbishop of York conduct the wedding service."

Charlotte's eyes widened. "I had not heard that was the case."

"Oh, yes. He is Lord Lyfford's godfather, you know. Naturally, he wishes to perform his godson's marriage to Jane. Mr Darcy and I are merely fortunate enough to share the ceremony with them."

"Well, then, Lizzy," Charlotte's eyes gleamed with amusement. "I believe I may safely guarantee that we shall indeed attend."

It had been arranged through correspondence that Lord Lyfford and the Darcys would dine at Longbourn on the evening of their arrival. When the day proved rainy and grim, there was some consternation, but late in the afternoon a note was received from Purvis Lodge that the travellers had arrived safely and fully intended to keep their appointment. Their arrival to Longbourn was not the warm and unhurried occasion the brides had envisioned, for the guests were forced to dash in from the carriage under umbrellas and mill about in Longbourn's small vestibule as they discarded their outer garments and swapped their muddy boots for dress shoes.

When they gained the parlour, however, Lyfford and his aunt were greeted as old friends by his betrothed's family. Lyfford clasped Mrs Bennet's hands and kissed her on both cheeks, causing her to blush and giggle like a schoolgirl. His future father was greeted with a firm handshake and that shoulder-clapping ritual so common among gentlemen who do not wish to be thought sentimental. His future sisters were addressed with warm affection but stricter propriety, even Lydia, who had hoped to be singled out in some fashion.

Mr Darcy and his sister were presented, she for the first time, and he for the first as Elizabeth's betrothed. Miss Darcy made all the usual expressions of pleasure upon the acquaintance and was soon engaged in an earnest discussion of the modern composers with Mary; Lydia sat near them, uninterested in the subject but enviously staring at her fashionable gown. Mr Darcy bowed gravely to Mr and Mrs Bennet, thanking them for the invitation and enquiring after their health. A few minutes of tame conversation followed, during which everyone attempted to pretend that no awkwardness existed between them, before Mrs Bennet came to the end of her very limited patience and spoke openly of the matter.

"Mr Darcy, I hope you will forgive us for any coldness of manner or other offences towards you during your last visit here. We were under a mistaken impression of your character, sir, but that does not excuse our incivility. We ought, at the least, to have been polite in company, and I hope very much that you can find it in your heart to put the past aside and accept the welcome to our family which we now, in all sincerity, extend to you."

Silence fell across the room; the Bennets had never heard her speak so eloquently on any subject save Brussels lace, while their visitors were merely surprised to have the subject canvassed so openly.

Mr Darcy bowed again to Mrs Bennet, saying, "Madam, I have been these last weeks seeking the words to convey similar sentiments to you. My forgiveness you may have, gladly—and if I may be assured of even the hope of yours, I shall be well satisfied."

Mr Bennet interjected here. "Mr Darcy, you have been entirely forgiven. Elizabeth has led us to understand your nature, and indeed we could not but joyfully welcome the gentleman who has made our Lizzy so happy."

Mrs Bennet added, "You must tell me your favourite dish, sir—for Lizzy does not know it!—so that I may be sure to have it some night or other when you dine here."

He confessed to being partial to roasted fowl, particularly pheasant, and the conversation from there became light and easy. They dined informally, and Mr Darcy was invited to sit next to Mr Bennet, who meant to make good on his promise to try to love this future son. Soon they were embroiled in a discussion of the Greek playwrights, which continued through the departure of the ladies and the dispensation of port, and only ended when they realised that they were excluding the only other gentleman present.

They did not tarry long in re-joining the ladies, and the younger gentlemen seized the opportunity to finally have some more or less private conversations with their betrotheds while Mary and Georgiana entertained the company upon the instrument, turning pages for each other.

"Your sister is much improved in her playing," Mr Darcy commented to Elizabeth.

"Yes, it is amazing what a few months with a master will do for a dedicated student," she said with a smile.

The wedding guests from London and other parts arrived the week before the wedding, setting in motion a whirl of entertainments as everyone in Meryton attempted to grasp their share of novel society. Sadly for Mrs Bennet's nerves, the Matlocks and the archbishop arrived on the same day, and she was forced to receive an earl, a countess, a viscount, and an archbishop in her parlour at the same time. Colonel Fitzwilliam, who would at one time have been of great interest in that room, was hardly noticed by anyone save Elizabeth and the Darcys. By taking refuge in the tea service and relying upon the interest her guests had in her two oldest daughters, she got through the trembling hour, and overhearing the archbishop telling Jane that her mother made a better cup of tea than his own housekeeper was her reward for fortitude in battle.

Elizabeth, having previously met with the earl and his family on several occasions, was all easiness, while before her sister Jane lay the fearful honour of being made known to the archbishop. He was a serious man, not given to mirth, though whether that was a natural tendency or a consequence of his weighty position was impossible to judge—he himself might no longer be able to say. He met Jane with a solemnity that would have frightened a lesser lady or one who had less confidence in the devotion of her betrothed. His manner softened by slow degrees as they conversed, Jane's intelligence and gentility combined with the obvious affection that lay between the couple impressing him as it had others.

Riding back to Purvis Lodge ahead of the carriage bearing the Darcys, Lyfford turned to his godfather with an expectant look. The older man's eyebrows raised, but he soon relented and said, "Very well, you young scamp, I am convinced. You have made an excellent if unconventional choice. Your father, God rest his soul, would have adored her."

"That is the shadow upon my present felicity," Lyfford admitted. "If only Father could be here, could meet my Jane and know that the future of the family is safe in our hands."

"I am quite sure he does know that, my boy. Quite sure."

Captain Markham was soon a very great favourite of Mrs Bennet. She had learnt not to fling her daughters at soldiers, but she herself would always have a place in her heart for a handsome man in uniform. For his part, the captain flirted with her in such an outrageous manner as to amuse the entire company and leave no doubt in anyone's mind that it was all in fun. Mrs Bennet enjoyed the attention for what it was and returned his overtures with all manner of winking and handkerchief waving. Her natural vivacity, which had so long ago drawn Mr Bennet to her side, weighted into mere nerves these many years by the demands of motherhood and the entail, shone in those moments.

One evening, shortly after the party from Purvis Lodge had departed, she turned to her daughters and said, "Girls, enjoy these carefree days. And you particularly, Jane and Lizzy, savour every moment while your relationships are new and full of ease and delight. Life will have its way with us all, and you will not forever be young and jubilant."

All of the girls, even Lydia, nodded and promised her that they would, and Mr Bennet took her hand and said, "Ah, my dear, you will forever be young in my eyes."

She rolled her eyes and swatted his arm. "Flatterer," she huffed, then glanced at him from under her eyelashes. "Do go on."

He bent towards her and murmured, "Later, I shall go on as long as you like, but you must give an old fellow a bit to work up to it."

None of the girls understood why their mother then turned red as an autumn apple but grinned as she replied, "I shall hold you to that, sir."

Mr and Mrs Gardiner arrived with Kitty two days before the wedding. The Gardiner children were left at home with their governess, nurse, and wet nurses. It was a wrench for Mrs Gardiner to leave the babies behind, but not for anything would she miss the wedding of her two eldest nieces, who had been almost as daughters to her even before her own children had come along.

Both Gardiners were delighted—and, despite the information they had from their nieces, rather shocked—by the changes in the Bennet parents and Mary. Even Lydia was slightly improved, as her desire to partake in company had melded with her deep sense of misuse to form a continual state of pouting which, though unseemly, was far less embarrassing to those who must claim a connexion to her than her previous wild behaviour had been. Mrs Gardiner was able to have rational conversations with her sister-in-law, while Mr Gardiner was pleased to be able to speak with his brother Bennet outside of Longbourn's book room. Mary's manner and performance on the instrument were now pleasing to all, and the sheer joy with which the third and fourth sisters greeted each other after their separation was a scene which would be fondly recalled by their relations forevermore.

To make room for the Gardiners, Mary and Kitty would share Mary's room until after the wedding, an arrangement which was in no way distressing to either. On her first night at home, Kitty presented Mary with a rubbing she had made of the inscription from the first bishop of Coventry's tomb, and a sketch she had made of the monument. Mary was moved to tears by the gesture and would not hear of merely sticking them up upon the wall; no, she resolved to have them framed.

With the Gardiners came the bridal trousseaux, which had to be unpacked and exclaimed over immediately. Mrs Bennet was in raptures over the new fashion for scalloped trimmings, and even Mary was seen to sigh over the fineness of the fabrics. Lydia watched the parade of lovely gowns, slippers, bonnets, reticules, wraps, and fans go by with increasing envy, until her jealous frustration burst its bounds.

"It's not fair! Why do not I get even one new gown, when all my sisters have?" she cried, stomping her foot. Her father turned with a face like thunder to order her to the nursery, but Mrs Bennet held up a hand to him, and he ceded the field to her with a curious look and a tilt of his head.

"Jane and Lizzy require new wardrobes to take their places in society and because they will soon be wives rather than maidens. You know very well that married ladies may wear a greater variety of styles and colours than unmarried girls. It would not do for Lady Lyfford or Mrs Darcy to go about looking like Miss Bennets." She paused and waited for an acknowledgment from her youngest, who nodded reluctantly. "As for Kitty, her aunt and uncle gave her a new gown to thank her for helping them with the babies after Jane and Lizzy returned to us, and she shall wear that as Lizzy's bridesmaid. Mary shall wear her ivory silk, which has only been refreshed and newly trimmed, when she stands with Jane. If one of the bridesmaids and I, the mother of the brides, are wearing gowns they already had, why should there be a new gown for you?"

"I could be a bridesmaid," Lydia said sulkily. "I wasn't even asked."

"Of course you were not!" her mother said sharply. "Mary and Kitty come before you, child, and what's more, they behave like proper young ladies and deserve the notice that shall come to them. Perhaps, if you learn to behave properly, Mary or Kitty will ask you to attend them when they marry."

"You are all horrid and I hate you!" Lydia screamed, startling them all. "I shall marry long before stupid Kitty, and horse-faced Mary shan't wed at all! And I won't have either of them for bridesmaids, so there!" She ran from the room, clattering down the stairs, and Mr Bennet hurried after. The ladies heard the sounds of a scuffle as he and Hill prevented Lydia from leaving the house, and the noise continued until she had been bundled back up the stairs and into the nursery.

When they looked at each other, they quickly realised that Mary stood rigid and trembling, still looking out the door and struggling to blink back tears. "Oh, do not listen to her,

Mary!" Elizabeth cried. "You know how she is when in a temper! You are lovely, and some lucky man will one day win your heart and thank God every day for his good fortune."

"I am very plain," Mary whispered, and as Jane wrapped her in a comforting embrace, Kitty also rushed to her.

"You are not," she said firmly. "You used to dress your hair in a very severe manner, and wear drab gowns which did not suit you. Now that you have learnt to make the most of your appearance, you are, as Lizzy said, lovely, and I shall fight anyone who says otherwise!"

That outlandish declaration resulted in a moment of silence followed by snickers and giggles from all the other Bennet ladies, and even Kitty, once she thought over what she had just said.

"I beg you would not, Kitty," Mary said jokingly, wiping her eyes. "For you bruise so very easily!"

Kitty kissed her sister's cheek. "There's my Mary, back again," she said with a satisfied smile.

CHAPTER THIRTY-ONE

O n the same day the Gardiners arrived, the Carterets made their appearance at Purvis Lodge. Mr Carteret was as he had ever been—ambitious, moderately clever, and thrilled by the proximity of the archbishop. His wife, the former Miss Julia Markham, was as Lyfford had expected—rather angry with him and struggling not to display it in company.

Deciding he had best get an unpleasant piece of business resolved as soon as may be, he claimed the privilege of an elder brother and bore her away to a sitting room, ostensibly to catch up on each other's lives. She turned a hard look upon him as soon as the door closed.

"So, when are we to meet this girl you have decided to waste the family's worth and position upon?"

Lyfford crossed his arms over his chest, leaned his

shoulder against the mantel, and fixed her with a glare that wilted her pretensions into anxiety. "You may, if you wish, accompany us to a musical evening at Lucas Lodge tonight. Jane and her family will be in attendance. But if you cannot keep a civil tongue in your head and remember who my godfather is, you had best stay here instead."

Her lower lip trembled, but she was not yet prepared to abandon her position. "You must understand that I fear for the family's standing in Society. It is why Godfrey married me, after all, and he is already cross because we have been wed these two years and I have not become with child. How could you risk not only your position but mine, by choosing a country nobody for your bride?"

"Do you truly believe that I would choose a lady without considering these things? Jane's family is not known by the *ton*, it is true, but she herself is everything a lady ought to be and more. She will win them over. Her sister is to be Mrs Darcy, which shall certainly not harm us. I am sorry if your marriage has not been as you hoped, but it was none of my doing—you made the match yourself. If he should ever mistreat you, he shall have to answer to me...as shall you, if you mistreat my Jane. Do you understand me, Julia?"

Reluctantly, she nodded. "I cannot like it, but I shall be civil to her."

"See that you do."

When the party from Purvis Lodge arrived with an unknown couple, Jane instantly comprehended that this must be the sister who was not pleased with Lyfford's betrothal and her clergyman husband. She gave Lizzy and Kitty, who were nearby, to know her supposition before going to meet Lyfford as he and his party suffered politely through Sir William Lucas's lengthy and enthusiastic greetings.

As soon as he was able to civilly extricate himself, Lyfford led the couple to where Jane waited just inside the room and with a smile he presented his sister, Mrs Carteret, and her husband, the Reverend Mr Carteret. Lyfford's sister greeted Jane with every politeness and not a jot of warmth.

Jane, for her part, smiled brilliantly and said, "I am so very pleased to meet you at last. I think I should have known you for Lyfford's sister anywhere, ma'am." Elizabeth and Kitty then joined them; all three Bennet sisters were at their most engaging, and it was only a few minutes before Mr Carteret was thoroughly charmed. His wife stood stoically by his side and listened to their conversation with an air of poorly feigned interest, contributing only rarely. When her husband excused himself to join the archbishop, Mrs Carteret asked, with a note of challenge in her voice, "I heard you have four sisters, Miss Bennet, was I misinformed?"

"Julia," Lyfford murmured in a warning tone, but Jane caught his eye and smiled, and with a brief inclination of his head he left the matter to her.

"Not at all, ma'am. My sister Mary sits over there, reviewing her music sheets," Jane said with a gesture towards the middle Bennet sister. "Sir William has asked her to open the performance this evening, and she is, just between us, a little nervous. I shall be sure to introduce you later, when the ordeal is behind her and she may give you the attention you deserve. My youngest sister is not yet out, and remains at home," she concluded, her smile never wavering.

"I see," Julia replied. "Well, I believe I shall join my aunt. She has secured an excellent seat, and I should not wish to miss a moment of your sister's performance, in particular."

With a shallow curtsey, she departed in the direction of Mrs Swindon.

Lyfford grimaced and looked apologetically at Jane and her sisters. "I am very sorry. I asked her to be polite, but perhaps I was remiss in not requiring her to be congenial."

Jane smiled and moved to his side, slipping her arm through his own. "Think nothing of it. I consider it practise for the Season!"

Lyfford and Elizabeth laughed, then Elizabeth took her younger sister's hand. "Come now, Kitty, do not frown so. It is simple reality that Jane and I shall encounter some people who do not believe we belong at our husbands' sides. We shall not allow them to destroy our happiness, and you must trust us to deal with them appropriately."

"Oh, it is not that I think either of you incapable of proving them wrong! But I do so dislike seeing anyone looking down their noses at you."

Lyfford said, "Dear Kitty, your loyalty does you credit. But you must leave it to Darcy and me to defend your sisters, should they ever require it, just as some perceptive young man shall one day wish to act on your behalf."

Kitty's romantic soul could not but be persuaded by that argument. "Very well, it shall be as you say, only give me leave to privately dislike anyone who does not love my sisters," she said saucily, and Lyfford laughed and agreed.

The night before the wedding, Jane and Elizabeth were scouring their room for any items they had neglected to add to their trunks when a soft tap on the door interrupted their search. They called out, and their aunt entered, bearing a tray with three glasses of cordial upon it. They thanked her for her consideration, and each took a sip of the sweet beverage before Elizabeth asked why she had come, for the third glass hinted that she planned to sit with them for a time.

"Well, girls, your mother and I have discussed it and decided that I should inform you of what to expect on your wedding nights. She does not know if her nerves can bear the frank questions she fears Elizabeth might ask," Mrs Gardiner replied, eyes twinkling, and the sisters laughed though Jane's was as much due to embarrassment at the subject as to the reason for her mother's hesitation.

"Well then, Aunt," Elizabeth said, sitting next to Jane on the edge of the nearest bed. "Tell us all, and I shall endeavour not to mortify you."

What followed was a gentle but clear account of both the necessities and possibilities of marital congress which left both young women red-faced and a little shocked. Jane would have been quite happy to end the conversation the moment her aunt finished, but Mrs Bennet was not wrong to assume that Elizabeth would have questions, and though Jane suffered a torment of mortification at both the questioning and the further details revealed by the answers, when her spirits had settled, she found herself secretly glad of the additional information.

While the brides received their aunt's gentle tutelage, Mrs Bennet made her way to the nursery. She paused to take a deep breath and a firm grip upon her resolve, then opened the door and sailed inside. Lydia was sitting up in her narrow bed, flipping idly through a copy of *La Belle Assemblée* that was nearly as old as she. She looked up at her mother, then sullenly directed her gaze back to the pages.

"If you have come to tell me that I shan't be allowed to attend the wedding, I had already guessed as much," she grumbled.

Mrs Bennet sat on the edge of the bed and looked steadily at her youngest child until Lydia finally met her eyes. "I have come," she said, "to give you a choice."

The look of surprise on Lydia's face was comical. "A choice about what?"

"Whether or not you wish to attend the wedding. If you do not, we shall leave you in the care of the servants and I will bring you back a plate from the breakfast. You shall therefore have a treat with no effort on your own part." Seeing that Lydia was still attentive, she continued. "If you wish to attend, however, you may do so. You will be expected to behave at all times as a proper young lady, and if you do not, when we return to the house, I shall take your pink bonnet—" She pointed to Lydia's prize possession, which she had invested many hours of work into perfecting. "—and you shall be made to watch as I burn it in the hearth."

Lydia's mouth fell open in outrage. "But it is mine!"

"On the contrary, Lydia, nothing is yours. Everything you have belongs to your father—that is the way of the world. You have a choice to make. You may take the easy path for a certain, small reward, or you may exert yourself to behave properly and receive not only that reward but also an outing and a party. You may tell me your decision in the morning, if you would like to think about it."

"I want to go," Lydia said hastily. "I shall be good, I promise."

"Very well." Mrs Bennet stood and plucked the pink bonnet from its peg. "I shall just take this for now, so that you do not get any notions of hiding it in the meantime." The furious look on Lydia's face proved the wisdom of that course, and Mrs Bennet grinned as she whisked herself away.

Jane and Elizabeth awoke on their wedding day to bright sunshine glinting off a thin sheen of frost which covered the landscape and would burn off before the sun had fully risen. They stood shoulder to shoulder at the window and watched the dawn creep over those familiar fields.

"Are you nervous?" Elizabeth asked.

"Not about the wedding," Jane replied. "But about being the wife of a great man? Yes, I confess I am. Managing two large households, and performing in Society in such a way as to bring credit to his name...I do feel some apprehension there."

Elizabeth sighed softly. "As do I. But we will see much of it through together, you and I. Darcy and I are decided to attend the major portion of the Season. He does not care for it, but I must be introduced into Society, and it is better done before Georgiana is brought out." She smiled at her sister. "Lady Matlock will be a help to both of us, I think."

"And we shall be able to call upon Aunt Gardiner whenever we are feeling beleaguered," Jane added lightly.

"Or upon Miss Bingley, if we find we are growing too conceited."

"Hush, Lizzy," Jane scolded, but immediately ruined it by snickering.

Later that morning, the archbishop raised his hand and silence descended instantly across the nave, which soon filled with the ringing tones of his voice, more used to a vast cathedral than this humble country church.

"Dearly beloved, we are gathered together here..."

As lovely as the wedding was, three of the four principals could recall little of its details. Darcy, for his part, would claim to remember every second of the service which bound him forever to the woman he loved above all things, and particularly the interminable blessings and prayers which continued after they had already plighted their troth and he wished nothing more than a moment alone with her. Lyfford would savour for the glorious moment when Jane's eyes met his as she answered with happy confidence, 'I will'. Jane and Elizabeth would both recall it as many brides do, through a haze of excitement and nerves.

When the last blessing had been pronounced over them, and communion taken, they were escorted by the two clergymen to a little room off the transept where the parish registry was laid out upon a table. There, the sisters each signed the name of Bennet for the last time, and the two couples were allowed a few moments of peace to whisper to each other before they were led back down the aisle of the now empty church, to appear on the steps before their cheering guests and many other residents of the area, showering the newly wedded couples with rice and seeds.

Elizabeth laughed and turned to her sister. "Well, Lady Lyfford! Until we meet again, at the breakfast!"

"Until then, Mrs Darcy!" Jane replied, laughing and leaning into her husband as he bore her away to the carriage which awaited them on the lane, the Darcy equipage poised behind it. She settled into her seat, trying not to crease her gown, and he took the place next to her. She had only a moment to absorb the novelty of being alone in a carriage with a gentleman who was not her father or uncle before the vehicle lurched gently into motion and Lyfford could wait no longer to kiss his bride.

A similar scene was enacted in the other carriage, and when the brides stepped out before the inn—the assembly rooms there being the only place in Meryton other than shuttered Netherfield with sufficient space for the wedding breakfast—they laughed again at each other's blushes and slight disarray. They entered the assembly rooms and there received the congratulations and well wishes of their relations as they poured in from the church.

Elizabeth's joking prediction of some weeks prior came true when Mr Collins, despite the best efforts of his wife, did in fact introduce himself to the Archbishop of York immediately upon his arrival to the breakfast, with all the pompous verbosity his relations and acquaintance had come to expect. He was entirely unaware that his manner gave the other man great offence, and the knowledge that the archbishop had never so much as heard of the inestimable Lady Catherine de Bourgh was to stand as one of the great disappointments of his life.

At last, the hubbub of arrivals faded, and the newly-wed couples and their guests sat down to the finest meal that Mrs Bennet, accomplished hostess that she was, had ever planned. It was, of course, quite lost on the brides and grooms, whose thoughts were consumed by their changed situation and its attendant happy concerns. Their relations, however, ate with relish and pleasure, and though for Mrs Bennet nothing could ever surmount the triumph of having two daughters so well and lovingly settled, being praised for her arrangements by the Countess of Matlock surely came close.

Mr Bingley and his aunt had quietly arrived the day before

the wedding and took the rooms at the Meryton Inn, which he had bespoken some weeks before. They sat near Darcy's relations during the ceremony and enjoyed the breakfast at table with the Collinses and the Longs. Mr Collins, of course, dominated the conversation when he was not gorging himself on Mrs Bennet's most excellent fare. Mrs Bingley, though greatly tempted to verbally eviscerate the garrulous clergyman, instead took pity on his blushing wife and thereby discovered the hidden gem that was Mrs Collins.

Lydia, who was kept firmly by her mother's side the entire day, did manage to make it through the events without misbehaving. Though she still did not understand why her boring, stiflingly proper sisters had such great good fortune while she —the only amusing person in the family, now that her mother had turned traitor—was dismissed as unimportant when anyone happened to notice her, she was thrilled to be out of the house, wearing a nice frock, and eating the finest meal of her life. She did several times come perilously close to saying something she ought not, but the thought of her darling bonnet always stilled her tongue.

Jane and Elizabeth embraced each other fervently as they parted, though this separation was to be of less than a fortnight, for they would meet again on Christmas morning to attend services at St. George and dine at Matlock House. It was not the length of their parting which caused them to cling to each other, but the knowledge that their lives had now fundamentally changed and that upon their next meeting, they would be even more altered than at the present moment.

Their grooms used the time to bid their farewells to Mr

and Mrs Bennet. Darcy was shocked to hear Lyfford call her 'Mother' and to see him kiss her cheeks, but even his resolute heart could not but soften further towards her when she took one of their hands in each of her own and beamed, saying with a fond sigh, "My sons! Oh, how well that sounds! Travel safely and take good care of my girls."

CHAPTER THIRTY-TWO

T he trip to London was slow, for a thin sheen of ice had accumulated along the low and shaded portions of the road. Lyfford's great Shire horses, stable and sure-footed in these conditions, saw them through it and delivered them safely to Markham House. When they disembarked, the groom reported that the Darcy carriage had been within sight almost to the edge of the city, so the other couple were assumed to be safe, also.

Therefore, it was with a light heart that Jane entered Markham House for the first time as its mistress, on the arm of her husband, to receive the murmured congratulations of the upper servants. Jane quickly wrote a note to her mother to assure her of their safe arrival, which was sent northward by express even before they made their way upstairs to change from their wedding finery.

"I hope you will be satisfied with the redecoration of your chambers, my dear," Lyfford said. "I thought your selections suited the space admirably, if a gentleman's opinion on such things is worth the breath required to speak it."

Jane laughed, "I am always interested in your opinion, and I am happy that you find my chambers pleasing." He quirked an eyebrow and Jane, realising that her statement might have been taken in an alternate light, blushed violently, which caused him to chuckle.

"Do not worry, my dear, I do not intend to pounce upon you the instant we are alone—that is, unless you should like me to," he added casually, and she sputtered with shocked laughter as he led her through to her chamber. The walls were newly papered in cream dotted with tiny yellow flowers and pale green leaves; that green was reflected in the fabrics covering the chair and settee, while the bed-hangings were of palest grey with thin, widely spaced green stripes. The ornate Oriental carpet had been replaced with a soft, thick rug of good English wool, and a set of cream velvet curtains over the room's broad south-facing windows kept out draughts while making the room seem bright even while they were drawn. Another set of curtains, sheerest muslin dotted in a soft shade of peach, awaited warmer weather. The vase on the mantel already displayed her bridal bouquet. It was a room made both cheerful and soothing by its new appointments, and Jane was very pleased with how it had turned out.

She said as much to her husband, who smiled and left her after several lingering kisses. Shortly thereafter, her maid entered from the dressing room and helped her out of the beautiful periwinkle silk and into one of her new day dresses, in a smart pattern of blue and white stripes.

"I've laid by some papers, my lady, if you should want to press any of these, or some from your bouquet," Roberts said as she carefully pulled the hothouse columbines and violets from Jane's hair without disturbing the elegant coiffure.

"Oh, I should not have thought of that until they had wilted, I am sure. Thank you, Roberts, I believe I shall." She saw the maid's brief, pleased smile in the mirror and began sorting through the blooms, selecting the most perfect for the purpose. She also pulled some cornflower and a single white rose from her bouquet, and she and the maid made quick work of laying them out between sheets of ironed newspaper and stacking several heavy volumes atop them.

Jane thanked the maid and dismissed her until it was time to dress for dinner, then tentatively knocked upon the door to Lyfford's chamber. He opened it with alacrity, and she apologised if she had kept him waiting, explaining briefly the need to press her keepsake flowers while they were still fresh.

Lyfford suggested that they take a spot of tea, and on the way down the stairs he said playfully, "Lady Lyfford, I have got you a wedding present, and it is in the parlour."

She blushed and returned in like tone, "Why, Lord Lyfford, what a coincidence! For I also have a wedding present for you, and it is in my pocket."

He grinned and ushered her into the room, an expectant look upon his face. She quickly spotted her very own work basket, brought from Longbourn, beneath a fine round rose-wood table she had never seen before. Its top was nearly a foot deep, inset with a drawer. Atop the table sat a mahogany box, also unfamiliar to her, which had been painted with scenes of chariot races in the ancient Greek style. Moving towards it, she saw that the lid bore a depiction of the Acropolis at Athens. She opened it to reveal a needlework set of surpassing beauty—silver thimbles, scissors, and needle-cases, mother of pearl thread-winders in the shape of snowflakes, ivory bobbins and bodkins, a little compartment full of pins and a velvet pincushion on a silver base. Beneath, three shallow drawers sat empty, awaiting her silks, ribbons, and other notions. She then opened the drawer in the table, expecting it, too, to be empty, but within awaited several short lengths of cotton and muslin in different weights and textures, though ample room remained for more.

"This is lovely beyond anything. I hardly know what to say, except thank you—I shall treasure it!" Jane exclaimed.

He came to her side, beaming. "Jewels are more traditional, but I thought you might prefer something you would use more often." He opened the lid of the sewing box and pointed out a detail she had missed—along the top lip of the box, between the hinges, was engraved 'Jane Markham, the Countess of Lyfford, 15 December 1812'. "There, I have ensured you shall never forget our anniversary," he teased, and she laughed, then pulled a little bundle from her pocket.

"This is neither so large nor so fine, but I hope you will like it," she said.

He opened the packet to reveal three handkerchiefs, each stitched with a large 'M' within which was entwined the initials 'H' and 'J'. On one, the 'M' was decorated with asters; on another, with yarrow; on the last, with red tulips. His face softened and he said with all sincerity, "I count these as far finer than what I have given you, my dear." He bent and kissed her, and several moments later the maid coming in with the tea tray got a bit of a shock and hurriedly retreated with a muffled giggle, leaving the tray for them.

Jane, red-faced, moved to the mirror above the mantel to smooth her hair. Lyfford laughed and commented, "I dare say the maids shall have to become accustomed to such scenes."

When they descended from the carriage, Mr Darcy had scandalised the servants and a few curious neighbours and passers-by by sweeping his laughing bride up into his arms and carrying her up the steps of Darcy House and across the threshold, kissing her firmly before depositing her upon her own feet once more. It was a blushing Mrs Darcy who greeted the startled assembly of upper servants awaiting them in the entrance hall, and for a moment, no one quite knew what to say.

Elizabeth quickly recovered from her embarrassment and greeted Mr Dunleavy and Mrs Hammonds, the housekeeper, both of whom she had met during her tour of the house some weeks prior. They, in turn, introduced her to the remaining upper servants. The chef, Mr Nevins, a stocky fellow with a distinct northern accent and wildly fluttering hands, was most anxious for her good opinion and threatened to detain her for much of the afternoon as he described in eager detail the menu he had planned for the evening, almost begging her to change any little thing that was not exactly to her tastes.

Understanding that he feared for his position with the advent of a new mistress, as must many of the upper servants, she went a long way towards winning the chef over when she said that she had such good reports of him that she would not think to interfere with the menu he had personally planned for their enjoyment on the day of their wedding. She then addressed all the assembled servants in saying that Darcy House was so beautifully run and tended that she hoped they would not be disappointed when she failed to make major changes, for she could find nothing wanting in its present state.

At her side, Darcy saw the relief of his loyal servants and beamed with pride at his wife. He had told Mr Dunleavy and Mrs Hammonds that his Elizabeth was not the sort of lady who would disrupt a well-ordered household merely to assert her authority, but it was only natural that they and the others would not truly believe it until they had met her. As the Darcys inspected the refurbished mistress's chamber and enjoyed the novel delights of an afternoon spent exclusively in each other's company, word spread from the upper servants to the lower of the new Mrs Darcy's kindness and easiness, and it seemed the very walls of the house breathed a sigh of relief.

The Bennet household was unusually quiet that afternoon, for all were tired after the joyous, hectic events of the morning. Mary even skipped her daily music practise, and Kitty her sketching, in favour of sitting quietly with their novels and occasionally falling into short periods of sleep. Lydia worked upon a bonnet recently discarded by Kitty, re-trimming it in blue and green to match the sash of her second-best muslin, while Mrs Bennet idly perused the last several weeks of the household accounts, set down in Mary's precise script, and Mr Bennet napped on the settee with a favourite translation of Plato open across his chest.

They all stirred curiously when a knock sounded upon the door as the sun was setting. Mrs Hill soon bustled in and handed a sealed missive to the lady of the house, saying, "An express come for you, mum."

"Oh, my, I hope it is not bad news!" Mrs Bennet breathed, and hurriedly opened it. Her look of worry quickly transformed to one of delight, and she beamed at her family. "It is from Jane," she said happily. "Here, I shall read it to you."

Dearest Mama,

We have arrived safely in town. The roads were a bit icy in places, but Lyfford's driver is very skilled, and I never truly felt unsafe. It is my hope that you will be pleased, not only by this information, but also to know that you have received the very first correspondence which I may sign
Jane Lyfford

After a truly splendid dinner to which neither of them had done justice, Darcy escorted Elizabeth to their chambers. "May I come to you in an hour?" he asked gravely.

Though she wondered at his sudden solemnity she smiled brightly and replied, "I believe that will be entirely sufficient, yes." With a last fond squeeze of his hand, she disappeared into her own rooms, newly papered in cheerful yellow offset by upholstery and curtains of smoky blue. A nervous upstairs maid, assigned to tend to Mrs Darcy until she might hire her own maid from the most exclusive agency in town—Mr Darcy had arranged interviews for Thursday—had prepared a gently steaming bath. After removing her rose silk dinner dress and the pearl and ruby necklace which had been her husband's bridal gift to her, she enjoyed the bath for a full half hour, a luxury previously impossible with four sisters in the house, emerging to be dried and dressed in the deliciously daring gown and wrapper her aunt had given her as a wedding present. The maid tended to her hair, taming the riotous curls into a shining, alluring mass with the merest dab of oil, and leaving her to await her husband with only minutes to spare.

On the other side of the connecting door, Darcy had attended to his own ablutions, including a fresh shave, before dismissing his valet for the night. Consulting the clock, he found that a quarter hour yet remained. Alone, with naught but a door separating him from the woman he had loved for so long, all of Darcy's joy in the culmination of his hopes dissolved into anxiousness over the one step yet to be taken. He rose and began to pace.

Elizabeth, for all her forthright speech, was a maiden gently bred and would no doubt be apprehensive of what was to come. Though Darcy was no Puritan, his busy life and many responsibilities had not allowed him the leisure to indulge his carnal inclinations as extensively as many men of his sphere, and he wondered now whether he possessed the necessary combination of restraint and experience to make his bride's initiation into married life a pleasant one.

It simply would not do, he thought, to give her a disgust of the process which might take weeks or months to reverse. Perhaps if he were to plan out their encounter, it might aid his self-control when the time came. Brow furrowed, he attempted to imagine approaching his wife, embracing her, kissing her, and caressing her with patience and care, but the images conjured in his mind were too exciting, and soon he had descended into a welter of helpless lust and anxiety.

He was not aware of the door opening on well-oiled hinges, or of his agitated pacing being observed with raised eyebrows and a bit of a smirk. He startled violently and spun around upon being addressed.

"Mr Darcy, am I going to be required to give you another hint?" Elizabeth was leaning against the jamb, arms crossed over her chest, her smile growing as her husband's expression only became more stunned upon seeing her there, with her hair about her shoulders and her shape only slightly obscured by her garments. With a significant look, she nodded her head towards the clock upon his mantel. It took him a moment, but he finally followed her gaze and saw that it was now over twenty minutes past the appointed time and groaned with embarrassment. He had kept his bride waiting on their wedding night. He turned back to her with an expression of contrition to find that she had moved closer, bare feet silent on the thick carpeting.

She smoothed her hands over the lapels of his dressing gown. "Fitzwilliam, I do not know what has led you into such a fretful state, and I am not going to ask. I suspect you have gotten some strange idea in your head that I have been awaiting you in fear and trembling." She twined her arms around his neck and looked up at him, still smiling, as his arms came around her waist and his expression of anxious surprise began to give way to one of interest. "But I will risk you thinking me fast to confess that my aunt's explanation of what is to occur has engendered in me a powerful curiosity, sufficient to overwhelm any nerves I might otherwise have experienced."

She tilted her face up a fraction more, inviting his kiss. Mr Darcy did not miss that hint and obliged his bride with great enthusiasm and no little gratitude that he had been fortunate enough to win the hand of this extraordinary woman.

"Remind me," he muttered against her lips as he carried her into her chamber, "to send your aunt a very nice Christmas present."

Jane's maid prepared her for her wedding night with great care and attention. First, she soaked in a warm bath scented with rose oil while enjoying a glass of wine, her hair piled atop her head to keep it dry. Then, she was dressed in a sheer nightgown and a wrapper hardly more opaque—a gift from her aunt Gardiner—and her hair was thoroughly brushed and left hanging loose about her. Roberts smiled at her in the mirror.

"You look beautiful, ma'am. And don't you worry none about the bed-linens. I'll be collecting and washing them myself, soon as you're up in the morning."

Jane blushed to think of her sheets being passed round belowstairs and inspected for evidence of consummation. "Thank you, Roberts. Your care of me is very much appreciated."

The maid stepped back and curtseyed. "It's a pleasure to serve you, my lady. Good night." She disappeared through the servants' door and Jane was left to wait in silence.

Her husband did not make her wait long, however. Only a minute or two later, a soft knock sounded on the door adjoining their chambers, and she called for him to enter. She blushed to the roots of her hair to be seen in apparel she privately found rather scandalous, and to see him in his dressing gown.

"Ah, Jane, you are beauty itself," he said reverently, coming to her and taking her hands in his, then rubbing them when he found them chilled though the room was comfortable. "You are not afraid of me, I hope?" he asked when she would not meet his eyes.

"Oh, no," she laughed nervously. "It is only that...well, it all sounds so very strange. But my aunt assured me that once one grows accustomed, it is pleasant."

"Your aunt is a wise lady, my love. Trust her, and please, trust me."

"I do," she said, finally meeting his gaze, and he smiled and bore her off to bed.

The couples passed a quiet week at their respective homes, venturing out only to join the Fitzwilliams on Christmas morning. When the Darcys entered Markham House, the sisters embraced fiercely, for no amount of domestic contentment could entirely obscure the lamentable fact that they no longer resided in the same home. Elizabeth then whispered, "Oh, Jane, is not being married wonderful?"

Jane threw her head back and laughed. "Indeed, it is!" she agreed joyfully.

The gentlemen, though less demonstrative than their wives, greeted each other with real pleasure. "I need not ask how you are finding married life," Lyfford commented with a chuckle as they shook hands, "for you smile almost as much as your wife!"

"When Elizabeth finally accepted me, I knew I should be happy, but I did not know that happiness would feel so very... effervescent," Darcy said in tones of great contentment. "It is all I can do not to grin like the veriest fool at every turn!"

Lyfford laughed. "I should like to see the reaction of Society if you did."

Darcy grimaced at the thought and turned the subject back upon his friend. "Lady Lyfford appears extremely well, and you seem no less happy than when last we met, so I must assume the state agrees with you, also."

"Very much so," Lyfford replied with a fond glance at his wife, who was speaking eagerly with her sister. "I pity the poor sods who look upon their wives as a leg-shackle, for if there is greater happiness than the love of a fine lady, I have never encountered it."

They soon made their way to the church, where they were

reunited with their families and subjected to the scrutiny of those worthies who had deigned to pass the holiday season in town. The meal at Matlock House was a more relaxed and joyous occasion, the company convivial and the menu beyond reproach. Georgiana Darcy and Ellen Markham were delighted to be once again in the company of their much beloved elder brothers and their new sisters, while Colonel Fitzwilliam and Captain Markham, acutely aware that their next Christmas was likely to find them across the Channel, celebrated with the slightly desperate gaiety of soldiers on the eve of battle.

At the conclusion of the gathering, Mrs Swindon and Ellen returned to Markham House with Lyfford and Jane, while Georgiana bid her aunt and uncle a fond farewell to resume her place in her brother's home. In the week between Christmas and the new year, they ventured out a bit more, paying calls upon their relations and occasionally strolling the shops, but still kept frequently to home where they settled into their happily altered family groups.

CHAPTER THIRTY-THREE

Too soon came the day when Lord and Lady Lyfford departed for Portsmouth to see Captain Markham off to war. They arrived in the bustling port city the evening before his scheduled departure and shared a dinner in their hotel's dining room at which everyone tried to have a pleasant time, and no one succeeded. The next morning, they saw Edward and his horse onto the H.M.S. Vanguard, which cast off into sunny weather, and they waved at the ship until it vanished from sight.

Arriving back at Markham House road-weary and heart-sore the following day, Jane sank gratefully into a warm bath. When she sat at her dressing table, Roberts did not immediately take up her comb to tame Jane's damp hair. Instead, she reached into the pocket of her pinafore and withdrew a sealed message and laid it upon the table.

"Captain Markham gave this to me just before you all left, my lady, and asked that I see you received it in private when you got back home. I hope I did no wrong by agreeing."

Brow furrowed with confusion and concern, Jane turned the featureless missive over in her hands. "No, Roberts, of course you have not done wrong. He is my brother, after all— it is not as though you have passed me a note from a stranger or an admirer." As the maid began to draw the comb through her hair, she broke the seal, unfolded the page, and read.

1 January 1813

> *My dear sister Jane,*
>
> *As my departure draws near, I find I must ask of you a favour. It is my earnest hope that you shall never have the opportunity to fulfil this request, but if I learnt anything from my wounding last year, it is not to leave to chance what I may instead arrange.*
>
> *You know, of course, that Lyfford and I have always been close. There are less than two years between us, and our temperaments are well-suited. I know him, I think, almost as well as I know myself, and having observed him after our father's death, I feel confident in saying that if I should not return from the conflict, he will attempt to pretend that he is not suffering. He will not wish to burden anyone, least of all you, with his grief.*
>
> *Here we come to my request: if I should fall, I beg of you, be his solace and safe harbour. Compel him if you must, by those gentle means which only a beloved wife can possess, to share his sorrow with you. Remind him that I have chosen this; our father wished that I should go into the Church or the law or, failing those, the militia. I and I alone chose the army, but Lyfford will blame himself for not dissuading me, though in truth he could not have done so—not then and not now.*

I will tell you a secret and leave it to your good sense to decide if and when it ought to be revealed to my brother: I was offered the opportunity to honourably withdraw from my commission after I was injured. I declined. I think at present he would be angry to know that for, good brother that he is, he wishes for nothing so much as my safety. But I shall serve the Crown all my life, however long or short it may be, and if I am able to do so with honour, I will be well satisfied. Do not allow my dear brother to regret that which I do so gladly.

May God bless and keep you and Lyfford both,

Edward Markham

Jane swallowed past a sudden obstruction in her throat and folded the page up again before she allowed a few silent tears to fall. She tucked the note into the drawer of her dressing table, beneath a stack of pressed handkerchiefs. Glancing into the mirror, she saw her maid regarding her there with a worried expression.

"I will thank you, Roberts, not to speak of that note. It is a request from my brother that I do certain things on his behalf should he fall in battle. I see no need to raise the possibility with anyone unless it should come to pass."

"Yes, my lady," the maid answered obediently. "A fine, brave fellow is Captain Markham."

"That he is, Roberts." Jane dabbed at her eyes and checked the glass to ensure that her husband would see no sign of distress upon her countenance when he came to her. "That he is, indeed."

Another farewell followed scant days later, as Lady Ellen was sent back to her school in Bath for what the family had recently decided would be her final term. Come summer, it would be Jane's role—with the able assistance of Mrs Swindon—to prepare Ellie for her future, while a small selection of masters and tutors put the finishing touches on her formal education.

The long-planned outing to the theatre happened to fall upon the evening after the opening of Parliament and Lyfford's investiture into the House of Lords. For the first time in living memory, the Darcy box at Drury Lane was entirely filled, and between the acts there was a constant stream of visitors eager to cast their eyes upon the sisters who had filched two extremely eligible bachelors from under the noses of Society's maidens, to speak with the influential Matlocks, or to congratulate Lord Lyfford on his ascension to the title.

None of this prevented the party from enjoying the special production of *Twelfth Night* or delighting in the portrayal of Viola by the American actress Marian Wilson, whose expressive face and changeable voice lent an unusual depth to both the comedic and the tragic aspects of the play.

Viscount Selfridge had mentioned at the start of the evening that he was engaged to view the final act with friends, so his departure during the break was not at all remarked upon. Just as the curtains began to part, however, Lady Matlock gasped audibly and clutched her husband's arm. In some alarm, he followed her surprised gaze to see his eldest son seated in a box across the way, next to Miss Vivian Ponsonby and under the chaperonage of her parents. Lady Matlock's shock quickly gave way to delight, for such particular attentions could not be misunderstood by anyone. Her eldest son was calling upon a young lady, and one she liked exceedingly well.

Witnessing the scene, Elizabeth Darcy whispered a question to her husband, who nodded and gestured for a servant to attend them. The man received his orders from Mrs Darcy with a bow and vanished for a time before resuming his post.

At the end of the play, after the roar of a succession of ovations had abated, Elizabeth smilingly announced, "I have invited the Ponsonbys to join us for dinner. I hope no one objects to their inclusion in this family occasion?"

There could, of course, be no objection, and when the viscount returned to the box, the Ponsonbys accompanied him. Mrs Ponsonby was all genteel delight as she expressed their thanks and acceptance to Mrs Darcy, and the viscount was seen to kiss his new cousin's hand and offer his own gratitude for her generosity.

"I hope," said Miss Ponsonby, when she was at last able to offer her own salutations, "that our addition to your party will not disrupt your arrangements, Mrs Darcy."

"Not at all," Elizabeth replied easily. "Mr Nevins, our chef, is always eager to perform for any number of guests. And may I say that I am so very pleased to see you again, Miss Ponsonby?"

"And I you, Mrs Darcy," the young lady replied warmly.

"Our cousin has been very sly, you know. We had not the slightest idea that he was wooing you," Elizabeth lowered her voice to say privately.

Miss Ponsonby blushed. "To be honest, Mrs Darcy," she murmured in return. "I was not entirely certain of it myself until he asked if he might join us for part of the play tonight. He has called upon us very regularly, but unlike the other gentlemen of my acquaintance, he treated me as a friend and spoke to me of things more interesting and important than the latest gossip. I had hopes, but..." She glanced at him, only to find him already looking at her. He smiled, and she blushed and smiled in return.

"Well-founded hopes, I should say," Elizabeth commented as the viscount made his way towards them.

"Miss Ponsonby, your parents have kindly invited me to ride with you to Darcy House. The carriage has been summoned, so, shall we?" She smiled and accepted his proffered arm, and together they left the box.

"Well," said Colonel Fitzwilliam to Elizabeth as her husband draped her shawl about her shoulders, "I cannot decide who is more delighted—my mother or my brother."

Both Darcys laughed, and Elizabeth said, "It would not be unfair to call it a draw!"

Dinner at Darcy House that night was the sort of triumph possible only when a capable hostess is further blessed with excellent servants, a fine chef, pleasant news to celebrate, and guests who are all eager to please and be pleased. The menu over which Elizabeth had agonised for days was praised by all, several bottles of wine put away by the old Mr Darcy were brought out by the new, and after the meal, the drawing room rang with music and laughter. If Mr Dunleavy, at his post outside the drawing room door, was seen to brush a tear away as the sounds of gaiety rang through the house, so long silent, it was never commented upon by anyone.

The next afternoon, Colonel Fitzwilliam called upon the Darcys and was invited to stay for tea. He gladly accepted, and they spent a pleasant hour discussing the previous evening's delights. Georgiana's talk was full of the play, while Elizabeth —newly married and happy—speculated eagerly as to when the eldest Fitzwilliam brother would propose to Miss Ponsonby. The colonel entered gladly into both subjects, and Darcy was happy to sit quietly and listen to his dear ladies and his favourite relation unless directly applied to for his opinions.

When these subjects had been exhausted, the colonel's expression grew serious. "Darcy, Mrs Darcy, Georgie...I came here a-purpose, to acquaint you with some news I received a few days ago."

Mr Darcy leaned forward, tensing. "Have you received orders? Are you to the Continent?"

"Yes, and no. We are to Canada."

The ladies gasped. "So very far away!" Georgiana exclaimed in dismay.

The colonel smiled faintly. "So it is. Our regiment is being sent to a place called Prescott, somewhat west of Montreal, where the army and the navy maintain a garrison defending British traffic along the river. The garrison is to become a fort, which we shall help to build and defend. It is entirely likely that I shall remain there until this conflict with the Americans ends."

"When do you leave?" Darcy asked quietly.

"We sail from Plymouth on the twenty-seventh, which requires that we depart London the Saturday prior."

"That is little more than a week from now!" Georgiana objected. Her brother laid a hand upon her arm, and she subsided.

As Darcy and Georgiana absorbed the shock of this news, Elizabeth's mind had already taken a turn towards the practical. "You must tell us, Colonel, what we may send with you to make your residence there more tolerable," she said. "There is little time to shop and less to make anything up, but I vow we will not see you off to the Americas without every needful thing."

He smiled gratefully at her. "I have heard that there are never blankets enough to go around in the Canadian garrisons, ma'am, and likewise cloaks, good wool stockings, and the like. I will be grateful for aught which may keep me warmer than my uniform alone."

Elizabeth did not even glance at her husband for approval of the expenditure; she knew he would wish this done at least as much as she. "You may leave it all in my hands, Cousin."

He remained another quarter hour answering their questions as best he could before he took his leave, though truthfully, he knew little more of his new posting than he had already said. Even Elizabeth was not equal to the task of cheering the Darcys that evening. Instead, she involved them in her plans for outfitting the colonel and allowed industry to slowly chip away at the weight of their concerns.

Having ascertained from the colonel that his parents had been informed, she called upon Lady Matlock the following morning, and that lady was pleased and grateful to be included in Elizabeth's scheme and to have something tangible to do to her son's benefit. The two of them, with Georgiana, spent several days dispensing Mr Darcy's money as well as the earl's liberally about the shops of London. New gloves, boots, cloaks, and flannel waistcoats were ordered, and a premium paid for their hasty completion. Mr Gardiner's warehouse was relieved of several bolts of fine, thick wool, which the maids of Matlock House quickly hemmed into blankets. The maids of Darcy House, meanwhile, plied their knitting needles and produced a tidy pile of stockings and several mufflers to further shield the colonel from the Canadian winds.

Soon, a trunk was filled to bursting with these items, and

to it Mr Darcy himself added an iron-banded lap desk suitable for the rigours of a military campaign, full of good plain paper, ink powder, and sticks of wax for sealing letters home. Purses containing what excess might be trimmed from the ladies' quarterly pin money were slipped in amongst the folds of blankets and waistcoats, not to be found until their dear soldier was well out to sea. Lord Matlock and Mr Darcy would attempt to press their own coin upon him openly, only to be refused.

During this time, the Darcys were also packing their own things and preparing to close Darcy House, for they had decided to proceed from Plymouth to Pemberley, to introduce Elizabeth to her new home and console themselves with the beauties of the country for a number of weeks before returning to London after Easter for the height of the Season.

"I am sorry we shall miss your first dinner party, Jane," Elizabeth said when she explained their plans. "But Fitzwilliam and Georgiana need to be at Pemberley to recover their spirits after we see the colonel off for God knows how long. And I confess, I shall be glad to spend some time in the country myself. Are you very disappointed, dearest?"

"Naturally I am a little disappointed, Lizzy, but I under-stand perfectly. To be home will no doubt be the greatest comfort to your husband and sister," Jane replied in all sincer-ity. "As for my dinner party, do not give it another thought. I shall have Lyfford beside me and the Matlocks and the Honingsbys in attendance. Together they shall see me through, I am sure."

"You must write me a very long letter afterwards and tell me everything," Elizabeth said. "And when we return in April, we shall take Society by storm, you and I."

Jane laughed. "I prefer to take Society by stealth, dear Lizzy, but I shall delight in watching you dazzle them all."

When Colonel Fitzwilliam's regiment departed London on a rainy Saturday morning, the Darcy and Fitzwilliam carriages made an odd addition to the ramshackle line of carts, wagons, and horses issuing from the barracks. They travelled with only the necessities, the bulk of their belongings already on the road north to Derbyshire. Sunday was spent in an indifferent inn near Aldershot, made bearable by the company of the colonel, who was able to pass the entire day with them. Over the following two days, he rode beside the carriages whenever the weather permitted and the Darcys and Fitzwilliams were happy to huddle under their carriage blankets with the window open for the privilege of conversing with him.

Late on Tuesday they reached Plymouth, and Wednesday's dawn saw them clustered on the dock, bidding the colonel a fond but hurried farewell, for the tide was fair and the captain eager to get underway. As the Lyffords had done at a different port only weeks earlier, they watched the ship until it had vanished from all sight before returning to their carriage and embarking in heavy-hearted silence for home.

The Darcys and Fitzwilliams parted two days later, when the London road and that to Derbyshire diverged. Elizabeth was heartily sick of travel; her companions, more used to long journeys, did not become impatient until the day before they reached Pemberley, a week out from Plymouth. All irritation was forgot, however, when the carriage halted at the top of a rise and they stepped out into the chill February air to behold Pemberley House across the valley, its pale grey stone a cool shadow against the blanket of snow which glittered in the midwinter sun.

"Oh!" Elizabeth breathed. "How perfectly lovely. I now

comprehend your willingness to brave the roads to return here." Her husband and sister felt their spirits lighten, being returned to their beloved Pemberley and knowing that their beloved Elizabeth would come to cherish it, too.

They descended the hill, crossed the bridge, and drove to the door, and while examining the nearer aspect of the house, all Elizabeth's apprehension of her new duties returned. "Goodness, Fitzwilliam," she said with some awe, "I wonder anew at your choosing me, of all the ladies of England, to be mistress of this place."

"Pemberley has run reasonably well without a mistress these sixteen years, my love," he replied comfortably, "and shall continue to do so as long as is required for you to become accustomed to the role. Which, I might add, I do not expect shall take as long as you fear. I have every confidence in you." He concluded this little speech with a kiss to her cheek, which was witnessed by the butler and housekeeper, who had just that moment opened the door to admit them. Though they had excellent reports of the new Mrs Darcy from their counterparts in town, this token of affection from the master did her no harm at all in their eyes.

The Darcys were ushered within and relieved of their outer garments, and though the proprieties and distinctions of rank were meticulously kept, it was clear to Elizabeth that her husband and sister were received with real warmth and affection by those in service to them. As had occurred on her wedding day, she was presented first to the butler, Mr Johns, and the housekeeper, Mrs Reynolds, and to them she made known her personal maid, Davis, who was whisked away to become familiar with her new domain.

Elizabeth then met the upper servants and, all the required forms and protocols observed, she arranged for tea to be served in an hour, after they had freshened themselves from their travels. She found her chambers there much as those at Darcy House had been—elegant but faded. Knowing that she would have ample time before their return to London to catalogue what was needed for their refurbishment, she put the matter from her mind and set about growing accustomed to her new home. In this endeavour Mrs Reynolds proved to be a treasure beyond price, for she was only too pleased to see 'the young Master' so happy, and there was no amount of time she was unwilling to spend with the lady who made him so, no question she would not answer with cheerful patience, no detail she would not happily convey.

The halls of Pemberley soon filled not only with the music from Georgiana's talented fingers, but also with the peal of the mistress's laughter and the low rumble of the master's. The servants, catching the mood of the family, hummed at their work and chattered gaily about the table in the servants' hall. The addition of Elizabeth Bennet Darcy brought sunshine into the elegant rooms and made 'home' a truer description of Pemberley than it had been for many a year.

CHAPTER THIRTY-FOUR

A s her eldest sisters settled happily into their new homes, so did Lydia adjust—poorly—to life at Madsen Academy. In little more than a fortnight she managed to lose every privilege. Her burlap dress, marking her as the most troublesome sort of girl, caused the other girls to avoid her. Without friends, without comforts, and regarded with universal suspicion by peers and teachers alike, for the very first time in her life she began to consider that perhaps her behaviour was not quite what it ought to be. Into this period of reflection came a letter from her friend Mrs Forster, now encamped at Basingstoke, which was to further disturb her equanimity with news of Mr Wickham.

He, who seemed such a gentleman, has been revealed as the veriest cad, and now he is gone forever! Would you believe, he was caught in a compromising position with General Forsyth's niece? It was not such a great scandal at first, for a man in his position could do much worse than to marry a general's beloved niece—it would have been a great boon to his career, and we all thought perhaps he had planned to be discovered. He claimed to be madly in love with Miss Forsyth, and deliriously happy to have won her hand, but then he ran off! Wickham told Denny that Miss Forsyth had only been a bit of fun, that he had no intention of making a career with the militia, and that he wouldn't shackle himself to any lady with less than twenty thousand pounds. Such cheek! A man in his position would be miraculously fortunate to get half so much!

Miss Forsyth was sent off to relatives in Nottingham, and not a week after Wickham vanished, an attorney appeared at our door representing a group of merchants from Brighton. Will you believe that in our five months there, Wickham ran up over three hundred pounds in debts? It is true! And it is said he left more than debts with several of their daughters! My husband has enquired of the merchants here and unearthed a further hundred and ten pounds of debt and two ruined shopgirls.

I need not tell you what a shock it has been to learn that our good friend is nothing more than a wastrel and a libertine, for I know that you are experiencing those feelings now! But there is one piece of good news in all this, and it is that Wickham has been caught. He got no farther than Reading and has been sentenced to transportation for his debts and deserting his post. And there you have it—he is for Australia on the next convict ship, with a sentence of twenty years at labour, and may never return to England.

I can hardly think upon it without becoming rather faint. My dear Forster says that I am too ready to trust a handsome

face and a pretty compliment, and though I have always
laughed at him before I begin to believe he is right...

The internal tumult with which Lydia received this information can scarcely be imagined. Even she was not slow to comprehend that her family had been right and she, wrong— that she had cast aside her comfortable life in Meryton for her present situation for no better reason than a stubborn refusal to believe that a handsome young man who had, she thought, paid her some quite particular attentions could possibly be false. If idle lies could tempt her into ruination, then her attractions and her worth were not what she had long thought them to be, and it must follow that all her grand dreams were naught but conceit.

Having not her elder sisters' quickness, it was some days before she had properly puzzled out her role in her own downfall and made the merest, humbling beginning towards acknowledging her true place in the world. She withdrew quite thoroughly into her own thoughts, and by the time she began to take more interest in events around her again, she had through sheer inattentiveness become so inoffensive as to win back the privileges of wearing her own gowns and dining with the other girls.

So delicious was the plain, hearty school fare to a palate that had subsisted for weeks on porridge that she spent her mealtimes enjoying the food rather than making conversation with the other girls. While she ate, conversations flowed about her, and after a little more time had passed, she absorbed the fact that a great deal of hushed talk concerned a Miss Oliver, who had left the school abruptly a few weeks into the previous term, and had recently died in childbirth, abandoned by the neighbour's son who had taken advantage of her, and disgracing her family.

Lydia was shocked. "A gentleman would never promise marriage to a lady and then leave her!"

Two girls burst out laughing but another took pity on Lydia and explained. "It is not easy to force a man to marry, you know. If he does not wish to and he is not honourable, only his own father can force the issue. Or maybe the lady's father if he is more powerful than the man. If some fellow trifled with you, how would your father make him marry you?"

"Well, he would go to the man and tell him he must," Lydia sputtered.

"And if he said he had made you no promises, that you were not betrothed and never had been? What could your father do then, if there were no marriage contracts to prove the man a liar?"

Lydia sat in stunned silence, trying desperately to think of some way in which her father—a squire of few means and little note—might force a man's hand in the absence of a binding contract, and could think of none.

"So, you must not allow a gentleman too many liberties before the marriage contracts are signed, in case he is playing you false?" she wondered aloud, remembering stolen kisses in the hedge behind the Meryton assembly hall and how several of the soldiers had tried to place their hands upon her bosom.

"You should not allow him any liberties at all. Some men don't persuade a girl out of her virtue, they take it by force," the second girl said, with a hard expression. "Never be alone with a man who is not openly obligated to marry you. You might go there expecting a stolen kiss, while he expects something very different."

Lydia wiped her eyes with the back of her hand. "I do not know what to believe, but I will think about what you have said."

"Mrs Madsen will tell you," the girls advised.

Mrs Madsen was a brusque, stern-visaged woman. All of the students were by turns terrified and admiring of her, for she seemed to know all that passed under her roof and though she was never vulgar, she spoke as she found and minced no words in the telling.

And yet, there was another, kind-hearted side of the headmistress which most students would at least glimpse in their time there, for Mrs Madsen spent much time comforting young ladies who had only just realised how close they had come to forever destroying their own futures and their family's good name.

Later that afternoon, Lydia stood before the door to the headmistress's domain for some moments before gathering the courage to knock. She was admitted by Miss Byerly, the secretary, and promptly shown through to Mrs Madsen's private study, where the lady herself sat behind a broad desk. The door bumped Lydia's skirts when it closed behind her, so little had she ventured into the room, and she stood there, hands clasped before her, wondering what her father would do if she was to be removed from the school.

"Come in and sit, Miss Bennet," the headmistress said. "I believe you have come across some information which has shocked you deeply, and I wish to discuss the matter with you."

Lydia sank into a chair before the desk, staring mutely at the woman who was spoken of with such awe by the other girls.

"I understand that you have now learnt that gentlemanly honour is not, perhaps, the unassailable bastion they would have the ladies think it is."

"Is it true?" Lydia asked in a subdued tone. "Do gentlemen

really ruin and deceive young ladies and suffer no consequence?"

"Every day," Mrs Madsen said flatly. "Young ladies are kept ignorant of many things, by those who believe that to keep them unknowing is to protect them. That very ignorance is often what makes their deception and ruination possible. As innocent and unknowing as sheltered girls are, it does not even require much cleverness on the man's part to lead a girl astray. I do not believe in perpetuating ignorance, Miss Bennet. You may ask me anything, and I will answer to the best of my ability."

Lydia thought for a moment. "They said that some men promise marriage but do not mean it, and others will force a lady to do what they want. How can it be that they can do such things and not be punished?"

The headmistress looked at Lydia with a serious mien. "It is because gentlemen are in charge of everything, and they protect each other. All of society is created to the advantage of gentlemen. Think on it only a moment, Miss Bennet—I am sure there is as much gossip in the town you come from as in any other. When a man and a woman misbehave together, what happens?"

"There is talk, of course." Feeling a bit more confident in the subject, she continued. "Last year at an assembly, Mr Watson and Miss Nesbitt were caught alone together on the balcony! No one spoke of anything else for a month complete, it seemed."

"And what happened to them? Did they marry?"

"No, Mr Watson was engaged to a lady from Devonshire. Miss Nesbitt went to live with her aunt in Cornwall."

"So, Miss Nesbitt had to leave her home and her friends, for the crime of being briefly alone with a gentleman, and—

do please allow me to conjecture—Mr Watson went on to marry his lady and is still welcome in your community?"

"Yes," said Lydia, her look of confidence slowly turning to confusion as Mrs Madsen seemed to expect something from her.

After a moment, the woman sighed softly and prompted, "Both of them went out there willingly, knowing it would not be looked upon kindly if they were discovered, and only Miss Nesbitt suffered any consequences?"

"Of course! She knew he was engaged and could not marry her, and she allowed herself to be caught alone with him!"

"Presumably Mr Watson also knew that he was engaged and ought not be alone with other young ladies," Mrs Madsen said drily.

Lydia had never considered it from that perspective before and found herself outraged. "Why, that scoundrel! That cad! If I ever see him again, I will punch him in the nose!"

Mrs Madsen was surprised into a laugh. "I would not recommend that course of action, Miss Bennet. But you will know him for what he is—a man who is, at the very least, selfish. And you will know that you must protect yourself from men who do not deserve you."

They spoke for a while longer, for Lydia had questions about those rules of propriety which she had long disdained but had begun to understand might have a deeper purpose. When she exited the headmistress's office and the door closed behind her, she felt as though she had left something of her foolish youth within.

EPILOGUE

J ane's entrance into society was not without impediment, for more than one lady of the first circles had cast her eyes in the direction of the young earl, either for herself or a daughter, and were not pleased to be usurped by some unknown country miss. But such was Jane's unshakeable gentility and grace in company that she soon won many friends and admirers among those less consumed with envy, and her detractors learnt to moderate their spite or face censure from many quarters. If, in those early days, she occasionally dissolved into tears upon reaching Markham House after a trying evening, none but her husband ever knew it.

Elizabeth Darcy did take the *ton* by storm, though she too had her detractors. Among the gossip and frivolity, Elizabeth and Jane each managed to find other women of sense and intelligence and began to build those friendships which would see them through the rest of their lives among England's elite. The Season ended with the wedding of Viscount Selfridge and Miss Vivian Ponsonby, and after the last toast had been made and the last slice of cake consumed, Jane and Lizzy bid farewell to their London acquaintance and left the heat and grime of the city with great relief. The Darcys proceeded immediately to Pemberley, but Jane and Lyfford made their way to Salcombe for a fortnight at the shore, by way of a belated wedding trip. On their way to Staffordshire, they retrieved Mary from Longbourn, to commence her promised visit to Lyfford Hall. A long summer of rest and country pleasures followed, punctuated by visits to and from the Darcys.

Together, and with the explicit support of the Countess of Matlock, the sisters would over the next several years become quite a force in society. Jane's elegance of dress and manner was widely imitated, and Elizabeth's wit and vivacity widely admired. To offend one sister was to offend the other, and likely the Countess and Viscountess, too; after that first Season, it was a rare occurrence indeed that anyone should deliberately slight Lady Lyfford or Mrs Darcy.

Some three years after Jane became Lady Lyfford, Kitty went to visit her eldest sister during the Season, for she wished to sketch a limited engagement of Grecian sculpture on display at the British Museum. At an exceedingly crowded ball, she was seeking her relations between sets and happened upon Mr Bingley, who was likewise in search of his lamentably still unmarried sister. Recognising each other, they exchanged greetings, which led to a request for a dance. Kitty offered her dance card and Mr Bingley scrawled his name in the next available space, which neither immediately realised was the supper dance.

They enjoyed their set and enjoyed their conversation over

the meal even more. Kitty had blossomed under the greater attention of her parents and elder sisters and the diligent practice of her artistic talents. She had become a sweet and cheerful lady, desirous of society but appreciative of the quieter comforts of home, not deficient in understanding but concerned with the artistic rather than the intellectual. Bingley, too, had altered in the intervening time. Though still garrulous and sociable, he was now very careful in his interactions with young ladies and had raised no reasonable expectations in any lady since his sojourn in Hertfordshire. He relied much more on his own judgment and had learnt to exercise his position as head of the family with a firm hand, to the continuing bafflement and dismay of his sister Caroline.

They would encounter each other at several events in the following weeks, and by the time the Season ended, Bingley was a regular caller at Markham House. Though his sisters were diligent in their efforts, he was not to be dissuaded from *this* Miss Bennet, and they were married eight months after their reintroduction. Soon after, Bingley purchased an estate in the north of Staffordshire, less than a day's journey from Lyfford and no terrible distance from his relations and continuing business interests in Scarborough.

Upon her brother's marriage, Miss Bingley was given the choice of making her home with the Hursts or setting up a spinster establishment with her dowry, for Bingley did not trust her to live peaceably with any wife of his, much less one who had previously borne the name of Bennet. She chose a third option, accepting the proposal of a nabob recently returned from India. Their well-matched fortunes and desire to cut a dash in society overcame the twenty-year difference in their ages as well as their complete lack of affection for each other, and they were each as contented as they had expected to be in the married state.

Miss Darcy, meanwhile, attended five Seasons and often despaired of meeting a gentleman she could love. She was three and twenty and seriously considering retiring to Pemberley and a spinster's cap when the extended families assembled at her ancestral home for Christmas, at Elizabeth's invitation. There she came to know the newly promoted Brigadier Edward Markham, lately returned from peace-keeping duties on the Continent. They had met briefly at their brothers' wedding and a few other occasions scattered across the years, but he was so rarely in England that their acquaintance had, until that time, not progressed beyond common-places. Theirs was a whirlwind courtship, culminating in an April wedding and a speedy departure to his new post ensuring the safety of diplomats in Belgium. They would return to England three years later, their young son in tow, with his reassignment to the War Office, where he would carve out a career attempting to ensure that troops in the next conflict would not be so poorly provisioned as he had been on the Peninsula.

Miss Lydia Bennet had inherited none of her father's cleverness, and self-interest would always be her guiding star, but having her illusions torn from her in such a short period of time proved to be exactly the spark required to kindle a flame of understanding within her. She wished to be liked and admired, so she learnt to take an interest in the concerns of others, that they might in their turn care about hers.

In her three years at the Academy, Lydia applied herself well enough to earn the required marks. Her great accomplishment, aside from the stitchery in which she was already well-versed from her love of bonnets, was that she learnt to speak both French and Italian with fluency and verve and developed an enduring love of gothic novels from both of those countries. When she left Madsen's for the final time, the worst that could be said of Miss Lydia Bennet was that she was not very clever and that she would give no countenance at all to any man who had ever damaged a lady's reputation.

At the ripe old age of four and twenty, Lydia—who had once hoped to be the first of the Bennet girls to wed—married the son of an associate of Mr Gardiner, a young man who had just purchased a small estate and knew the value of a gentle-born wife with connexions to the peerage. She had asked her aunt and uncle to help her find a husband, for the morals of the middle class as they related to the treatment of women were much more to her liking than those of society. They introduced her to a number of upstanding men before she chose Mr Northrup. He was reasonably wealthy, undoubtedly intelligent, neither handsome nor ugly, and prepared to be kind and indulgent, within reason, to a pretty wife whose connexions raised his own consequence and whose reputation was pristine. She kept his home well and presented him with four healthy children, while he gave her his respect and a generous allowance. Though theirs was no great love story, they both were able to truthfully claim happiness in their union.

The Lyfford and Darcy families prospered, side by side, while many other aristocratic fortunes were diminished or lost as the agrarian economy of England shifted to one of industry. When an investment opportunity arose, it would be investigated with all of Lyfford's perception and Darcy's caution. If they found the principals honest and the terms fair, they would give the numbers into Jane's clever hands, proceeding only if she also declared the scheme reasonable.

Mr Watts, the thieving steward, was never apprehended. Every so often there was a 'sighting', prompted no doubt by the five hundred pound reward which Lyfford maintained, but all came to naught.

"My dear," he said to Jane, one ordinary night over dinner, "I have been thinking of withdrawing the reward for Mr Watts's capture."

"If you think it best," she replied placidly, for nearly a decade of marriage had taught her that his thoughts often ran along lines she could not predict. "Have you lost all hope, then? I suppose after all this time it is unlikely that you should recover anything, even if he were apprehended."

"Ah, Jane...his debt has been repaid, and more. If it were not for his thieving, you and I should never have met and married and produced three lovely children together." He smiled at her in that way that still made her catch her breath.

"It is true," she said, with a smile of equal affection, "that we have gained much more than he. Let us do as Lizzy always urges and think on the past only as it gives us pleasure."

ACKNOWLEDGMENTS

A big thanks to my beta readers Melissa and Elaine, who gave of their time and energies to make this story better.

The lovely community at A Happy Assembly read the first, unpolished draft of this work and their encouragement, questions, and suggestions were invaluable. A particularly deep curtsey must be made to the admin/mod team, who take very good care of the authors and readers there.

Thanks to the Quills & Quartos team, who took a chance on a first-time author, and in particular Jan, who ground down the rough edges of this novel and spurred me to fill in the gaps. Also to Mary McLaughlin, who found and excised every unfortunate word choice and misplaced punctuation mark.

To my spouse, Ryan, who isn't much of a reader and is baffled by my love of Austen, but encourages me anyway.

And last but not least, I could not forget those who have patiently borne with my excited ramblings on characters, plot twists, and settings, while urging me to keep writing, keep revising, keep dreaming: Jessica, Rebecca, AJ, and Aaron.

ABOUT THE AUTHOR

Frances Reynolds fell madly in love with *Doctor Who* at the tender age of seven. This, in turn, led her to embrace other quintessentially British delights such as tea, scones, Dickens, and Austen. When she is not wrangling wild data for a large financial firm, she is generally to be found reading, writing, or watching her favorite series (*see above*) while knitting.

Frances lives slightly south of Canada with her spouse and a small herd of cats, in a house which is continually upset that it has been obliged to remain standing since 1916.

 facebook.com/FrancesReynoldsAuthor